engaged

engaged

A NOVEL

K.L. GILCHRIST

ISG PRESS

Library of Congress data available upon request.

ISBN 978-1-7341705-1-1

eBook ISBN 978-1-7341705-0-4

Cover design by Stefanie Fontecha for Beetiful Book Covers.

Interior design by ISG Press.

Second edition.

also by k.l. gilchrist

leave a review

Dear Reader,

Hi! I hope you enjoy this story. Just a reminder here that book reviews are a wonderful way for readers to connect with authors, and they also play a crucial role in helping us spread the word about our stories.

Whether you love the story or even like it a little, a quick review on the platform where you purchased it would be incredibly helpful. Even if you received a complimentary copy, your honest feedback is valuable.

Of course, I'd also love to hear your thoughts directly. Feel free to reach out at kl@klgilchrist.com.

Warmly,
K.L. Gilchrist

In loving memory of my precious daughter, Jordan Niambi Broomes, who loved these characters from the very start.

So, chosen by God for this new life of love, dress in the wardrobe God picked out for you: compassion, kindness, humility, quiet strength, discipline. Be even-tempered, content with second place, quick to forgive an offense. Forgive as quickly and completely as the Master forgave you. And regardless of what else you put on, wear love. It's your basic, all-purpose garment. Never be without it.

COLOSSIANS 3:12-14 (THE MESSAGE)

contents

drone

I CAN HANDLE A LOT. For real. I've been through some serious situations in my twenty-something years. And not in a I'm-a-millennial-struggling-with-adulting-but-I'm-stuck-living-with-my-parents-and-my-boyfriend-is-a-nut kind of way.

Nope.

I'm talking intense stuff: battle back from the edge of death, accept a new life in Christ, live independent and strong even with an occasional panic attack, conquer my toughest temptations, and win the heart of the dopest bachelor at Rise Community Church.

Been there. Done that. Got the pics on the Gram to prove it.

This afternoon, though? I am not in the mood to tangle with a ridiculous, whirring, midnight black drone hovering too close to me and my man, John. A minute ago, we turned down the concrete path through the park behind the Philadelphia Museum of Art. My only thoughts then were about how warm and rough John's fingers feel holding my hand, and how the air smells springtime fresh, and how those purple flowering azalea bushes look glorious.

See, this is our absolute favorite spot. We regularly walk or run through here on bright sunshine-filled days. Even if the sky is gray and overcast, we might still stroll this jawn wearing our matching fleece hoodies. Cold day. Hot day. Doesn't matter.

Right by the parking lot, two sun-faded brown benches sit beneath a narrow wooden gazebo. My heart zings because that's where John and I experienced our first delectable kiss—in the center of the city like cool urban teenagers, except we're grown. We're in love and blessed in our cherished little patch of Philly, so we *should* continue to hold hands and grin and reminisce.

But we can't because that doggone drone zooms over and hovers above us.

So I do what any courageous queen would.

I make a break for it.

"Chablis! Get back here!" John hollers when I sprint away. "It's a machine. It won't hurt you. Come on, now!"

"It's a drone. So no!" I yell back, twenty steps closer to my goal— the safety of his black Jeep.

His long legs carry him to my side in a flash. He's not even breathing hard.

"Just so you know," he says. "It'll be your fault if I have to wrestle you to the ground. If one of my contacts pops out, I won't see you good and you'll mess up the moment. Slow your roll, there's a reason for that drone."

I squint at the sky, jump into a fight stance, and stare that whirring robot down like I'll roundhouse kick it if it flies any closer.

"Bae," I point at the drone. "I think some weirdo teenager is flying that thing, trying to tape us."

"A teen isn't flying that, but it *is* taping us."

"You got a BB gun or something to shoot it with? You know I have issues."

"No, now just listen. Will you please stand still?"

I'm bouncing around like I'm about to go six rounds with Manny Pacquiao. I stop.

John steps in front of me. His megawatt smile is everything. "Chablis, I love you so much—"

"I love you too—"

"And if you'll have me." He gets down on one knee and pulls a small black book from his jacket. "I would love for you to be my wife. Will you marry me?"

I freeze. I'm not breathing.

He pushes the book, a worn Bible, into my hands. A crimson ribbon hangs from the top.

"Open it." The smile grows larger on his toasty brown face. Joy glows behind his eyes.

I do as he asks, and the ribbon is a bookmark for 1 Corinthians 13. Love is patient. Love is kind. All that good stuff. In the middle of the crease, tied to the satin ribbon? An exquisite, sparkling, princess cut diamond and platinum engagement ring.

If God pressed the stop button on my life at this exact second, I'd be happy to launch straight into heaven, knowing my final earthly moment had been the most phenomenal one I'd ever experienced.

But I'm alive. My heart is still pumping.

John gazes at me, still with one knee planted on the concrete. He stays in place, even as a lanky, red-haired woman wheels a baby carriage past us and mouths, "Aw."

Eyes on the ring again, I blink once, twice, then three times.

That promissory jewel shines like a star in the sky.

Forget a stupid drone!

"So? Will you?" John stands and gently takes the Bible from me.

"Oh my God!" I throw my arms around him so tight I'm probably cutting off his circulation. My face smashes into his shoulder, and he murmurs something and tries to pull my body to the side. I can't stop squeezing him, though. *His wife! He asked me to be his wife!* Right here, in the middle of green grass, purple azaleas, and the smell of fresh mulch.

"Sunshine?" He uses his special nickname for me, then lands a moist kiss near my hairline.

My mouth stays smashed against his body. "Yeth, honey. Yeth, I wilfth be your wife. Foreverth and everth!"

"I love hearing those words, and I need your hand. Let's do this right."

I let him go, and tears fill my eyes. My hand shakes when he grasps it. He pulls the ring from the ribbon and slides it on my finger. Smudges of MAC Viva Glam lip gloss decorate the front of his jacket, but he doesn't seem to mind.

"You just told me yes and I don't believe in divorce." He leans down and kisses me softly on one dimple, then the other. "Whatever happens between us from this day forward, we're going to work it out. No matter how hard it gets. Promise me?"

"I promise."

"Good. Now can you do one more thing for me?"

"What's that?"

"Give me a Hollywood-style kiss for Facebook and the Gram."

John moves in close and I breathe deep with his face next to mine. His fingertips stroke my cheeks. I tangle my fingers in his bushy beard. When my mouth meets his soft lips, a magical feeling rises inside me, like I'm saying yes all over again, but differently. *Yes. I'm yours. Yes. You're mine. Yes. We will take this journey together.*

He tastes like peppermint Trident because he's always chewing gum. But this may be the best kiss of my life.

Only the one I get at the altar can top it.

Calm is John's middle name. With no frenzy at all, he sends a pic of the ring on my hand along with a *SHE SAID YES* message to all his loved ones. Then he climbs inside the Jeep.

Look up the term 'act a fool' and that's me after the proposal. One picture from me? Oh no no no no no. Uh-uh. That won't work. I take multiple shots of the ring, my face, John's smile, and the two of us posing together and send them to my favorite folks with a two-word message: *WE'RE ENGAGED.*

We speed away from the parking lot and by the time we reach the first stop light my phone chimes with back-to-back return messages.

Wow.

I'm riding along feeling like every sentence of every happily ever after paragraph at the end of a chick lit novel. Chablis Charmaine Shields, the Jesus chick with purple highlights through her wild hair, gets to marry her best friend and the love of her life, John Leonard Gerald.

Eleven months of steady dating led me here, strapped in the passenger seat of John's Jeep while we drive to the Northeast to tell his mom we're jumping the broom.

"Hey?" I scan texts. "Nikki wants to know how long before the wedding."

He merges us onto I-95 North. "You busy next month?"

"Next month?"

"All right. What about next week?"

"For real, John?"

"You know we can do this tomorrow. That good for you?"

"Ha ha ha. And I thought I was the funny one in this relationship." I finger-comb my curls. "Seriously, man. When?"

"I don't want a long engagement, that's for sure. What works for you?"

Wedding timing. Hmm? We'll need enough time for event planners to work their alchemy for our special day. It's late March. A summer wedding? No. Too soon for what I'm envisioning. Philly will still be warm in early October, though. My ladies can wear strapless gowns. And the fellas won't overheat in their tailored designer suits.

Oh yes, we can pull this off in less than a year.

"Six months?" I tap my calendar app. "First weekend in October?"

"Six months it is." He shows me that heart-stopping smile again.

My thumbs text that answer to Nikki before I slide my phone into my bag and finally sit still. Nikosia Perry is my closest buddy besides John. It goes without saying that she's my maid of honor, but in case she has any doubt, I'll message her again later.

Inside, I'm still shaking. I gotta calm down. I need to be cool, and collected, not crazy emotional, when we see John's mother. Her name is Patricia Gerald. I call her Ms. Pat. I hope she'll be happy for us because she acts snooty whenever we visit her. On my end? Well. It's hard to have warm fuzzies for a woman who calls me 'John's church friend'. On Valentine's Day I overheard John talking to her, keeping his tone respectful when he told her to please stop mentioning his former fiancee's name because it's disrespectful.

But anyway.

After we see her, we can take our engagement tour to my parents' house. And after that, some of my friends and family will be at eatLARGE restaurant down in South Philly tonight. I'll ask John if we can flash the ring over there.

Then.

I don't know what we'll do after that.

Maybe we'll do what we haven't done?

I shift around and take a good hard look at John. Butterflies perform Simone Biles somersaults inside my belly.

"You all right, Sunshine?" He asks.

"Uh, yeah." I crack my window. Fresh air pours in. "Six months, huh?"

"Six months."

seven hours and two guardian angels

WHY DO romance writers always describe a male hero's eyes as green or blue? That makes no sense to me. Are a man's eyes only gorgeous when they're ocean-colored? They must call it fiction for a reason because John's golden-brown eyes are flat-out striking. They're the kind I look into and they make me wanna say *um-hmm* like I hear a jazz-funk rhythm and I'm already swaying.

Darn shame his eyesight sucks.

John wears contact lenses because he's insecure about his glasses. I can't imagine him as a scrawny elementary schooler with Coke-bottle thick spectacles, but that was his reality. Stupid kids picked on him on the daily, and since all the crap that happens to folk when they're young merges into their emotional DNA, no one will catch him wearing glasses in public. Life gave my man lemons, but he crushed them into lemon water ice. He pushed past those dorky kid issues by building more muscle every year that he grew taller, doubling down on being smart, and sticking close to God. He's still sensitive about his eyes though.

I couldn't care less about his sight. If it grows worse, we can pick out a seeing-eye Siberian Husky. Cool with me because a large animal might protect me when I have panic attacks. I get those on occasion. If anyone creeps up and surprises me from behind, I'll tremble, gasp, and try not to melt like a snow cone dropped on a summer sidewalk. My mom once told me I shouldn't joke about sensitive issues, but it's my life, and for real, sometimes I have to laugh to keep from crying.

Ten years ago John joined Rise Church. I did the same thing a few years after, and we met while serving in the Help Squad ministry. Back then, I had some health issues brewing, and I needed a trainer. Since he loves exercise and all things healthy, I asked him to guide me to a life without blood pressure meds. It turned out we had a lot in common and we became friends. We both work with technology—I do software testing and he architects cloud network solutions. He turned me into an exercise junkie and now I like weightlifting more than he does. Biking sets him free. Line dance does the same for me, and we both dream of raising a family to the glory of the Lord. Shared interests made us buddies, mutual attraction drew us together, and God took care of the rest.

So, yeah. We're a real good couple.

Unfortunately, I don't think John's mother sits on our side of the aisle, so to speak.

The minute we show up on Ms. Pat's porch, she hugs John and lands two loud kisses on both his cheeks. When her eyes rest on me, she nods without speaking and opens the door wide enough for us to step inside.

I hold John's hand in the middle of Ms. Pat's pristine, off-white living room. It's like Antarctica in this place: beautiful and cold. And beneath the Arctic blast, we give her our engagement news.

"Congratulations," she mumbles, her body motionless.

Seconds pass and no one speaks a word. But so what? Ms. Pat will be my mother-in-love in a matter of months. It's okay we need to grow our relationship. And that we must do. John's father passed away from heart failure when he was seven and Ms. Pat raised John and his brother, Nate, by herself, with help from his grandparents. I understand life hasn't been easy for her. I can forgive her for showing her chilly side.

And that's why I drop John's hand, skip over, and throw my arms around her. When I kiss her cheek, her body stiffens. She pats my back with a light touch.

John hugs me when I return to his side. "Mom, we'll let you know as soon as we start the wedding plans."

"Oh, fabulous," Ms. Pat says. Her growing smile reminds me of a sliver of moonlight emerging from behind slow-moving dark clouds.

So, I guess that's... good?

My parents? Sonny and Charlene Shields? They're a *whole* different story.

As soon as John and I touch down on their front steps, Mom practically pulls the door off the hinges.

Inside my parent's overstuffed living room, Mom holds my engagement jewel to her face and tears drip down and soak her flowered blouse.

"I love you both so much! Congratulations!" Mom chokes out and race-walks her tiny frame to the powder room to grab a Kleenex.

Meanwhile, Daddy locks future hubby in a bear hug and claps him on the shoulders. "What took ya so long, young blood?"

This I expected from Sonny Shields. A man who started calling John his son approximately sixty-six minutes after they met at the family summer cookout.

One tight group embrace and dozens of #FutureFamily pics later, my beloved and I backtrack to Philly.

The friends know.

The parents know.

Heck, Instagram knows.

The next stop on our whirlwind tour? My friend Towanda's South Philly restaurant, eatLARGE. It's a healthy food spot she manages with my older cousin, Mariah, and the second tallest executive chef in the world, Gabriel Seay. John and Gabriel get along great because they're both addicted to clean eating. They ingest foods no human should want for dinner, like grass-fed bison and pickled seaweed.

John and I stroll in holding hands, I flash the ring, and people yell congratulations. My heart swells with every face I see—I picture everyone dressed in their finest, standing in the Rise Church pews on our wedding day.

Marvin Gaye and Tammi Terrell's voices float through the air, and Mariah cranks up the volume.

"Your Precious Love."

I'm chatting with family and John stands and extends his hand to me. I accept it. At the front of the restaurant, he coaxes me into the wingspan of his embrace. We dance, rocking each other slowly.

"I love you, precious lady," he whispers.

"I love you more, my precious man," I whisper back.

The lights dim and I clutch his body tighter and we sway to the impromptu serenade. Mariah paces around us with my phone in her hand. I bet she has us on Instagram Live. It's all right, though. Completely and wonderfully, all right.

Pure love courses through my body and when I tilt my head to look at John's face this incredible sense of peace flows from my scalp to my feet. It's a sacred moment, like we're cradled in the arms of angels. The song fades out and all my thoughts scatter. The crowd claps when John and I break our embrace, and a shiver runs down my spine when he steps back and kisses my hand.

Tonight will be our most delicious night ever.

I just know it.

ॐ

At midnight, Towanda and crew kick everybody out. On the sidewalk outside eatLARGE, I bounce around, grinning, when John strolls out clutching his keys.

That song! That dance! I'm hyped!

"Um, where are we going now?" I bat my eyelashes. "The Ritz-Carlton? Wyndham? You're the romantic. Scattered rose petals and lavender-scented candles gotta be lined up on a carpet somewhere."

"You don't want to wait anymore?"

"Hey man, I waited." I raise on tiptoe and whisper in his ear. "You put a ring on it. I'm yours forever."

John's eyes hold love and kindness, but the downward turn of his mouth and the way he rakes his fingers through his beard makes me brace myself for bad news.

"I promise you," he says. "I want you more than I've wanted any woman, but I need you to hear me out now."

"*Okaaaay*." I settle back to earth.

His lips move in slow motion. "I want us to keep waiting 'til after the wedding."

I blink, and each time I close and open my mascaraed eyelids, there he stands, quiet and still.

Wait.

Uh-uh.

He needs to quit playing!

Marvin Gaye and Tammi Terrell just serenaded us. Gleaming platinum and shiny diamonds grace my finger, probably courtesy of Kay Jewelers. John confirmed he loved me in front of the entire Instagram universe. And to top it off, it felt like our guardian angels gave a dap while it happened. My skin still tingles because of it. I'm flying so high, I might never come down.

John must have sensed that, so he's gotta give me something better than, *oh, I want us to keep waiting*.

I wave my new jewelry in his face. "Hello! We just got engaged. Engaged! Aren't you excited?"

"Of course I am." He takes my hand and leads me alongside him down the block.

"When we danced? Didn't you feel—"

"Like something spiritual touched us?"

"Yeah!"

"Felt so good it actually scared me."

"So, no flowers. No candles. Nothing else for us tonight?"

"The experience we had in there?" John stands still again and drops my hand. "That's how I know God's giving us a genuine gift, Chablis."

Uh-oh. He's calling me by my government name.

He's serious.

His eyes drift toward fast-moving traffic. "The Lord wants us to bless one another the right way... and I want us to honor that. We have to wait until after we take our vows."

I love the Lord and John knows that. What's the game changer? This ring on my hand, making me feel like I won the golden ticket, and it's my time to check out the chocolate factory. Still. A diamond shouldn't weaken my commitment to walk upright before the Lord.

That's what I *know*.

That's not how I *feel*.

When I study future hubby's face, with his smooth skin, and his dark beard, and his gorgeous eyes, my heart melts like Valentine's Day chocolates opened on the Fourth of July. I am so ready to be his completely. He's right, though. Whatever wrapped around us when we danced, it came straight from heaven.

Only an idiot would mess that up.

I will not be that idiot.

Lord, I pray, *please cover me during this time. Thank you for giving me John to have for a lifetime. Just don't let me be too thankful tonight. Amen.*

"All right." I say, trying hard to keep disappointment from strangling me. "I've been discipled and I know how to behave. I'll be good."

John smiles. "Sunshine, we've got so much to take care of these next few months. We're never gonna get another time like this, so let's just enjoy it. Let me know what you're dreaming about and we'll fantasize together. What do you want for our wedding?"

Wedding? Now he's talking! "One word. A-MAZ-ING. Whatever we do, it's gonna be—"

"Unapologetically dope. What do you think about a destination wedding?"

"Beautiful idea, but we can't do it."

"Why?"

"My dad's afraid of airplanes, and a lot of our Rise folks probably wouldn't make it."

"Yeah, you're right. We'll stay here and have something elegant and romantic." His golden eyes twinkle. "But that's with a budget, okay. We need to hire a planner and follow the recommendations. "

"You trying to say I'll be extra with the big day?"

"I think you'll try, but we'll work it out." John's soft lips land a kiss on my forehead. "What we won't do is let a bunch of shenanigans mess with our relationship. We've got a lot of peace and joy between us, and I don't want to lose it."

"But elegant? Romantic? Sounds like code for boring."

"How about I leave out any other adjectives and say I'm trusting God for a blessed wedding day? How's that?"

"That'll work. For now."

We stop talking but keep walking and my mind stays on the grind.

Our. Wedding. Day.

Months away, but I can already picture myself on Daddy's arm, marching down a white rose petal covered aisle. At the altar, my sweetheart will wait for me with tears in his eyes. As our friends and family support us, they'll see our union, but they'll also witness a new me. The strong, smiling, lovely and saved Chablis. The one dressed in a white silk gown, clasping hands with her beloved while orchestra violinists play love songs in the background.

Everybody will see that image and forget about beaten, abandoned, broken Chablis.

The Chablis I don't like to think about.

So, yeah, we need to have the most memorable nuptials in the history of Rise Community Church. An event that makes us stand out like the king and queen we are, especially in the eyes of John's mother. And I agree with my man, we will stay as loving and joy filled as we are in this moment.

"Ahem." I prompt the future hubby. "Tonight?"

He unlocks the Jeep and opens the door for me. "I'll drive you back to your place. Give me ten of your best kisses and we'll call it a night."

"Make it fifteen." I flutter my eyelashes again. "I do have standards."

He laughs so much he's still cracking up when we cruise down Broad Street.

And I'm glad he's grinning, even though he just dropped an ice-cold water balloon on my expectations. He's a good man. Integrity. Priorities. Intelligence. All that. That's why I'm proud to marry him.

John drives and I have a ball on the Gram. Takes less than a minute to follow three different wedding influencers and a cool account for inspirational marriage quotes. On that one, a pretty pink and white graphic reads: *Your wedding is one day. Marriage is a life-time-long sacrificial journey.*

I heart that post, then switch to John's Instagram. His pic of us smiling and showing off the engagement ring gathered a bunch of hearts and comments. Lots of love from friends, family, church members, and co-workers. Yay! I scroll down further and a comment from someone named VSweetBoss gives me a funny feeling in the pit of my stomach.

VSweetBoss didn't write *Congratulations* or *God bless your union.*

Nope.

She wrote, *Guess you found another innocent victim you want until you get tired of her.*

flashing lights

HATERS ARE INEVITABLE. Discouragement is a choice.

I pin that graphic to the *ENGAGED* Pinterest board I create on the drive to my West Philly apartment. I also add the Serenity prayer, ten tips for a dream wedding, and the top five exercises for brides-to-be. Deep cleansing breaths soothe my nerves while Jonathan McReynolds sings "Cycles" through the car radio.

Yeah, the Instagram comment bugged me, but this is still engagement night.

Nothing will rob me of its sweetness.

My apartment building has a chipped and faded red brick walkway leading from the tiny parking area to the front door. An old Pennsylvania mansion converted into individual efficient living spaces, it's only large enough for six grateful singles. The Main Line sits two miles down Lancaster Avenue, where twittering birds awaken rich folks at five in the morning. At my location? I wake to the sound of rumbling trash trucks and rushing commuter traffic. I can't wait to move.

John follows me down the walkway. "Why so quiet?"

"You want me to chatter?"

"I love your chatter."

"All right." I stop moving and face him. "Who's VSweetBoss?"

"What?"

"Check the Gram."

John blinks like he has no clue who I'm talking about. That's a good thing. If he'd flashed a sly smile and stuttered an explanation, I'd twist my new ring off, pop him in the noggin with it, then run upstairs to write my *Today's Christian Woman* testimony about how God rescued me from marrying a cheating fool.

"Hold up." He whips out his phone and taps the screen a few times. "Veronica Sweets? I didn't know she was still following me. If it bothers her I'm getting married, I can't do anything about that."

"Any direct messages or scandalous late-night escapades I need to know about?"

"No, come on now."

"I had to ask."

"I promise, you never have to worry about me for anything like that." He slides his device into his back pocket. "Remember when we talked about people in our past? I know I told you about Veronica."

Veronica? Veronica? "I can't remember, so let's say you did. She seems mad."

"Maybe she is. I mean, we were in a relationship, then we broke up after a couple of months. It's crazy if she's holding on to old memories."

"Did you break her heart?"

"Listen, I don't think tonight's the right—"

"I'd rather know."

"I was twenty-four, and—"

"And that sounds like yes." I look to the overgrown forest green hedges. Gardeners cut the shrubbery each week, but uneven branches always return—messy as ever.

It would be stupid to get mad about one of John's exes. Until a few years ago, John had an extremely active dating life. Before he graduated from Drexel, he was even engaged to a woman named Trina Greene. They broke up and never planned a wedding. I also know he slept with some ladies he dated after his split from Trina. He repented and dedicated himself to sexual purity and has always promoted celibacy for us though. And when we started our relationship, he changed his phone number so none of the women from his past could call or text him.

No doubt—future hubby comes with some baggage.

But I'm dragging a bucketful of Birkin bags behind me, so I can't judge him.

"Sunshine?"

"I'm good." I shake my feelings off and ease into his warm embrace, because I'm still celebrating our engagement. Forget Instagram. "I think you owe me some affection, Mr. Gerald."

Those fifteen kisses become a reality and he walks me to my apartment door, and that's it. The end of engagement night.

Alone inside my personal comfy cozy cave, I drop on my couch and meditate on Proverbs 19:11. *A person's wisdom yields patience; it is to one's glory to overlook an offense.*

I drum my fingers against my thighs. John *is* my man. It might not be wise to clap back at Veronica, but she must understand I'm in his corner.

I grab my phone, launch Instagram, scroll to that ratchet comment and tap out: *Hello, I'm Chablis! I'm the grateful future wife, not so innocent, and in no way a victim.*

I wait a few minutes.

No more comments appear, so I shut my phone off and go to bed.

Rise Church is located less than a twenty-minute drive from my apartment building. It's a mega church, so you'd think it would have a mammoth front parking lot. It doesn't. When we arrive Sunday morning, I'm restless and fidgeting as John navigates the Jeep to overflow parking behind the building.

He helps me from the car. "Sunshine, you look gorgeous."

I adjust my gauzy blouse and smooth my silk skirt. "Thank you. So do you."

John wears charcoal-colored pants and a light slate gray sweater. I raise on tiptoe to kiss his bearded cheek and smell aloe and grapefruit from the Soft Like Butta beard balm he loves.

"You ready?" I ask him.

"Let's do this."

We stroll hand-in-hand through the glass church doors like local celebrities. Church family give us hugs. Some of them watched the "Your Precious Love" dance on Instagram Live. Others tell us they adored the drone video John posted on all his accounts.

News in our church spreads faster than a California wildfire.

Before service starts, our senior pastor, David Downes, waves at us when we settle three rows from the front.

"We have a betrothal here at Rise Church," he announces to the congregation. "John Gerald asked for Chablis Shields' hand in marriage."

Applause and whistles fill the air before Pastor speaks again. "Settle down, family. Y'all know she said yes. You're all on Instagram." He chuckles, looking our way. "So, Marvin and Tammi, kindly take your happy selves to the church office and visit Sister Gunning before you leave today. Thank you."

For the rest of service, I grin like Pastor gave me a whiff of laughing gas.

And that smile drops from my face when John and I step into Sister Gunning's office.

Mary-Gladys Gunning serves as Rise's official church secretary. She's ninety-eleven years old, weighs a hundred pounds soaking wet holding a brick, and stands about four feet five inches tall. And that's with heels on. Nevertheless, she runs the show around here. She remembers even the smallest details of a congregant's life, and she can put the fear of God in you by leaving a voicemail saying, "Pastor Downes wants to speak with you."

Gray-haired and wrinkled, she rests behind her colossal mahogany desk like a teeny female version of Oz the Great and Powerful, peering at us over her bifocals.

"If it isn't Marvin Gaye and Tammi Terrell." She looks us up and down. "Nice dance."

"Thanks," we say.

"Have a seat and complete this form." She passes John a pen and a clipboard with a white form on it.

We sit on the hard wooden chairs opposite her desk.

"You have better penmanship." John pushes the clipboard to me.

I raise an eyebrow. "My first wifely role is to fill out all our forms?"

"Yup."

I scan the paper. *Rise Community Church Application for Counseling Services.* What the what? "Sister Gunning? I thought we were filling out the form to ask Pastor to marry us?"

"You are. Pastor Downes will only marry you if you complete premarital counseling. Your assigned counselor will e-mail you detailed questionnaires you'll fill out on your own."

John nudges me, whispering, "It's all good. We should do it."

I select the box for *Premarital Counseling.* Beneath that, I enter our full names, contact info, and our requested wedding date. I also check that we are full-fledged members of Rise.

The next question stops me, and I tap my pen on the clipboard.

He pats my hand. "What's up?"

"They want to know if either of us has had therapy before."

"So?"

"Should I say something? Dr. Jerrica?"

Dr. Jerrica used to counsel me because of my tendency to panic. When I was nineteen, my boyfriend at the time somehow found out I'd cheated on him. After modern dance class one Friday night, he followed me down the alley leading to the main street, beat me

19

senseless, and abandoned me for dead. Gave me a concussion that took a year to heal from. I recovered fully—no lasting brain damage, but I'll still panic if I have enough reminders of the assault.

John wraps his warm arm around my shoulders and pulls me close. "Don't mention it if it's uncomfortable for you." He keeps his voice low. "They might want to know if either of us is being counseled for addiction, anger, or sexual issues."

"Got it."

I write *no*, finish the rest of the form, then pass it to John. He reads it and slides it to Sister Gunning.

She peers through her bifocals. "Six months? You don't want to wait a full year?"

"No," we say.

Her eyes switch from me to John and back to me. "Your counselor will e-mail you those questionnaires and other information, so check your messages. If you attend a church life group, let the leaders know you'll be absent until you finish counseling."

We nod and say thank you and stand up to leave.

She holds up a hand. "Oh, one more thing, Marvin and Tammi."

"What's that?" I ask.

"You must successfully complete all counseling sessions or Pastor Downes will not marry you." The corners of her mouth turned upwards into a smile. "Now have a blessed afternoon."

Five-thirty, John and I return to Wilmington for Sunday dinner with the parents. As soon as we walk through the door, they smother us with hugs and kisses. Feeling their arms around me and the man I'm about to marry fills my heart so full of joy, I never want to break the embrace. I could do this forever.

Mom ends the lovefest. She pulls away and grabs my dad's car keys off the coffee table. "Steve, we don't have dinner rolls. Go pick some up. You can take John with you."

My daddy's full name is Stevenson Otis Shields. Everyone calls him Sonny. Everyone *except* my mom.

I kick off my heels and place them on the rugged black plastic mat by the front door. "Mom, we don't need rolls. Who needs all that bread?" I look at John.

He has his body positioned to follow my father. "Huh? I'm going with Dad. We'll be right back. So Dad, how's that knee?"

Daddy opens the screen door. "Not so bad, son, not so bad. Can't complain. I've been stretching my leg and foam rolling it. Just like you told me."

"That's what I want to hear," John says, shutting the door behind him.

Their growing relationship is so sweet , I can forgive my man for ignoring my comment.

Mom and I hang out in the kitchen. She used to smoke, but she's been cigarette-free going on five years. Cooking is her major pastime now, and she goes all in with it. She pulls roaster pans out of the oven while I sit at the table and scan Instagram.

"Are you gonna make his plate tonight?" She peeks under aluminum foil. Aromatic steam makes the room smell like baked chicken and seasoned vegetables.

"Whose plate?"

"Don't get cute."

"Mom, John is grown. He has two working hands."

She gives a quick grunt and cuts the oven off. "He told you that?"

"No."

"Then listen to your mama and start treating your husband special from day one."

"Fix his plate, though? That's so old school."

"Why do you think old school couples are still together? Tell me that." She sits across from me, scanning my face. "What's the matter?"

"I'm looking for something." I scroll through John's pictures faster. "It's not here anymore."

"What?"

"An engagement pic from yesterday. He posted it and I wanted to see the comments again but it's gone and—" I bring my head up. "He must have deleted it, but he didn't tell me."

"Maybe he wants to post a better one."

"Yeah. Maybe." If I explained why I need to see that post, and the reason I'm sweating now that it's missing, she wouldn't understand. "I'll ask him about it later. Anyway, you're going to help with the wedding, right?"

"Yes, just understand our money's not that long. Your dad won't tell you that, but I will. He's going to want you to have the dream wedding."

"A dream wedding to me means having everyone there. Family. Friends. Our church fam and our co-workers. My line dancers and his training buddies. I'd love to invite them all. I'm thinking at least three hundred guests or more and at least fourteen bridesmaids and groomsmen. At a classy reception location, not a cramped Philly banquet hall."

"Do you and John have a budget for all that?"

I shrug and glance around the room. My mom and dad's kitchen has needed a fresh paint job for years. The living room too. And their hot water heater and furnace are on their last legs—Mom complains about it all the time. They both work at the local post office, and they should use their extra cash for their home and retirement fund. I don't *even* feel right asking for money, but traditionally, the bride's family pays for the wedding.

"What do you think you can give us toward the ceremony?"

"I'm not sure. Let me talk to your dad first before you pass us a wish list. Start small because you can always scale up."

"Duly noted."

"Does John understand you want a huge wedding?"

"Does it matter? It's the bride's big day and I'm the bride."

Mom taps her red fingernails on the tabletop. They're pointed with fake bling on the tips. I used to get bling designs, then I started fitness training. Now I keep mine short and French-manicured.

"Chablis, there's no room in your marriage for selfishness. Without sacrifice and forgiveness you'll tear each other apart."

John and me? Tearing each other apart? Can't happen.

"That's impossible. We're two of a kind." I tap my phone screen, turning it around so she can look at it. "You've seen my Instagram."

My Instagram account is like a romance movie with over three hundred pictures and videos. John took the first photo of us the day I picked him up from Philly International after he returned from months of working in Germany. After that, he snapped pics of us at every outing, including our first official date at The Chart House restaurant.

"You want a picture of us together this soon?" I had asked John that evening after he handed me roses and posed us for a picture at the front of the restaurant.

"Yes." He took his phone back from the hostess and kept his warm hand on my back when we moved toward our table.

"And what if things don't work out for us?"

He pulled out my chair. "I'm a positive thinker and I'm loving the way we flow. The way we're going, I need a picture of this date."

"You sound confident."

"Nah, I'm just direct." He sat and took my hand. "We vibe so well together, and I'm falling deeper for you each day. If you don't want a future with me, please say so now. I'm serious, because I don't do drama or games. From this moment on, I'm making it my job to learn the real you and I want you to get to know the real me. So we're going out everywhere, exercising, visiting people, and worshipping together. Expect random gifts and cards from me. I'll pray for you daily, and I want you to pray for me. You're my lady, and I'm your man, we're in a relationship and we're exclusive, unless we decide

23

otherwise. Now, that's how *I* see us—two people moving forward to find out if marriage will work for them. But I'm not in this alone. So, Ms. Chablis Charmaine Shields, would you like to keep going?"

That whole gushy soliloquy turned my insides to Jell-O, and I clutched his hand and nodded *like, yeah, okay, we're doing this.*

That was last April.

And he delivered every single thing he mentioned.

He picked me up Sunday mornings for church.

He joined my YMCA so we could work out together.

He visited The Grandstand Dance Hall & Social Club at least once a month to watch me line dance.

He took me to the movies, bowling, and out visiting friends and family.

He bought us matching t-shirts to wear when we sat court side at Sixers games.

He held my hand when we walked along the beach in Cape May.

He replaced my worn-out Nikes with brand new ones from Zappos.

He shared his reading plans with me on the Bible app.

He prayed with me on FaceTime every night and asked about my concerns later.

He let me watch Devin the Ink Czar tattoo Psalm 37:23 across his back.

He let me see him wearing his thick-lensed eyeglasses.

He saw me without concealer hiding the scar on my right cheek.

He cared for me with so much concern that on New Year's Eve, when he told me he'd love me forever, I shouted the same thing back, which made him laugh instead of kiss me when the ball dropped but it kind of worked for us.

Mom places her hands on top of mine, covering my phone screen. "It's nice you enjoyed yourselves. Are you sure John is the man you want to sacrifice your time, money, and energy with for a lifetime?"

"I'm sure. Believe me. I am so sure."

"Good." She keeps her hands still, but her voice wavers. "Because Daddy and I... we need you to be okay."

The weight of her words sinks into my soul.

My parents sheltered me after an angry boyfriend tried to take me out. They were the first ones to race to Wilmington Hospital after the EMTs scraped me off the pavement. These precious people sacrificed a year watching me heal. They quietly cared for me while I lost my dignity and self-confidence, and all my childhood friends drifted away.

Last night they celebrated with light in their eyes, communicating words they didn't speak: *our only daughter grew past the trauma of her younger years and she's getting married.*

And I didn't bring them just any guy. I presented them with a new millennium Samson for a son-in-law. Someone to love me and keep me safe. Short of having a son playing in the NFL, this ranks number one for them.

The look on Mom's face confirms what I already know.

If John and I don't get married, one of my parent's biggest dreams will die.

And we wouldn't break two hearts.

We'd break four.

count the cost

I'M GETTING ready for work when John FaceTimes. He's on screen, walking along outdoors in his biking gear, probably smelling like sweat and twenty miles of dusty road. A moist sheen covers his skin, and a white reflective helmet sits on his head, the black straps dangle beneath his chin. His standard look after he finishes cycling from the Schuylkill River Trail to the Manayunk Towpath.

Those trails scare the mess out of me.

Travis, John's biking and CrossFit buddy, told me he once wiped out on a sharp, leaf-covered turn. That was all I needed to hear. I prefer my cycling stationary inside the YMCA, thank you very much.

John owns a Cervelo Caldonia 105 road bike, that he named Samantha, which cost $2900. The price shocked me when he first told me about it, but hey, if he has the money to pay for it, he should enjoy it. Long as he stays safe. That's all I care about.

"I had to block Veronica on the Gram." The soft clicks of his bike accompany his voice. "I'm thinking about temporarily disabling my account."

"You took the picture down. I was waiting until you said something." I stand in my beige-tiled bathroom and my phone lies screen up beside my bathroom sink. This way, John can see me finish my hair and makeup.

"That was damage control. I read your response to her first comment, though."

"She had more to say?"

"Nothing worth worrying about. She was tripping. Leaving comments about me and our time together. Disrespectful, considering. I had to get rid of it."

"John, if I didn't know your character, we'd be having issues." Curly purple hair strands decorate the front of my white silk blouse. I brush them off and grab a small container of olive oil hair gel. He's watching me groom myself like I'm cucumber cool, but if he stood in this bathroom, he'd hear me grinding my teeth.

"You can trust me, you know that." Gray clouds threatening to block out a bright blue sky frame his head. "Hey, we've got a wedding and a future to plan, so let's keep things positive. I thought about the wedding during my ride. What do you think of us performing a dance together at the reception?"

"Eh... I don't want to."

"What? My dancing queen doesn't want us to have a choreographed performance. I'm shocked."

"Don't be. You know when I dance, I go all in, and I'm not trying to worry about timing and steps on my wedding day."

"Yeah, I see what you're saying."

"Speaking of weddings, I wanna call Luxurious Events today. They're the event planners my cousin Diamond hired." I use the gel and a toothbrush to sculpt my edges. "Contacting them is first on my agenda today. If we can get them, we don't need anyone else."

"Can you wait until tomorrow? Until we talk over money and budgets. Actual numbers."

"Numbers would be good. Last night Mom and I talked money, but she wants to run stuff past Daddy first. I'll be happy about anything they can provide. How much can you dump into our wedding budget?"

The trail winds behind him. He uses one hand to hold the phone and the other to push Samantha.

"I'm taking care of the honeymoon," he says. "And I don't want to brag, but you'll love your surprise. All-inclusive, adults-only, tropical utopia... and that's all I'm saying. Renew your passport and shop for a red bikini. With all that, plus the clothes for the ceremony... the wedding ring set... count on me for two thousand."

"Two thousand? For an unapologetically dope wedding?"

"Listen, the wedding is one thing, but I got the honeymoon. I'm focused on the most romantic time we've ever had. It's not cheap, but I'm booking it because that's my gift for us. How much can you put toward the wedding?"

"Around three thousand and that's pushing it."

"All right. Can we go out tonight to talk? I can pick you up at seven and drive to MochaBlacCoffee."

"Coffee? This evening?"

"Yeah. Something serious is on my heart, and I feel like God is prompting me to be transparent."

I stare in the mirror, silent, arranging my purple curls. Something serious? We've only been engaged for two days—neither one of us has been behaving badly enough to break up. But he wouldn't take me out for no reason. When he says something is on his heart, he sits me down to discuss it face to face instead of on a call or text. If I ask him to talk about it now, he'd say no, because he respects me enough to be in a room with me while I'm processing the issue. He could come to my apartment, but MochaBlacCoffee is another favorite spot of ours, so he must want us to be in a better atmosphere than my shoebox-sized place.

"Are you going to take that much time to get ready when we live together?" He asks.

"You like the results?"

"I love the results."

"Then don't worry about it." I drop my hair tools in their

container and grab my phone to take with me. I give two air kisses. "Gotta go."

"Love you, Sunshine."

"Love you right on back." I say and end our connection.

Outside in my kitchen area, all dressed and ready for work, I lean against the breakfast bar. John's been up front about everything Instagram-related, but still.

What if he cheated with Veronica, and he needs to confess?

Or what if he's still in touch with Trina and wants to admit that?

Or, what if Ms. Pat called him last night and tried to get him to renege on the engagement?

"Stop, Chablis." I shake my head to knock those thoughts away. It's better if I cast my concerns to God. "Lord, thank you for always keeping me. I trust you, Lord. I trust the man you've given me to marry. Reveal his heart and remove any insecurities before they take root. Amen."

I look around my living room. My beat-up Ikea furniture fits fine in this space, but John and I can't live here. We need an apartment, not a closet. Maybe we can find the perfect townhouse? New construction with stainless steel appliances. I can fill the place with better furniture and kitchen items from Williams Sonoma. With our combined incomes, we'll find a glorious spot. Maybe all he wants to talk through are future living arrangements.

Arrangements! Almost forgot!

Phone in hand, I send a text message to Nikki:

> Good morning beautiful and blessed best friend and MAID OF HONOR. Put mani-pedis and dinner on your calendar for next Saturday. You be great today!

. . .

"Love your purple hair," the young barista with two silver nose rings says when I request a small dark roast with room for cream.

I thank her and shuffle to the right so John can request a medium original blend and pay for us. We're ordering hot drinks, getting ready to swallow strong caffeine like we're gonna hit the gym later. MochaBlacCoffee's artsy atmosphere and rich java smell help me relax a little. Still, good sleep might not happen for me tonight.

After I drown my beverage with cream and Splenda and John laces his with nothing, I follow him to an empty wooden table in the back room.

He sits back and takes a swallow of his drink. "Before we go any further. Before we talk about wedding plans, there's something I need to share."

My body doesn't want to stay still, so I cross my ankles and let my toe tap against the floor.

"Look, it's okay." My toe continues to tap. "I mean, if something happened with you and Veronica while we were dating, as long as it's all over now, we'll move past it. But I want to understand when and how it happened. I'll be upset, but it doesn't change my love for you."

He raises an eyebrow. "What are you talking about?"

"Engagement night. Remember? VSweetBoss and her comments on Instagram?"

"No, that's not why we're here." John wipes a hand over his face. "But since you brought it up, our marriage will be trash if you don't trust me. I meant what I said when I told you she was tripping. I haven't seen her face in five years and I'm not a cheater. Dudes who cheat are bored with their lives or with their women, or they have serious character and self-control issues."

I exhale my relief. "I'm sorry, I shouldn't have thought that. Okay, so, your mom is the actual issue for us, so I guess we should—"

"Chablis, I need you to listen. Please?" John's face sags. His eyes beg me to stop chattering.

Brown/red/orange/yellow/ivory canvas paintings hang from the walls. The round abstract faces in them mock my attempt to sound upbeat.

"You look scared," I say.

"I'm trying to find the right words." John slumps in his seat and tugs his beard. Then he pulls himself back up and fumbles with his phone. Then he lays his phone down and messes with his watch.

I've never seen him so vulnerable.

I swallow coffee and the hot liquid warms my insides. "Are you sure you want to marry me?"

"What kind of question is that?"

"The question I ask when my fiancé asks me to listen, even though he dragged me out at night to drink strong coffee that will send me to the bathroom in thirty minutes."

He picks his phone up again. "If we weren't walking down the aisle in October, I wouldn't have a hard time talking about this."

"We have these devices right here." I wave my phone. "On the count of three, tap out what you're having a hard time with and send it to me."

"Seriously?"

"Unless you have a better idea."

His eyes are a mystery for a moment, but then his gaze meets mine. "All right. I'll do a countdown."

A chill runs through me, but I pull myself up straight and grip my phone.

John's thumbs tap his phone screen, entering information. He stares at me when he finishes. "One... two... three."

Seconds later, I tap to read his text:

I still have more than 50K in private student loans. I've been trying to pay those down, but I also have a lot of commercial debt. Between Amex, my two Visas, and my car loan, I owe around 40 thousand dollars.

A quick tally and my heart beats faster than it does after I finish a set of burpees, followed by squat jumps and donkey kicks. Another chill slides down my spine.

"This is a joke, right?" I point my phone at his face. "You're ninety-thousand dollars in debt? And you're telling me this *now?*"

He moves his lips like he wants to say something else, but no sound comes out.

The chill disappears only to be replaced by an angry heat that feels like a thousand degrees. I wanna thank him for being transparent right before I reach across the table to pluck every single hair from his thick beard while screaming at him for ruining my dreams of new townhouse living.

No Williams.

No Sonoma.

And zero chance of a dopalicious over the top wedding.

"What happened, man? Talk to me." I jog my knees up and down. "I know how much you make and you can't be in that much debt, John. You just can't."

"It's hard to hear, but I am. I came out of school with over a hundred thousand in private student loans, and most of what I owe is that."

I shake my head, still in denial. "I don't believe it. You're the most disciplined person I know."

"I pay my bills. But I went through a few years when I'd pay the minimum on my loans and use my money to buy road bikes, sports stuff, obstacle course fees, food and supplements. And then you and I got together."

"How do I figure into this?"

"What's on your feet right now?"

"Steve Maddens. The baby blue ones."

"Those cost ninety-nine bucks a pair. How many pairs are in your closet?"

"Three pairs, you sent them to me, and I get the point." This is nuts. He's in debt and he's bringing up *my* shoe game. "John, you didn't have to buy me all those gifts, especially the shoes and clothes. And you don't have to bring me groceries from Whole Foods each week."

"Listen, I enjoy buying presents for you because it makes me feel good to see you happy. The organic food and vitamin supplements are my way of taking care of you. Real men treasure and nurture the people they love."

"You're trying to tell me I'm to blame?"

"No, I made my own spending choices. I'm saying though, God doesn't want us to keep heading down this road."

I drum my fingers on the tabletop. "And you want to get out of debt *now*?"

"Yeah. I mean, what I did with money as a single, I don't want to do that in my marriage. Dr. Jones told me to have a debt sit down with you months ago."

Dr. Brian Jones is John's mentor—he directs the Health & Wellness ministry at Rise. If Dr. Jones coached John to survive on tree bark, sea kelp, and calcium supplements for the rest of his life, John would try it, so who knows why he didn't listen to the money advice.

"He had a point." I study the inside of his wrist where Devin the Ink Czar tattooed Joshua 1:9 in small graffiti block letters. "Why didn't you tell me sooner?"

"Thought you'd turn me down for marriage. And we just vibe together so well... when it got to where it hurt to leave your side every night... I don't even have the right words to explain it. With you, I knew in my heart I had my queen, my rib, and my favor and—" He studies my eyes. "The debt bothered me, but I couldn't erase it fast enough."

I glance down at the shining jewel on my finger and know the answer before I ask the question.

"My ring?"

"Maxed out my Visa for it." His eyes drift from my face to the wall behind me. "But living with Nate helps me make big payments on my cards, so I should be able to pay that off soon."

I start twisting the ring off.

John snaps out of his daze. "Don't!"

"But—"

"That ring has to stay on your hand. I'm dead serious."

"You still want to get married this year?"

"Yes, because I promise you, I'm paying off bills left and right before we get married...and... I can't put much toward our wedding ceremony."

"The honeymoon?"

"I have a different plan for how to take care of that."

I'm out of questions so I say nothing else. Two teeny brown dots of spilled coffee rest on the table in front of me. I stick my pinky in one and swirl it around the wood.

"Sunshine, I'm so sorry I didn't tell you sooner," John says.

I keep swirling coffee drops. Coffee. Wood. Coffee. Wood.

"Chablis?"

Coffee. Wood. Doggone coffee.

"Chablis?" He reaches across the table and grasps both my hands. The skin on his fingers feels rough, like someone who does pull-ups off his brother's garage roof. "I know this changes your thoughts about our finances, but it doesn't change our relationship. Will you look at me, please?"

I raise my head and stare at the man who stole my heart. Sure, he's being transparent about his finances *after* I committed to marrying him. It's like he locked me in before I could say yes or no to his plan to pay off principal and interest. Doesn't seem fair, but I don't wanna fight about it. Some women would, but I'm not some women. John still has my heart on lock. He's my hard-working guy who loves the Lord, and when he commits to a goal, he's all in. He once tried out for *American Ninja Warrior*—our growing relationship was the only thing that stopped him from trying again. Future hubs *already* sacrificed a dream for me.

I agreed to take this journey.

I'm *not* changing my mind now.

"You need me to be in this with you?" I wiggle my fingers against his palm. "I'm in."

"I love you."

"Love you more." I tug his shirt sleeve. "Just promise me I can shine on the big day."

"You shine every day."

"You know what I mean."

"All you have to do is to be who you are. You shine regardless."

I stop talking and finish my coffee.

In the Jeep, Kirk Franklin's "Love Theory" plays on Philly's Favor. Lyrics about a better love sail past my ears, and even though I adore the song, I don't sing along.

I have my own love theory.

Genuine love means accepting truth.

No matter how hard it is to hear it.

sticker shock

MY DRAB OFFICE resembles two cubicles glued together with a glass door in the middle. New carpet scent permeates this space, no matter how much sandalwood oil I add to the diffuser on my desk. No one will ever catch me complaining about my gig, though. It took me five years to earn a Senior QA Lead position and I enjoy working to develop and document the test data for software deliverables. SourceTech LLC is a startup, so my salary isn't all that high. I accepted this position for the growth potential, not the money. Thank God for my affordable apartment and a Ford Focus I paid off two years ago.

I'd never marry for money, but I gotta be honest. I *was* looking forward to the day John and I blend our finances. Now that I'm woke to my beloved's financial situation, I have to think differently about our lifestyle. However, future hubby *said* our wedding will be unapologetically dope. I'm gonna hold him to that.

Ten o'clock arrives and I call Luxurious Events. Lorenzo and Luna St. James, the company owners, agree to consult with me and John this Thursday at six. When they ask me for budget numbers, I bite the tips of my nails and tell them I'll call back.

Lunch hour. I shut my office door so I can chat money with Mom.

She talks the second the call connects. "Yesterday I talked to Cousin Vivian. She says hi. She's looking forward to the wedding. She just knows it'll be as nice as Diamond's."

"What a coincidence? What's up with Di? She disappeared off Facebook last month."

"Oh, she's separated."

"She hasn't been married that long."

"I know, but Devonté had some crazy idea about being polyfactimous and he brought a girl home to meet her who was supposed to live with them—"

"Polyamorous. The word is polyamorous."

"Your generation and your new terms, I swear. Anyway, she left him and re-enlisted in the Marines. But that's her, not you, and my new son-in-law bet not think about making you live with some woman he wants to—"

"You don't have to worry about that. Trust."

"Good. So you called about money for the wedding, right? Daddy and I can give you about three thousand."

I drop my water bottle and it hits the floor with a splash.

"Baby girl? You there?"

"I'm here." I snatch the bottle from the floor and brush water droplets from my pant legs. "I might have been hoping for more. John and I had a talk and it turns out he can only provide a few thousand for the wedding budget."

"Why?"

"It's a long story, but he's still paying off student loan debts and other stuff. But anyway, neither of us has enough cash sitting around to feed hundreds of people."

"I know three grand doesn't cover as much as it used to and our folk like to eat a good meal when they give you gifts, but we're looking at retirement soon—"

"Mom, I get it. Thanks for telling me what you can provide. I'm guessing Luxurious Events will work with us on any budget. How does Dad want to send the money? Can he CashApp or PayPal me?"

"He won't PayApp or CashPal nothing. Stop down and get a check from him like you got some sense. And explain that polyamorous thing to me. It sounds interesting."

I glance at the time on my computer. "I don't have time right now. Gotta finish this salad and get ready for my one o'clock meeting. Call you later?"

"You better. Bye, baby girl."

"Bye."

Next time I see her, I'll have fun watching her face change colors when I explain polyamory.

I put my phone aside and twirl around in my chair. Numbers. All right. Two thousand from John. Three grand from the parents. Three from my personal savings. That's eight thousand to communicate to Luxurious Events. Whatever I do, I won't ask John for more. He looked me dead in the eye last night and told me he's focused on two things: paying off debt and securing our honeymoon. Besides, if I bug him for more cash, he'll reiterate his desire for elegant and romantic. Not *extra*.

But we'll need a bigger budget if we want to have a large guest list. There's no getting around that. The more heads we have, the more money we have to pay the caterer. So what options are there, really?

Second job? No. Exhaustion and I are not BFFs. Whatever side hustle I took, I'd start chowing down on coffee and Tastykake Krimpets at night just to stay awake. Full and curvy is fine, but I worked hard for a tight shape and I plan to keep it.

Raise donations through crowdfunding? My parents, John, and all of Rise Community Church would think I lost my mind.

Beg for help from our extended family members? That could embarrass me and John. Can't do that.

I pull my salad container from my lunch bag. "Welp, Lord." I whip out a napkin and lay it over my desk calendar. "Eight thousand is what we've got. You'll have to help our planners turn water into wine."

. . .

Thursday afternoon I arrive, prompt and smiling, at Luxurious Events.

John hasn't shown up yet. I call him. "Where ya at?"

"Westchester Pike. I'll be there in a minute. Don't start without me."

"Would I do that to you?" I tease.

"Hey, don't start without me!"

"Fine, fine. See you soon."

After I hang up, I tell the receptionist my name and walk around the reception area. What a beautiful office! Gold framed awards decorate the marble mantel. Sweet-smelling rainbow roses in tall cut glass vases grace the tabletops. The walls are salmon-colored and this ivory carpet I'm walking on is so plush I have the urge to slip off my heels and dig my toes into it. But I don't do that because a man who resembles a deeply tanned Chris Evans walks in from the hallway with a smile worthy of a game show host.

"Chablis Shields?" He says.

"Lorenzo St. James?"

He shakes my hand firmly. "Yes, we talked on Tuesday. So good to meet you. Purple hair highlights make you positively regal. You're going to be a lovely bride."

I blush. "You're so sweet. Thank you."

"You're quite welcome. Now, where's the groom-to-be?"

"He should be here in a few minutes."

Lorenzo moves to take a folder from the receptionist, then turns to me. "We can wait together and chit-chat. Luna said to tell you hello. She had an appointment tonight, but we'll work with you as a team for the wedding."

I check out Luna's picture on wall. She looks like a petite Gabrielle Union. I am *dying* to find out their love story.

"Diamond raved about your company after her big day," I say.

"Yes, she had requested a classic Hollywood theme. Dorothy Dandridge-styled dress. I remember. Do you have a theme for your day?"

Hmm? I don't think *make us look dope* is a theme. "No, but I lean toward contemporary."

"She means romantic. It has to be romantic."

The glass door swings shut behind John. He and Lorenzo greet one another before Lorenzo points us toward the hallway. "Let me show you to our conference room. I'll have Jennifer bring us some water and we'll get started."

Inside the room, the future hubby pulls out my chair before we sit at the table.

"What's that?" He eyeballs the notebook I slide from my backpack.

"My event notes." I flip a few pages with magazine pictures pasted on them. "What you got over there?"

He scrolls on his phone. "My notes."

"Exactly how long have you been writing stuff down?"

"Since New Year's Day."

"So you knew I was going to say yes?"

"If you didn't, I was going to keep asking until you did. I love a challenge." He reaches over and fingers one of my notebook pages. "When did you start clipping things from magazines?"

"Am I in trouble if I answer that truthfully?"

"Maybe."

"Valentines Day."

"You know what, I'm offended." John gives me a pained look, grabbing his chest. "I am genuinely hurt. I thought you were feeling the same way I did on New Year's?"

Before I can react to him, Lorenzo returns along with a woman I assume is Jennifer. She passes out bottles of Aquafina and leaves.

41

"I, for one, am glad both of you decided to marry," he says, sitting down across from us. "If you hadn't, Luxurious Events wouldn't have had the chance to work with you." He scoots to the table. "I've been over the number you emailed us, along with the timing you presented. Wedding for the first Saturday of October. Budget around eight thousand dollars. If costs rise based on your requests, would you consider wedding financing?"

John turns to me. "We probably should have talked about this too, huh?"

"Yup," I say. "I'm guessing you're against it?"

"We're making our decisions together, but yeah, I'm against it. I don't think we'll need it." He turns to Lorenzo. "Nah, we'll stay out of financing. We're good."

Lorenzo sips his water. "That's perfectly fine. Luna and I once worked on a dazzling Center City wedding on a tight budget. We planned and executed that event within three months. If we did that, we could do this."

That's a relief because if I had to coordinate everything, I'd panic every day for the next six months.

"I want to let you know, we need you as much as you need us." Lorenzo rests a Cross pen on his black leather notepad. "For years, Google listed Luxurious Events in the top ten of Philadelphia-area wedding planners. But we parted ways with a difficult bride last year, and she was an elite YELP commenter. She spread the word that she didn't like our services. Suddenly we received one star reviews and unsubstantiated opinions. So, your approval of our work is vital. We must build our brand again, one client at a time."

What a Bridezilla! "I'm so sorry," I say.

"Thank you. I didn't mean to burden you, but I wanted you to know we have extra incentive to make your day a masterpiece." Lorenzo brightens. "Now here's the fun part. What did you have in mind?"

John taps my thigh. "Ladies first."

"Age before beauty."

Lorenzo clicks his pen. "I'll break the tie. Chablis, you have a lovely notebook there, so you go first."

I flip through pages. "Three hundred guests. I'd like seven men to stand with John. Seven women with me. The Rise sanctuary should be filled with imported deep orange, red, and yellow flowers—they'll make our Instagram pictures come alive. A Philadelphia Orchestra cellist to play "Your Precious Love" when I walk down the aisle. A huge, rented mansion for our reception with a PHILADANCO! performance before the dinner hour. The reception entrance draped completely in white flowers. Luxe fabric draped against a ceiling made entirely of twinkling white lights. Inside the reception, every area should be draped in luxury decorations. Long reception tables with dangling orchids hanging from the chandeliers. Our dating and engagement photos should be black and white blow-ups as a huge reception backdrop—a total celebrity move. The first dance should have an ethereal atmosphere from a fog machine. White flowers bursting from every tier of our wedding cake. Artist-designed menus and food entrees. And last but not least, exiting in a hot-air balloon as Vivaldi plays in the background."

I'm out of breath when I finish and look up.

Lorenzo has both hands over his mouth.

John looks stunned.

"Baby, um," he stammers. "You're throwing things out there for fun. Right?"

"No." I shut my notebook.

Lorenzo clears his throat, sips more water, then nods at John. "John, would you like to share your ideas?"

John glances at his phone screen. "Rise Church ceremony with plenty of greenery and white rose arrangements at the altar. Incorporating the Pantone color of the year: Living Coral. Seventy guests. Two men and two women to stand with us. Suspended greenery and mini park benches at the reception. Oh, yeah, and we need a healthy food buffet and a traditional wedding cake."

When he finishes, he winks at me.

I stare back at him.

How does he know the Pantone color of the year?

"Thank you both for sharing," Lorenzo says, taking notes. "Now we need to strike a balance between a sweet romantic wedding and New York City during fashion week."

John holds up both hands. "Honestly, I'm flexible as long as we stick to our budget. If I fight for anything, it'll be the Art Museum park decorations."

Lorenzo directs his azure eyes to me. "Chablis, some things you mentioned are quite expensive. A hot-air balloon rental alone will swallow ninety percent of your budget. Add on professional performers, a mansion rental, excessive luxury decorations, a large wedding party, and artist-designed food, and that's a fifty-thousand dollar price tag." He stops to write something inside his folder "John's ideas fit your budget much better, but we'll definitely work to include glamorous, contemporary touches. How does that sound?"

I tap my toe and wait patiently for John to tell Lorenzo he changed his mind, and he's open to the financing option. He doesn't. I catch him turning off his phone alarm—the one that tells him he needs to drink a protein shake soon.

This *is* the biggest day of my life and everyone wants to keep things simple and understated. That's easy for them, but I was left for dead years ago. Broken and shattered and weak. I'm alive and kicking today, and I need our wedding day to shine, doggone it!

Staying cool at this moment is the name of the game though. I clasp my hands together and say, "Yes, that's fine."

No disrespect to future hubs, but somehow, I *will* figure out how to make our day more spectacular.

mother-in-love

"MY COMBAT STRATEGIES ARE SICK, I'm telling you."
I fire laser beams from my virtual rifle. "See there! Check out how I
protected you. I'm unstoppable!"

Tonight, John's older brother Nate is my teammate as we battle
giant zippy robots in Gundam Versus. He should show gratitude for
me being on his side because he can't win this fight without me.

"Stop yapping and play!" Nate's fingers fly across his game
controller.

"I'm just saying—"

"I get it. Keep firing!"

All this goes on in Nate's living room while John showers and
changes upstairs. He promised to cook dinner for us. As long as he
doesn't have us eating turtle eggs and wheatgrass, I'm down.

The smell of Dove men's body wash and John's thudding footsteps announce him when he approaches the couch.

"Ready for dinner?" He leans over to give me a forehead kiss.

Oh no! A robot threatens to defeat our two-man team. I employ
Boost Dash. "Take that!"

"Sunshine?"

"Uh-huh."

"Come on, keep me company while I cook."

"Oh, all right." I slide my game controller onto the coffee table. A bionic representative just beat us. The loss stings, but I won't let it show. "I'll redeem myself later."

Nate resets the game. "Redeem yourself? Girl, you know you can't play as good as me. I'm too smooth with it."

John's already heading into the kitchen, so I yell over my shoulder as I follow him. "Next week, all right. Same time, bro, I'll be right here fighting in style!"

Nate is a thirty-two-year-old, clean-shaven, wiry version of my beloved who has no problem wearing his rimless glasses. I adore him. He makes me feel like the little sister he's never had.

His Bala Cynwyd townhouse is wonderful. I hang out here a lot because John has lived here since he moved back from Germany. Nate owns butter-soft cappuccino-colored leather couches and chairs, CB2 cane glass coffee and side tables, and of course, the large screen Smart TV. He also has satellite service, a PlayStation 4, Xbox 360, a Keurig K-Supreme coffee maker, and other items my minimalist lifestyle doesn't include.

Nate works as a sales rep for CapGreen Pharmaceuticals. When he's not traveling, gaming helps him relax. Marriage didn't work out for him, and I've never met his ex-wife, Sarah. John told me she wasn't loyal to his brother. I looked her up on Facebook last year. She's a kindergarten teacher who looks like a Nigerian supermodel, and when she's not displaying pics of colorful art projects her students made, she posts photos of herself posing with one hot guy after another. If she did that when she was married, I understand how the habit wouldn't sit well with her husband.

Inside the kitchen, John stands by the stove prepping sirloin for the broiler. Soft gray lounging pants embrace his legs and a thin, white t-shirt hugs his muscular shoulders. For a few minutes, I watch him play the role of my personal G. Garvin. A beautiful man who prays *and* cooks for me? Yes! God truly loves me!

"I have something to run past you." I take a seat at the kitchen table. "But first, do I need to check your Instagram today?"

"Nah. Everything's good. What about you? Get any comments from brothers saying more than congratulations?"

"Oh, please. Miss me with that, okay. You know my history." I switch my gaze to the window so I can stop staring at his physique. "I figured out a solution for the wedding. There's a way for us to both have what we want."

"No hot air balloons this time, right?" He laughs.

"How about I save that for our baby announcement in a few years?" I roll my eyes. "Anyway, Nikki told me we can request a combination worship service slash wedding. Since the Rise sanctuary seats up to two thousand, we can invite everyone we know to worship with us as we get married. After, we can still have that garden reception dinner with the roses just like you asked for, but that would only be for a small group of people."

"Sounds fine to me, but have you talked to my mom at all?"

"I'll text her tomorrow or something."

"She hates texts and she might not like the idea of us inviting everyone to a wedding worship service, then only feeding dinner to a select few."

"How come?"

"Cause she's still mad Nate eloped in Hawaii." John sprinkles garlic salt over the steamed broccoli. "I know my mom. She's gonna want all my family and most of her friends at our reception."

"If she'd like to contribute money to the budget so she can have that, that's cool. But it's our wedding. It's supposed to be what we want."

"Oh, I thought that too." Nate walks to the refrigerator, sliding in right on time for this conversation. "I was the black sheep for a year after I got married."

I keep my mouth shut, but I'm thinking that might have been because of the wife he chose.

"You know what, I'll ask Ms. Pat about it." I stand and move to the cupboard by the sink. We need some glasses on the table. "She might surprise us and love the idea."

"Okay, get your phone and let's call her." John reaches into the overhead cabinet and pulls out a stack of white plates.

I place drinking glasses on the table, then rush to the living room and pull my device from my bag. I've missed five texts, three of them from Nikki. And two voice mails, one from Luna and one from Mom. I send a quick return text to my best friend. I'll call Mom and Luna later.

Back in the kitchen, my stomach growls. The aroma of broiled steak with mushrooms and onions floats through the air. Our dinner is almost ready.

Instead of calling Ms. Pat, I sit down and dash off a message to her:

> Hi! This is Chablis. What do you think about me and John holding a huge wedding worship service and then having an exclusive reception for a small group of guests?

John serves our food, we pray together, and we're busy chowing down when I get her response.

> Stop it with the silly texts. Come visit me like a grown woman.

I drop my fork.

This is from my future mother-in-love?

John glances at my face. "What's the matter?"

My phone lays face up on my lap, so I swipe it and lock the screen fast. That text was from the woman who gave birth to him. If I fuss about it, it'll cause a different type of problem for us. One even bigger than salty comments from his ex-women or clashing wedding ideas.

"You know what?" I grab the shaker and sprinkle pepper on my steamed broccoli. "There's time in my schedule tomorrow before dance class. I'll swing over and pay your mom a visit and describe the new wedding option."

Nate and John quit chewing and stare at me.

"Guys." I pick up my fork. "Everything will be fine."

They glance at one another and communicate without words. Then both of them say, in concert, "All right then."

Ms. Pat is a substantial woman. Flat-chested with wide shoulders but nonexistent hips, she's built like a walking exclamation point. She always pulls her wavy hair into a tight bun that gives her an instant facelift. She's also pretty tall, like John, so she looks down on me with her protruding light brown eyes, and when she does, it actually *feels* like she's looking down on me.

This is what she does behind the metal screen door while I stand on her old-fashioned wide front porch, waiting for her to invite me in.

"May I come in?" I force a smile onto my face and kindness into my voice.

She says nothing and pushes the screen door open wide so I can finally step inside.

I like her luxurious, white swivel barrel chairs, but she covered the snow-colored sofas with clear plastic. People still do that? Glass frames hold Nate and John's sports, high school, and college graduation pictures across her wooden tables. No clutter or knick-knacks. According to the brothers Gerald, she loves to cook just like my mom, but I don't smell food. No Glade or Yankee Candles either. If I wasn't looking at the human who owns this home, I wouldn't think anyone lives here.

"May I sit?" I point to the loveseat.

"Certainly."

"I'm glad I caught you today." The frigid plastic chills me when I sit on it. I clutch my bag in my lap and ignore the feeling. "How are you doing?"

"Fine." She brushes imaginary lint from her tan pants.

"Uh, I stopped through today to get your opinion about our wedding plans. We have a small budget for the wedding. My parents are providing all they can and John and I are grateful for their contributions, but we know lots of people and we'd like to have as many there as possible. What we can do is ask for a marriage worship service we invite everyone to, and then we can have an intimate reception later for a select group. To me, that seems like the best way to have something large and small at the same time. We sure would like your view on everything before we talk to the wedding planners again."

"John? He wants my opinion?" She rolls her eyes. "Really?"

"Well, um, it's my alternative plan and I want your opinion."

"I can't believe either of you stopped to ask me anything." She crosses her arms against her chest. "All winter, I hardly heard from him. Then he leads you in here with a diamond on your finger and I'm supposed to jump for joy. I didn't know he wanted to marry you."

"Apparently he does." I sit up straighter. "I love your son. He's a wonderful man."

"I thought he was only casually seeing you." Ms. Pat's arms stay strapped across her body, creasing her white button-down shirt. "Can I be honest with you, Chablis?"

"Of course."

"No offense. I'm sure you're an okay person, but I spent years praying he would connect with Trina again and marry her. They had something special."

I don't know what to say to this. It's hard to ignore pictures of John and Trina on the marble mantel above Ms. Pat's fireplace. There's John, holding Trina's hand as they pose at some party. Another one of them from a Royal Caribbean cruise vacation.

There's even one of Trina and Ms. Pat hugging and smiling. Hearing Trina's name doesn't shock me. But the look in Ms. Pat's eyes tells me it crushes her to peep the engagement ring on my finger.

"John and Trina? They were meant to be together," she insists, still looking at me like I'm a mistake. "But ooh! That son of mine can be so headstrong. Him and his life plans—"

"Life plans?"

"Oh, you didn't know?" Her eyes zero in on mine. "He plans to be married before he turns thirty because he doesn't want to be too old when he starts his family. I can certainly understand why he chose you. You're the right age. You share his faith. Healthy, just like him. And you're his close buddy. You'll do."

I'll do?

Like I'm number two? John's second choice?

Is that the real reason John only wants a simple wedding?

Uh-uh! No! The devil is a lie, and I *will not* plug into Ms. Pat's obvious attempt to rattle me.

"John and I love each other deeply." I stare back at her. "If he has a life plan, its designed by God to include me. Now, what do you think of my wedding idea?"

"I hate it." She finally uncrosses those arms. "This will be the first time I'll see one of my sons marry. I want to experience something better than that."

In five and a half months, I'll be this woman's daughter-in-law. Why do I have to call her Ms. Pat?

"I see. Well, uh. Ms. Pat, would it be okay if I call you Mom now?"

She brushes away fake lint again. "No, you've been raised. You have your own mother."

I bite my lip so hard I'm surprised it doesn't bleed. And I'm only doing that because my parents and the Bible taught me to treat elders with respect. Now if I was orphaned and unsaved? John might ask for the ring back after I cuss his mother out.

"Ms. Pat, I have a line dance class to go to, so I'm gonna leave now." I stand. As heavy as I feel, I will walk out of this house with my head held high.

She walks me to the door and seconds later, I escape the ice queen's realm. On the sidewalk, I walk past neat brick homes and inhale fresh April air while exhaling negativity.

Ms. Pat considers me a second choice, prays for John to change his mind about Trina, and won't let me call her mother. Unreal, but I'm more shook up about Ms. Pat's attitude than about John's former relationship with Trina. I know why they broke up: Trina didn't really want to be married. From what John told me, she only took his ring because she didn't want to hurt his feelings. She wanted to focus on her career—and when she shared that with John, he ended their engagement.

I climb into my car and sit for a moment, closing my eyes and letting my emotions die down. I'm fine. Hurt and shaken inside, but fine. She'd have to chase me down the street and threaten to beat me up before I'd panic.

When I whip out my phone to scroll through my calendar app, a reminder pops up, telling me about practice for a special event at The Grandstand in June. My line dancers are producing a benefit for the Philly Social Dance scholarship fund. When will I have time for that? Point blank, I won't. Whatever I thought I was doing before, I'm canceling. From now on, I'll double-down and show Ms. Pat, and anyone else who thinks I'm so little of me, that I'm not some second-rate choice.

I tap to play my one voice mail message. It's from John, asking about my private chat with the woman who birthed him.

I press for callback.

He answers.

I squawk. "What do you wanna know first, huh? Which heart-breaking thing do you want to hear? Take your pick!"

"Whoa, whoa, whoa! What happened?"

Streaks of white bird poop decorate my windshield. That's funny, considering what Ms. Pat just told me.

"Did you know she's been praying you'll fall back in love with Trina and marry her?" I say with a sigh. "It's the John and Trina show in living color all over her fireplace. I've seen those pictures before, but now she pushed them to the front like a shrine."

"You can't be serious!"

"John, something's off about this. What is it about Trina that your mom likes so much?"

"They like the same things. They used to hang out even when I wasn't around. She was like the daughter my mom always wanted, but she never had, and Mom always loved that Trina became a lawyer. I think our breakup hurt Mom more than me. Listen, none of that is about you, so don't take it personal."

"Oh, I know she has nothing against me personally." I stare at those messy white splotches on my window. "In fact, she told me she's sure I'm an okay person. Do you have a life plan?"

"A what?"

"A life plan. Stuff you want to do before you turn thirty. Like a bucket list."

"Bucket list? I mean, I have goals, but you know those. What's your point?"

"Your mother said she understands I fit right into your life plan so that's why you proposed."

"Aye, yo! Now I'm getting mad. She can't talk to you like that!"

"Wait, there's more." I hold the phone in front of my mouth and shift my position in the driver's seat. "She told me I can't call her Mom because I've been raised and I have my own mother."

"I promise you, I'm handling this." His baritone voice morphs into a deep growl. "She's my mom and I honor her, but you're going to be my wife, and I'm not letting her disrespect you. I should have taken those pictures and trashed them years ago. We'll all be family soon and if she doesn't know you enough, she'll get to know you and love you like I do."

It would tick him off more if I tattled his mother's exact words about me.

Just thinking about that makes my heart ache.

"I'm packing up my stuff and driving over there," John says. "Listen, please don't dwell on what she said. Enjoy your dance time. Can you do that for me?"

"I'll try. Just, when you see her, don't go off on her." I say, still hoping I wake up from this nightmare. "It's better if you let her know how you really feel about me, so she understands your heart. You don't want her to have any hard feelings about us. Okay?"

"Okay. Message me when you get to the Grandstand. Let me know you're safe."

We end the call, and I sit in silence. I'm calmer now. Future hubby is on my side. Mine. When I look through the windshield, somehow the bird poop doesn't bother me as much. It takes a second to click the lever that sprays blue cleaning fluid and sets my wipers in motion.

A moment later, and that crap is gone.

worth it

"NIK?" I open one eye and peek at my best friend.

"I'm listening," Nikki says.

"Don't fall asleep in that chair."

Two brown women, one long and lean, one athletic with curves, relax with their feet inside sudsy warm water—me and Nikki at Modern Nails. The gel manicures are complete and neither of us wants to mess them up. We rest our hands lightly on the tan massage chair armrests and breathe in the scent of fresh nail polish.

Mani-pedis on a Saturday afternoon with my best sister-friend. Nothing like it.

Nikki's eyes are shut, her head tilted back. "I'm awake."

"We got numbers back from Luna. She and Lorenzo are talented folks, but they're not magicians. With a formal meal, hors d'oeuvres, and a cash bar, we have to cap the invites at eighty to stick to our budget. They found us a banquet hall with a private garden, and that fits in with John's ideas, so no mansion." I jump when the technician slides her fingertips across the sole of my foot. "I have my eye on this lace sheath Allure Bridals gown I found online; it has beading throughout it and a chapel length train. I'd look like royalty in it, but it costs seventeen hundred. And I want to invite at least another hundred people to the wedding... and I know this sounds bananas, but... to make a long story short, I'm thinking of getting a small loan. Like fifteen thousand dollars?"

She points a pale, pink-painted nail at me. "That is the *dumbest* thing I've ever heard you say."

If anyone else had said that to me, I'd have gotten mad. From Nikosia Perry? I'll let her slide. She's the first friend I met at Rise and there's no malice in her heart.

But, I'm sorry, this queen ain't eating hotdogs and Fritos at her wedding.

"Not dumb. Just a different way of doing things. Nik, I've got my one chance to be a dope queen for a day. You want me to play small? I hate that it even comes down to this."

"I still hate the idea," Nikki says. "And I'm not letting you start your marriage with a lie."

"It's not a lie. I love John, and I'll tell him. There's no way I'd deceive him like that."

"I thought he told you no financing."

"He did, but I think I can handle this on my own. It would be a bank loan with an interest rate lower than my Visa and I'd start paying it back with my own salary."

"Girl! Get up! Right now!"

"Whassamatter?" I stand with my feet still in the water.

"Your pants are on fire!"

Both the petite technicians working on our feet hide their smiles, trying to stop giggling. Okay, I'm a little humiliated. Whatever.

I ease back into the comfort of the massage chair. "I'm going to sit and enjoy this girlfriend time and feed you a delicious dinner later on, even though I might leave you on the curb afterward."

"No, you won't."

"Watch me."

"Some best friend."

I reach over and pinch her bony arm. "Help me figure out what to do. I told you John's mom treats me like I'm nobody."

"We prayed about her earlier, and you already told me John set her straight." Nikki admires her beautifully manicured nails. "If you try to do anything else and bring drama into your own life, you're going to suffer."

I settle into silence. Both of our chairs rumble and massage away while technicians pamper our feet. I'm almost back in relaxation mode when Nikki pulls me out.

"It's only a wedding." She reaches over and pinches me back, then strokes my skin. "You know your worth, and that loan idea is prideful."

"Did you have to use the P-word?"

"Want some scripture to go with that? Highlight Proverbs 11:2 in your YouVersion. When you're done with that, move on to James 4:6."

On an average day, it's okay being close to a preacher's kid who was raised in the Church of God in Christ. That kid grew into a kind-hearted, sweet-voiced high school counselor. She doesn't hit anyone with a Bible verse until she feels she has to convict them. Today I am that person. But she wasn't in the room when Ms. Pat told me I'm an 'okay' person. That still stings.

I'm beyond torn—time to change the subject.

"Doing anything next Saturday?" I ask her.

"No."

"What if we have dinner next week? Me and John and you and Terry? It'll be fun."

Terry, aka Terrence Weeks, is John's best friend. He and John have been buddies since middle school. They're a lot alike. Both of them are undercover blerds. Black nerds. One time I walked in on them having a heated argument over who has more money: Bruce Wayne or Tony Stark.

"Oh no, I see what this is," she says with a laugh. "You want Terry and me to join you in marriage land next year?"

"It could happen."

"He's nice, but he's a package deal."

Terry has five-year-old twin daughters with a woman named Roslyn, who he broke up with two years ago. He adores Nikki, though, and they always have a great time when they're hanging out with John and me.

"He likes you a lot." I remind her.

"That's... flattering."

"You still holding out for a man with no kids?"

"I don't have any. Why should I settle for a man who already has them? Men with small kids who don't love the woman who made them confuse me. Terry's a decent brother, but I can't look him in the face without thinking about Roslyn. The lady had twins with him and didn't marry him."

"Sometimes relationships don't work out."

"And sometimes brothers need to try a little harder, that's all I'm saying. And why are you playing matchmaker suddenly?" She removes her dripping feet, and the tech drains the basin.

"So when John and I have our babies, you'll be Auntie Nikki and Uncle Terry."

"We'll be that, anyway. Just make us the godparents."

"You have an answer for everything."

"Sure do. Ask me where I want to go for dinner."

"Where you wanna go?" I pull my feet from the fragrant water.

"HoneyGrow."

HoneyGrow salads are a quintessential blend of healthy and delectable. After we select custom toppings, they make them fast and fresh right in front of us. We receive friendly service with a smile, which I'm sure is cleverly designed to keep us from wondering how we spent forty-five dollars on lettuce leaves, fancy toppings, and bottled water.

We choose a table at the back of the restaurant and FaceTime Stacey Robins-McClain, so she's here with us having the first bridesmaids dinner even though she's out of town with her husband. Stacey is good people. For years, we served together with the Help Squad ministry. Last December, she got married and joined her new hubby at a church outside of Philly, so I don't see her as often as I used to. But she's another great friend I've known since I joined Rise, so I added her to the bridesmaids crew.

My cousin Mariah will be my third bridesmaid, and her daughter, Binky, will be my junior bridesmaid. I wanted them here at dinner too, but Mariah is working at eatLARGE tonight, and Binky had plans with her friends.

"Living Coral?" Stacey's voice echoes through the phone as Nikki and I eat our salads.

"It's the Pantone color of the year," I explain.

"He knows the Pantone color of the year?"

"We're talking about the man who planned a drone video proposal thingy. Luna told me coral goes well with gold, so those colors will work for us."

"Also goes good with ocean blue."

"How do you know?" I ask.

"I'm on my laptop, Googling coral bouquets and other stuff. So, for our jewelry, are you thinking—"

Stacey's voice gets cut off by my phone buzzing. I jump slightly when I see the caller ID.

Patricia Gerald.

Nikki's eyes grow wide. "Chablis? Your face!"

"Stacey, we'll call you back in a few minutes." I scoop up the phone and stand, tapping to end FaceTime and switch to the new call. "I should take this outside."

Nikki nods, watching me as I make my way out of the restaurant.

With my hand on the glass door, I take a deep breath and put a smile on my face, forcing myself to sound pleasant. "Hi, Ms. Pat!"

"Good evening. Did I catch you at a bad time?"

"I'm having dinner with my bridesmaids right now, but I can take a minute away."

"Chablis, I'll keep this short. I just ended a call with John."

Oh no!

"And we talked about the wedding."

Dear Lord!

"He explained the budget and how you specifically requested performers and other features. Is that true?"

I pace back and forth, trying to figure out how to admit I'd like bigger and better without seeming needy. When I look through the window, Nikki gives me a thumbs up and motions prayer hands. She's praying for me. I appreciate her.

"That's right." I force myself to stand still. "Our budget is tight for some things I mentioned to Luxurious Events."

"Yes, well, the bride's family usually pays for everything."

"I know."

"But in this case, I think you should hold the wedding you truly desire."

Do I hear right? Are Nikki's prayers working?

"At our meeting the other day, John said my words may have upset you. He's since been clear with me about how much he loves you. He knows you want to invite more people to the wedding, and he asked if I could help with a few thousand. I can do that. I'll send him money for the wedding budget. If you need more, I'm here."

"I... uh..." I stutter. "I don't know what to say. Thank you."

"You're welcome. There's just one thing. Would you mind if I had input into the guest list?"

I breathe out my relief. I don't care who Ms. Pat adds from John's family. The more the merrier.

"We'll definitely invite as many family members as we can." I tell her.

"Oh, this is a friend of mine."

"Friends are fine too."

"So you wouldn't mind Trina attending? She's still a close friend of mine, and she wishes nothing but the best for John."

Wait a minute! Hold on! I'm not insecure about my relationship with John, but I do have standards.

Future hubby's former fiancée? At our wedding?

Oh, what the HECK NO!

I glance through the plate-glass window at Nikki as my cheeks burn. The next thing I know, she's out of her seat, dashing toward the door.

I whip around, clutching the phone to my ear. "Ms. Pat, thank you," I say cautiously as Nikki's hand lands on my shoulder. "But no, thank you. We'll be fine. You can keep your cash!"

"But John said—"

"I'll talk to him later about it. Goodbye."

I end the call as Nikki mouths *why, why, why*.

Ignoring her, I step away so I can circle the building to walk out my anger.

That woman! It's like I can't ever talk to her without hearing an insult or Trina's name. That's not normal, and she's messing up every warm feeling I thought I'd have for my mother-in-love. Okay, I definitely want to build a great relationship with her and the rest of the Gerald clan. I should probably call her back about that money, but I won't. Nope.

So what if she is John's mother?

I wouldn't take that witch's money if she owned Fort Knox.

control issues

I'M that chick who submits everything to God in prayer, so I'm *definitely* praying for guidance and strength. Peace, too, because I have feelings and Ms. Pat hurt them. I don't get her obsession with Trina, and it's crystal clear: the future mother-in-law does *not* care about me.

Despite all that, the Lord probably gave me a shot of wisdom through Nikki's words—if I want to listen.

Nikki's such a dope friend—she deserves a good man to treat her like a treasure. One who can have her feeling like God scoured her prayer journals and vision boards and delivered her heart's desire.

And Terry is like John's brother from another mother. He's a real smart guy with an African meets metropolitan style—short, neat afro, full beard, and beaded bracelets. It was an easy decision to introduce him to Nikki last August. They both work in academia. Terry is a Curriculum Director for a charter school. So, yeah, I still think it would be incredible for Nikki and Terry to jump the broom.

Tonight Nikki doesn't mention what she said about Terry last week, and I don't talk about it either. They sit next to one another, joking like they go back to dollar movies and Tahitian Treat. So funny. She hates me playing matchmaker, but if she hadn't pushed me to ask John for fitness and nutrition advice years ago, we wouldn't even be here.

Inside SOUTH, the four of us share appetizers and entrees. Cornbread and collard greens and duck breast and crab cakes and classic mac and cheese. I eat a little of everything and it makes me way too thirsty. When John excuses himself to go to the restroom, I sashay to the bar in the front room to buy an extra bottle of water for the drive home.

"Chablis?"

I turn around fast, and Mike Roberts approaches with a sly grin. Mike is this guy who runs a gym in Manayunk and rides motorcycles as a hobby. He's also *fine* with a capital F. I dated him for a minute back when John worked in Berlin, wasn't sure he'd return to the states, and besides all that, we were still only friends.

"Hey, Mike." I lean close to the polished wood bar, remembering his passionate kisses and how I almost let myself drive to his apartment for more than kissing after our date.

He steps to me with open arms. "I'd know those curves anywhere. What up? Can a brotha get a hug? You still dancing all over Philly?"

I lean in for a quick, loose, embrace. "Oh, every chance I get. What're you up to lately?"

"Studying physical therapy now and I'm still riding with my boys on the weekend. I see you changed your hair from pink to purple. Looks nice on you. Yeah. Real nice." His grin spreads wider and he licks his lips. "Been a minute since we talked. You ever get someone to keep that body warm at night, 'cause I'm available anytime. Who you here with?"

My eyes scan the restaurant. John's not the jealous type, but I don't want him to walk out and get the wrong idea. "Actually, I'm here with my fiancé and friends." I stretch my hand out so Mike can peep my ring. "I'm getting married in October and I've never been happier."

"Good for you, girl! Man, I missed my chance." He whistles, then stares in my eyes like he means what he's saying. "Make sure he treats you good, darling. Because if he don't, Imma be here waiting. A brother could hold your sweetness all night long, know what I'm saying?"

And I should say goodbye and step away from the bar.

But for some reason, I don't.

I stare in Mike's dark eyes for a long moment, and one word enters my brain as we practically occupy the same space.

Easy.

Some things are too easy.

Like co-signed by Satan and seven demons easy.

John wants me to wait for intimacy with him, but this guy wouldn't. This brotha with the texturized mohawk and customized motorcycle jacket and those luscious lips? A wink from me. A whisper. A secret phone call. Just that quick we could meet late at night, light fragrant candles, and listen to sultry love songs. He'd flirt. I'd laugh. He'd get closer. I'd free myself to do more. We'd make a this-is-not-a-love-thing agreement. Use a condom. Drift into satisfaction. Walk away the next day.

And that disgusting split-second thought turns my stomach inside out.

I need air. Right now.

"You take care of yourself," I blurt out and push past Mike, moving faster with each step, until I almost fly past Nikki standing by the hostess desk.

She passes me my purse. "Where's your water? And who was that talking to you? Do I know him?"

I don't answer because John walks out of the restroom and he appears larger than normal. Even though he's yards away from the front of the restaurant, I know he sees sweat beads on my forehead.

With or without my friends, I gotta go.

One step, then two, three, and I'm outside on the sidewalk, cruising away from the outdoor tables, heading anywhere in the fresh air.

Keep moving.

Get air!

Nikki rushes to my side so fast it shocks me and I stop. Warm wind. Ground beneath my feet. Hard city concrete equals pain if I land on it and mind turns inside out and I'm the me I used to be strutting around with an incredible body and wicked thoughts that lead to sinful actions and something could happen and somebody's gonna get hurt and it'll be me and Lord please Jesus help me God.

My purse crashes to the ground and the world fades before me.

"Chablis!" Nikki grabs hold of me. "Guys! She's panicking!"

Air. Please. More air. Breathe in. Hold for seven. Out. No dirty alley. No beating. No broken body. Breathe in. Hold. What's real? Nikki. She smells good. Like Prada perfume. Breathe out. What else? Window with the white SOUTH menu pasted on it. SOUTH. Yes. We had dinner. Breathe. Real. Hold. This is my life today. Out.

No danger. Forget the past. Breathe. Live.

John's powerful arms peel me from Nikki's grasp, and he presses me to his chest. "I've got you, Sunshine. I'm here."

Fresh oxygen flows in and out of my lungs when my beloved holds me and my friends surround me.

"Chablis, we can drive you home so you can rest." Nikki rubs my back.

John squeezes me tighter. "No, this is my life right there in my arms. I have to take care of her." One of his arms leaves my back and I hear his keys jingle. "Terry, take my keys and bring the Jeep around. I'm in the Broad Street lot."

"You got it, bruh." Terry grabs the keys and takes off in a rush down the sidewalk.

I'm still trembling and I wish the whole thing had never happened, but in John's embrace, I keep breathing and settle down. In his arms I experience two things no stolen moment of passion could ever make me feel.

Chosen and treasured.

In bed, John and I gaze at one another.

Thank God for FaceTime.

John wears his glasses with the thick lenses. He's comfortable with me. Other than Nate and I, no one sees him transform from Superman during the day to Clark Kent at night.

The bottom of John's face is slack, full lips turned down. It's like he's processing events that happened before today, plus the panic attack tonight, and maybe even the next four months and beyond.

"I wanted to stay with you tonight," he says. "But, you know—"

"Yeah, I know the deal. I might call Dr. Jerrica tomorrow."

"Want to talk about what happened?"

Colossians 3:9 fills my brain. *Do not lie to each other, since you have taken off your old self with its practices.* Still, I don't want to panic again. I'll keep it simple.

I hug my pillow. "Saw a guy I used to talk to and something about him triggered me. I ran out for air and... that close to the dirty street, then Nikki ran behind me... it was too much."

"Share something else?"

"Okay."

"Me and Terry and Nate and the men at Rise and your job. How come none of us trigger you?"

"Men in general don't bother me. When I was little cousin Aaron walked me from elementary school to Memaw's house every afternoon. Daddy and Grandpop. My wild uncles and crazy cousins—they all loved and protected me. If God hadn't placed them around me, I couldn't have opened my heart to you. You're one of the good ones." I breathe in deep, and blow air out slowly, my pillow twisted in my grasp. "The beating... wasn't... all men don't snap and—"

"Shh, you don't have to say anymore, it's all right." He flips around on his bed and turns off his lamp. Darkness behind him. The screen shakes and his phone slips down. When he appears again, his glasses are gone.

"What are you doing?" I ask.

"Showing you something. Can you turn off your light?" He blinks and pulls his phone further out.

I do what he asks, and except for the soft moonlight that peeks through my venetian blinds, I'm in the dark now too.

"Can you see me?" He asks.

"Yes."

He closes his eyes, then opens them. "In the dark, without my contacts in, you're a blur to me. But it doesn't matter because I can still see the shape of you. I see you with my heart and I love you more than you can imagine, and it's always going to be that way for me. You know what I'm saying?"

This man knows my sensitive issues, and I know all of his, and we're still here for one another. If I could reach through the screen, I swear it feels like my fingertips could brush John's soul. This type of intimacy is so much more than our bodies; it's about vulnerability and acceptance.

I could curl up here forever.

He slides his black-rimmed glasses back on and the screen shakes again. "I've been thinking. Tonight you broke down, and I wanted to do anything to make sure you were fine. I need to make sure we're good from now through the wedding and beyond. What I'm doing for us right now isn't good enough. You know how much the dinner bill was tonight?"

"No."

"Two hundred and five dollars."

"Yeah, but that was between you and Terry."

"Nah, I carried the whole thing, plus the thirty for our parking. Terry didn't have it because his cash is low this month. I figured I'd cover it so we could all have a good time, but see, that's the same attitude I had when I let my debt build up."

"Don't beat yourself up."

"No, Chablis." He shudders, looking like he's searching for the right words. "I know what you wanted for the wedding, and how you want us to live later. If I don't get practical fast—"

I bring my phone closer so he can't miss the serious expression on my face. "You listen to me. You work hard, you train hard, and you're my rock. Anything, and I mean *anything* we need, we'll figure it out."

"I'm about to get emotional. I don't have the words to describe how much I love you."

"We're two imperfect folk trying to make it through. That's all. Now pray for us so we can go to sleep and get up for church tomorrow."

He does that and we end the call.

I shut my phone off and toss it to the other side of my messy bed.

I know one thing; I don't want John to worry about me. Sometimes panic happens, but I refuse to let it control me. I have less and less of it each year. And what I'd like for our wedding? I'll have to think of a solution I can carry on my own.

My pink body pillow does a wonderful job holding me up, but honestly, I'd love to press a hyper-speed button, say I do, and rest my head on my husband's shoulder at night.

If I cried, my tears would become his tears. My joys his as well. And his sorrows?

Mine.

money moves

OUR WEDDING SITUATION? I must take the reins for a few reasons. First, I don't want John to stress about my grandiose desires for the big day. He contributed what he could. Second, my precious parents gave us the money they could spare—I'm not going back to them. Third, no way on God's green earth will I accept a darn thing from Ms. Pat.

I'm taking it all on me.

I've been over and over and over this a million times and every time I dismiss the thought, I see the transformed fantasy wedding vision of myself slipping away. I only have one actual option left to keep the dream alive.

I woke up this morning, and emailed my team to tell them I'm taking paid time off until noon.

Bright and early, I'm in Southwest Philly, headed straight into the QwestLife Federal Credit Union. At the main desk, I tap the glass screened kiosk to enter my information and take my confirmation.

My appointment? Nine-thirty with Ms. Gloria P. Clark.

Four black plastic chairs section off the area, and I plop into one of them. My conscience kicks and I pull out my phone and play Wordscapes for the distraction factor. Three levels later and I'm about to match letters to spell C-A-N-C-E-L-E-D when an older woman with curly gray Sisterlocks steps to me.

"Chablis Shields?"

I drop my phone in my bag. "That's me."

"I'm Gloria Clark. Please follow me and how can I help you today?"

"I need to apply for a personal loan." I trail after her, then sit in the small metal seat in front of her desk. "But I want to ask something first. That's why I didn't use the website."

"What would you like to know?"

"Is there a penalty if I pay the loan off right away? I'm getting married in October, and I only need this money to pay for items for my wedding."

A big smile lights up her face. "Congratulations."

"Thank you."

"If you're approved for the personal loan, our credit union doesn't charge you for paying it back early. We encourage early payback on low-interest loans for people trying to build their credit rating."

"Will I receive the seven percent rate I read on the website?"

"The amount we loan you and the interest rate depends on your credit score. We have to check your credit first. How much would you like to borrow?"

"Fifteen thousand."

Forty minutes later, I step through the sliding doors into the bright sunlight. I'm done. No more asking for wedding funds. The bank will send me a message about the loan approval.

Cool. Good. All I need to do is figure out how to tell John. I'm not trying to lie to him. I have a strategy to pay the money back. My automated bill payer can apply two hundred to the loan each pay period, starting next month. My budget will scream bloody murder for a while, but when John and I merge into a single household, my salary can cover it. At least I'm not using my Visa, racking up charges at a seventeen percent interest rate.

If the bank rejects the loan request, our current wedding plans stay the same. We'll work with the existing budget. But, if I am approved, I'll nicely take future hubs to dinner at Real Food Eatery, and while he's busy chewing his grass-fed braised beef alongside golden cauliflower and chopped kale, I'll level with him about the loan. He will ask why I took it upon myself to borrow money. I will tell him the truth: this is our *only* option for upgrading our wedding day. And while he drinks Fiji water and narrows his golden eyes at me, I'll explain he's *not* on the hook to pay off anything I borrow.

Luxurious Events isn't open yet, but I whip out my phone and call Lorenzo anyhow.

"Good morning, Lorenzo. It's Chablis Shields. When you have a spare moment, can you please call me? I'd like to discuss our guest list and reception details again. Perhaps a few other things? Talk with you soon."

If QwestLife loans me 15K the extra cash flow should cover a designer wedding gown, artistic desserts, and a few other choice items. I can ask Lorenzo to hire PHILADANCO! dancers for the reception. Maybe even include those professional violinists for the moment I walk down the aisle?

I can practically smell the tropical mix of imported orchids waiting for us at the altar. I put my phone away and hum "I Got That" while strolling down the sidewalk to my Focus.

Oh yes, our wedding *will* be unapologetically dope, Instaglamalicious, sanctified, and glorious.

And we'll keep the Living Coral color.

Maybe.

Jamie calls me this afternoon to ask if I can substitute teach her Overbrook Arts Center line dance class. I practically hug her through the phone. Of course, I'll do it. Dancing illustrates joy, and music and fun will help me relax and release. The extra money won't hurt either.

After work I drive into West Philly wearing Capezio dance shoes, my East Coast Line Dancer t-shirt, and leggings. I keep a dance bag in my trunk for times like these. Bible Study starts at seven sharp, but I can throw my jacket over this ensemble before I walk into Rise tonight.

After I fight through thick traffic on Lancaster Avenue, I glide into a parking spot in the small lot beside the KFC, then dash over to the gray building. The garden area is in full bloom outside. Indoors, women file into the big air-conditioned multi-purpose room. I plug in the speaker, connect my phone, and flow right into teaching *AIM*, *Act Like You Know*, and *Showstopper*.

In the middle of the third dance, a student raises her hand. "Can we go over the swirl part again? I keep missing that."

"Sure." I position my feet on the aged linoleum and run through the complicated step that switches feet several times. "Let's try it from the seven-count. Five, six, seven, eight."

I turn and watch the women repeat the steps. Not bad. They can practice a few more times, then move on to the next step.

"Who's ready for the music?" I ask, encouraging them. I walk to the table and press the Play arrow. "Showstopper" by Brandon & Leah fills the room.

After the intro plays, I call out, "Five, six, seven, eight."

The women stumble through the first attempt. When I play the song again, they perform it once more, looking smooth.

"You ladies are doing fantastic." I cheer them on, and they reward me with shy smiles. "The next step is a half turn. Step on your left, then turn toward the back." I show the move. "Ready?"

Three notifications chime back-to-back from my phone. What the what?

"Keep practicing for a second, y'all." I pick up my device.

"Excuse me." An older woman with false eyelashes and a long auburn wig calls to me. "Jamie has a rule! No texting or talking on the dance floor during class. Do we get a break now?"

"No, you don't. And don't you dare tell Jamie!" I scan my texts. From Nikki:

> The Alfred Sung open-back tie satin trumpet gown. That's the one I'm co-signing on. 😊

From Stacey:

> Nikki just messaged me about the dress. I liked the other Alfred Sung better, but I'll go with it. :-)

From John:

> Got a few things to chat with you about after Bible Study. Something I'm planning, but I won't do it unless you agree. CU at Rise.

I can message my bridesmaids back later. *OK* is what I text John before I return to the dance floor. He probably wants to talk wedding details. I bet he decided on the suits for the groomsmen. That's cool. Whatever he needs to say, I'll listen and support him. QwestLife Credit Union hasn't responded to my loan request yet, so there's no need to discuss what I don't know.

"I'm sorry about that, ladies." I push my thoughts aside and take my place in front of them. "We're right at the half-turn part."

John rushes into Rise twenty feet ahead of me.

"Hey!" I yell to him.

"Hey, you." He stops and holds the door for me. "Thought you were already inside."

I raise up on tiptoe and brush my lips against his bearded cheek. "No, I taught a line dance class at Overbrook Arts. Jamie had an emergency root canal today, and she needed a substitute."

"You have to tell me where you get all this energy. You exercised this morning, worked all day, and taught a dance class. Now you're here at church. When are you going to rest?"

"Soon as Pastor Hargrove finishes teaching."

"No. Uh-uh. After Bible Study, we need to talk. Remember?"

"Yeah. Right."

We head inside and sit near the back. Our buddies wave at us from the balcony, and we wave back but stay put.

Pastor Hargrove moves back and forth in the front of the sanctuary, but I'm half-listening to his teaching. I open the Bible app on my phone, but I don't highlight any verses because my mind grinds away.

John remains quiet next to me, tapping out notes on his own device. Tonight he's a mixed bag. I can't read him. His tone seemed serious when we stood in the foyer, but he seems his regular self now.

Guess I'll have to wait to hear what he has to say.

Pastor Hargrove closes out in prayer, and I turn to John. "What's up?"

"Mom called me today to talk about our wedding—"

I roll my eyes. "Ugh. You know what, I know she's your mom, but she can't invite Trina. I'm not allowing it and I'm not changing my mind so she can just—"

"Not my mom. Your mom."

"Oh? Okay?"

"Seems she's got some opinions on my money flow, especially as we head into marriage."

Oh Lord! "Look, our business is our business, so whatever she said—"

"Aye... she's right."

I must have heard that wrong. I blink at him. "What?"

"She's right. She kind of surprised me, but then again she didn't. She's like you—scrappy and direct. She said I blindsided you with my debt and I have to step up and change things."

"So what're you saying?"

He wipes a hand over his face and gives a sigh. "I need to take care of it, and I'll get another job. It's not like I can't do Uber or Door-Dash or something where I can set my schedule. I won't do anything that'll interfere with SynerCloud or worship on Sunday."

"You're a tech guy and you want to deliver pizzas?"

"I'll do what I need to do to take my debt down. Should've done it before, but I was busy courting my future wife."

"Working two jobs, though?"

"Sunshine, I'll work three jobs for us, if that's what it takes. Every Saturday. Every single holiday. I'll take the money and put it all on my debt. I promised you I'd take responsibility for clearing more away before we get married."

"And that means? What?"

"Our private time... uh... I won't be around a lot. Are you okay with that?"

I search for an answer, but all I blurt out is, "I'll have to be."

Prayer meeting starts in five minutes and I should grab my bag and head toward the front pews with John, but I hang back when he stands and moves to the center aisle.

My body feels heavy, like I'm holding a fifty-pound bag of concrete. I should have told him about the loan application the second he said he wanted to get a side hustle. What did I do? Sat here acting all innocent when I'm guilty of something I can't quite name.

John calls to me. "Chablis? You coming?"

I stand and nod and follow future hubby to gather with other believers for prayer.

Something tells me I should ask them all to pray for me.

my peanut butter chocolate cake with kool-aid

MONDAY NIGHT I'm sitting in my apartment studying bridal accessories online. Homemade garlic-salted kale chips are my snack since future hubby's habits have rubbed off on me. I take a potty break and come back to my laptop and see an email notification from someone named Ariana Thompson. I click it.

To: JGerald, CShields
    From: Ariana Thompson
    Subject: Premarital Counseling

Good day and congratulations!

My name is Ariana Thompson and I am a Licensed Marriage & Family Therapist. I partner with Rise Community Church to provide marriage and family counseling. I will lead you through exercises and information intended to help you grow your bond and strengthen your partnership for a lifetime. You will also complete assignments from the workbook *Forever Together Faithfully*. The workbook and other support materials cost $40.00, payable during the first session.

Seven hour-long sessions will be held on Tuesday evenings at 7:00 PM at the Center for Family Counseling in Philadelphia. Your first session will occur next Tuesday. Our final meeting will be a dinner fellowship at your pastor's home.

Information about the center is attached to this message. Because you are both members of Rise Community Church, there is no direct charge for counseling services, but Rise encourages a freewill offering.

Please click the link and fill out the confidential questionnaire I've provided. I look forward to meeting you both.

In His Service,
Ariana Thompson, LMFT

I click and a browser tab opens with an online survey. Premarital counseling. Confidential answers. All I gotta do is fill out the form and click the Send icon.

The survey doesn't ask me for my name, only my initials. I type those in and answer the top set of questions. Have I been married or divorced before? *No.* Kids or pregnancies? *None.* Still living at home or on my own? *On my own.* Have I been baptized? *Yes.* Do I pray regularly? *Yes.* Do I consider Jesus my Lord and Savior? *Absolutely.*

The next set of questions address personality. *Active or a couch potato? Optimistic? Ambitious? Impulsive? Introvert or extrovert? Lonely? Personable? Nervous?* I click the boxes that tell our counselor I'm an optimistic, personable extrovert with occasional impulsive tendencies.

The last group of questions ask about my relationship with John. How long have we dated seriously? *A year.* Have we ever broken off the relationship? *No.* Have either of us been engaged before? *Yes.* Do our parents approve of our relationship? *It's complicated.* Are we living together? *Heck no.* Are our parents married? *Yes.*

I don't wanna think too hard about letting a stranger know all our business, so I click Send before I change my mind. The form makes it seem like premarital counseling is for couples who have problems with God, life, or each other, and that doesn't apply to me and John.

Do we need to do this?

Five forty-five in the morning and I'm in the zone. Dim lights and pulse pounding music. This dark blue cube of a room reeks of rubber floor mats and sanitizer spray, but I don't have a care in the world. Thoughts of wedding budgets, Instagram comments, and future mother-in-law issues don't trouble me. I'm pumping fast and sweating hard. Feeling alive and strong as ever while my heart beats double-time.

SPRINT class. Oh, yeah!

My friend Daisy shoots me a look when I climb off my bike celebrating like I won the Tour de France.

"You want to ease up there, speedy?" She dismounts her lithe body from the ProForm frame. "Are you planning on doing a triathlon soon?"

"I'm just feeling so pumped this morning."

"Give me some of your energy then." She takes a sip from her water bottle. "I was barely hanging on today. I needed more caffeine before I came in here. I was going to brew some, but I dashed out of the house when I looked at the baby monitor and saw Brooks rolling around in the crib."

Daisy Worthington and I bonded at this YMCA a little over a year ago. She could double for a forty-year-old Meghan Markle if the Duchess of Sussex had green eyes and sandy brown hair. She's so light-skinned that when we met, I swore she was white. She isn't. She's just light. Her parents are civil rights lawyers and her grandfather once walked with Dr. King in Birmingham. She's actually named after Daisy Bates, the civil rights activist and journalist. Her mom wanted to name her Olivia, but her father snuck and asked for Daisy on the birth certificate. I can't see how, but they stayed married after that. Daisy comes from a whole different world than me. Old money and debutante balls and summer vacations on the Vineyard. She's married to Tripp Worthington and is the mother of three little ones: Brooks, Tucker, and Caroline. She writes women's devotional journals, and she's growing a ministry for young ladies. Stand us side by side and she's about as different from me as they come, but she's *still* my sister.

That's why she's my unofficial accountability partner.

After John and I had the "define the relationship" talk, I wanted a Christian woman to chat with about my relationship from time to time, but my Mom said I shouldn't run my mouth to my church buddies about what I have going on with my man. She told me it's all good until a favorite sister-friend spreads my business through Rise Church. I'm no dummy. I call and text Daisy about the deep stuff.

"What's up with you? Still being good?" She drapes a pink towel around her slim neck.

She's talking about my sexual desire for John, which I text her about. On the daily. But, yes, John and I are still holding off. Our bodies have not yet collided.

Yay.

I nod and pass her a paper towel so she can wipe her equipment.

She cleans the handlebars. "I've been praying for you."

"And I appreciate you oodles. Hey, did you and Tripp have premarital counseling before you got married?" We roll the bikes to the side of the room and grab our jackets and bags from the wall pegs.

"No, at Princeton, the church we attended didn't recommend it. You and John have to do it?"

"Yeah." I zip up my running jacket.

"You don't want to?"

"Our pastor requires it, but I went through the questionnaire last night and I felt like I was filling out a job application. I don't know if I want some stranger dissecting my relationship."

"Maybe you shouldn't look at it that way," she says when we head down the hall to the staircase.

"It's just more work. We need to find a place to live in a few months. I don't know. John and I get along so well and we've never had relationship problems."

"At least you have the counseling option. Tripp and I were so young and in love and we didn't think to ask." A grin spreads across her pale face like she's thinking back to those early days. "On our wedding day, all I wanted was for us to arrive at the church on time so I could show off my grandmother's antique dress and hug my family in the pictures. But you should thank God you have a pastor who cares enough to direct you to counseling."

"Really?"

"Marriage gets rough sometimes. Whatever you learn now will help you later."

"Office sessions and workbooks, though? More stuff to take up time."

Daisy pulls her hair back with a Burberry band. "But you *could* make time for something that important, right?"

"Well, yeah."

"Then purple-haired one, do it."

I roll my eyes, but my lips turn up in a smile when we stop beside the front desk.

Across the room, John sits with three other men in the rest area, their heads bowed. A Bible lays open before them on the blue metal table.

Four powerful gentlemen praying before the start of their day.

And one of them belongs to me.

Daisy wraps an arm around my shoulders and squeezes.

"Sweetie, you've got a good one. Looks like God's already given you what you need. Follow his lead, all right?"

"I got you." I hug her back and release her. "See you next week?"

"Yes. And you text me later, all right?"

"I will."

Ten minutes later, John and I climb into his Jeep. He's driving me back to my apartment so I can get ready for work.

I know what Daisy said. But *still.*

"John?"

"Yeah."

"Um, you can only pick one." I tell him while he starts the engine. "Just one artist to listen to when you lift weights. Andy Mineo, Trip Lee, or KB?"

We play the "pick one" game all the time. It's random and fun and no matter who starts it, the other person smiles.

"Shoot, that's easy. The one you didn't mention: Lecrae."

He's laughing. Time to launch into the premarital counseling question.

I shift closer to him. "You read Ariana Thompson's email?"

"Yeah."

"So, ahem, counseling? How are you feeling about it?"

"All right. I mean, every engaged couple at Rise does it. There's not much to think or feel about it. It's part of the process."

"What if we don't need it? I reviewed that questionnaire and the books we need to buy. And we'll have to do homework assignments. How are you gonna do all that when you're working multiple gigs?"

"We're not canceling, if that's what you're thinking. I already asked Dr. Jones about it and he said it's the best thing."

"Really?"

"Even if Dr. Jones didn't give me his opinion, I still want us to do it." John adds. "We've been given a counselor to meet with seven times. That's nothing. Plus Pastor Downes won't marry us unless we do it. He's like family to me, just like Dr. Jones. Let's submit. It'll be over faster than we think."

. . .

I could kick myself for not leaving work sooner.

Today was beyond busy and my director insisted on starting a meeting close to five and it lasted a full hour. Sometimes Sue acts like an obsessive-compulsive field marshal. Rush hour should die down now but tell that to the cars clogging 76 while I'm trying to escape King of Prussia. I'm so glad I asked John to meet me at the Center for Family Counseling. He can represent for us.

There's only off-street parking in this rapidly gentrifying neighborhood past the Philadelphia Zoo. I park two blocks away from the center address. With my fuchsia heels on, the ones that squeeze my toes but match my cute outfit, I'm limping when I spot the sign that reads Center for Family Counseling in block letters on the glass door between the Grind House Cafe and the Super Suds Laundromat.

Inside, I slip my heels off and sprint up the narrow flight of stairs. I'm not breathless when I run down the hallway because, yes, my daily workouts serve me well.

I push through the main door and enter a quiet waiting room, facing three doors in a row. One is open, and I can see John's long legs, so I slide my shoes back on and stroll in.

A desk and three cocoa-colored armchairs fit into the warm, cedar wood-smelling office. Immediately, I feel relaxed. A woman who I assume is Ariana Thompson stands beside a floor-to-ceiling bookshelf on the opposite side of the room. I step in and offer her my hand to shake.

"Hi, Ms. Thompson!" I smile. "I'm Chablis Gerald. Nice to meet you!"

She has a big friendly face, a gap-toothed smile, and long dark hair that's been permed and layered. She shakes my hand and giggles. "Nice to meet you as well. Call me Ariana. And I thought your last name was Shields? Did you get married over the weekend?"

"Nope." I drop my bag next to an overstuffed chair and have a seat. "Just wanted to see if you were on top of things."

"You know, we can go to City Hall tomorrow," John says. "I mean, since you're ready to take my name and everything."

"Ya got jokes, but that's okay. I can take it." I stretch my body over and smooch him on the cheek. What I really want to do is run my fingers through his thick beard and hug his broad shoulders. Mmm. He is my peanut butter chocolate cake with Kool-Aid.

Ariana shuts the door and sits opposite us. "We've just met, but I have to put on my professional hat for a moment. If you can do your best to be on time for our sessions, I'd appreciate it."

Her voice sounds kind as she says this, so I nod like, *okay, duly noted*, and pull a notebook from my overstuffed backpack. Lateness isn't a habit of mine, so I'm not stressed about it.

She holds two red folders on her lap. "First, I have to say this, John and Chablis, you are one good-looking couple."

I'm blushing when we mumble our thanks. She's right. I'm not being vain. We do complement one another. John works so hard in the gym, he's like a walking CrossFit ad. I almost match his toasty brown color, with hard-earned muscles of my own, and well controlled curves. What Ariana really means is we look good *together*. Like we should put on matching Reebok outfits and strike a pose for the cover of *PhillyFIT Magazine*.

She passes us each a folder. "I'll work to support you both as you transition from singles to marrieds. We'll cover communication and your core beliefs and values as a couple. We'll also discuss honesty and boundaries in your relationship. My teaching and your work-book, think of them as tools to help you build a strong relationship foundation. But I have to say, of the two, that workbook will be your most valuable investment. You'll give answers about the events that shaped you as people, like the manner in which you grew up, and your families of origin. You'll also look at how you manage things today. The way you handle stress, loneliness, job issues, extended family, desire, your outlook on children, household tasks... all of it affects your marriage."

My phone vibrates in my bag. Thank goodness I remembered to mute it before I got out of my car. I can still see it lighting up, though. Who's calling? Could be one of my friends. No, it's probably my mom. Or maybe Luna or Lorenzo because I left them a voice mail today.

John elbows me. "Sunshine?"

"Huh?"

"Focus."

Focus. Right.

I kick my bag to the side.

"I'm not big on paper," Ariana says. "That folder will be the last set of papers you'll see from me. The packet contains a syllabus and counseling expectations and guidelines. It also has a confidentiality statement. You'll sign that and give it back to me. If you have questions as you read, let me know."

I flip through pages. "I don't see it here, but Sister Gunning told us Pastor Downes won't marry us unless we complete all the sessions. That can't be true."

"Oh, that's definitely true." She says with a nod. "What your pastor told me, is that couples who were unwilling to take guidance were the same people in his office asking for help after a separation. He wants all new marrieds to get off to a good start, but even he's wrong in his timing."

"What do you mean?" John asks.

Ariana points at us. "You've already picked each other. No counselor could change your mind now. But if you intentionally chose a mate with similar life goals and faith, and you understand that love is a verb and marriage isn't 50/50, it's 100/100, you should be fine."

"What if something happens and we don't make all the sessions?" I ask.

"If your schedules become an issue we can arrange an alternate time or meet through Skype," she says.

John nods toward me. "So, no turning your phone off."

"Turning your phone off?" Ariana's face holds a questioning look.

"Sometimes I get so many texts and notifications, I need to turn it off for a minute." I glance at my beloved. I know he hates when he can't reach me, but must he tattle so soon? "I'm getting married, I'll adjust."

"Ah! Adjust is a grand word. Respect for your partner is crucial," Ariana says. "The love that builds a marriage is called agape, and that's love that seeks the welfare of the other person. It's the type of love God has for us. Speaking of that, let me skip ahead and give you your first assignment. I want you to read Chapter One together. Write out what your commitment means to each other and why respect is important in your relationship."

Easy enough. If all the homework is this straightforward, we can get it out of the way fast.

Ariana continues. "As you journey into marriage, you'll discover your partner struggles with sins you never knew about. It's inevitable you'll go back and forth over money, family, and career decisions. Your finances will be intermingled, and if you made poor decisions in the past with money or credit, your spouse will take those on."

I glance at John, and he doesn't flinch. Why should he? He took me out for coffee shop confessions and told me all about his debt. I know what's up. He's planning on working an extra job. His conscience is clean.

Me? I'm sitting here like Ms. Perfect Future Wife and each word Ariana speaks becomes a needle stabbing my sense of right and wrong.

Love. Honesty. Commitment. Respect. Decisions.
Money.

"Where'd you park?" John asks when we step out of the Center for Family Counseling.

"Two blocks down."

"I'll walk you over and you can drive me to the Jeep. I parked past the zoo."

We walk side by side and we're only one block away from my Focus when I trip on a crack in the sidewalk. John catches me and helps me upright again. I move forward, understanding the Spirit just kicked me right in the ego.

Whether or not I'm justified, it's time for me to tell John about that loan.

"Future hubby?"

"Um-hmm."

"Pick one?"

"Okay."

"Five, ten, or fifteen?"

He scrunches his face. "Five, ten, or fifteen? You asking my favorite numbers?"

"No. But just pick one."

He slows his pace. "Ten."

"Nope, you're wrong. The answer is fifteen."

"Fifteen what? Help me out."

I swallow hard. "Fifteen thousand—the amount of loan money I applied for at my bank for our wedding day."

John stops and turns to me. "You're joking, I know you are. Come on now—"

"No, bae, it's not a joke."

He turns away and paces the pavement. When turns back, his jaw is clenched.

"Are you deliberately trying to cause drama between us!"

"No, and stop yelling, that's not cool and you're being a hypocrite." I cross my arms and stand my ground. "You shouldn't be hollering at me when you kept me in the dark about your money for a year. You know that wasn't fair!"

He wipes a hand over his face. "It wasn't, and I don't want to be a hypocrite, but why would you borrow more?" He asks in a normal tone. "We agreed we wouldn't finance the wedding. I mean, you said you'd be in this with me."

"I am in it with you, and you told me you wanted an unapologetically dope wedding. Average wedding cost is like twenty-six thousand and we don't have anything close to that."

He steps closer. "Chablis, do you know what dope is to me? Dope is you and me saying I do before God and the people we love the most, and we can do that at Rise with a simple ceremony. I don't want or need anything more than that."

"What about what I want?"

"Lorenzo and Luna are helping us, and they're pros at working with any budget. Even if we gave them more money, they can't make you look any more lovely than you already do. If you want more than that, you lied to me."

"How did I lie?"

"The entire time we dated, every time we discussed our future. I mean, we talked about faith and God, and we talked about being partners, and having a vision for raising kids. You never mentioned a big extravagant wedding. And it's not like you're some materialistic chick because you're cool with your apartment and your Focus." His voice drops lower. "You gotta tell me, why are you pushing so hard for an event that'll only last a few hours?"

Old gum plasters the pavement beneath my feet. I stare at a round, dark mark and my mind drifts to the image of an abandoned, beaten teenager who would have been forgotten if she'd died. But she lived to see many more days, and she's yearning for the most spectacular day.

The day that should change the image forever.

I shake my head because that stupid image has to fade.

It can't be the main reason for my actions, even if it is.

I clear my throat. "John, I hear you. What do you want me to do?"

"You gotta cancel that loan application. Can you do that?"

I give a slow nod.

"And can you be grateful for what God has for us, right now? Today?"

I bring my eyes up to look at future hubby. Love and concern color his face.

"Yes," I say. "I can."

new rules

TUESDAY IS LEG DAY.

Six AM and I drop into my third set of goblet squats when my phone vibrates inside my shorts pocket. Probably John. For the past three weeks, instead of hitting the gym with me, he drives Uber around Philly. He also works for the ride share service most evenings. All the money he makes, he funnels to his debts.

His driving for Uber doesn't make me insecure. I pray for God to keep him safe on the road. And... well... the day he started I asked the Lord to chase away any over-eager females who might wonder if their bearded Adonis Creed lookalike chauffeur is available for anything more than a car ride.

I peek at my device and sure enough, it's a message from the future hubs:

> GM, my fine and luscious black queen!
> Praying u have a great day. Looking forward
> to 20 kisses tonight before counseling.
> Finish ALL the squats on the list—Love u.

I text back:

Love u more.

I miss our Y time together, even if we spent most of it sweating. Now John squeezes in workouts at the Planet Fitness close to his office and does CrossFit on Saturdays. I'm on my own fitness-wise. If I don't have an exercise class to attend, he'll message me a workout. Like he used to before we started dating and I drafted him into helping me drop pounds which my doctor later told me I shouldn't have done because John isn't a certified trainer but whatever because I earned a future husband out of the deal and God is good, okay.

Anyway, John thinks he's slick.

Every workout he sends includes squats and lunges.

Outside the wellness room doors, Daisy passes by with her sandy brown hair pulled into a high ponytail. I wave with both arms so she can see me.

She waves back and mouths, "Call me later."

I definitely will. A chat with her is a chance to vent my feeling to someone who listens, crack jokes, and prays for me afterward.

"Hey, hey... uh... a little help. Help, please!" A voice pleads.

I turn around and a wisp of a lady with blue-tinged white hair struggles to hold fifteen-pound weights in her delicate hands. She lies on the weight bench, trying to keep her chest press form steady.

Two big leaps and I'm by her side, snatching the metal dumb-bells so they don't crash down to her neck and chest.

"Thank you so much, sweetheart. I appreciate that." The lady sits upright, relief on her reddened face.

"You're welcome. And next time, be careful about the amount you lift, okay? You can always ask a trainer to help you."

"You're not a trainer?"

"No, ma'am."

She breathes hard and pats her chest, looking me up and down. "My goodness, you sure look like one. Thank you."

I take her dumbbells back to the steel rack and glimpse myself in the mirror. Navy blue Under Armour shirt, shorts, and socks. Under

Armour athletic shoes. Plantronics flexible waterproof headphones. Yep. I'm impersonating a trainer today.

Wish John was here. He would have loved hearing that. But, he's working two gigs because he's in debt. I'm marrying him. That means *we're* in debt, and I feel it more than ever. John doesn't buy my groceries or supplements anymore, so my shopping bills are higher. Who knew organic women's gummy vitamins cost $16.96 a bottle? I need to start couponing!

Oh yeah, John and I are sticking to a tight spending plan now.

We crunched numbers after our counseling session covering money and finances. The one when Ariana told us, "Marriage is a business in and of itself. Marriage will make you the co-CEOs of Gerald, Inc. Co-CEOs work as a team and make beneficial decisions for the company. See it that way, and you shouldn't have any issues with salary transparency, addressing debt, money goals, financial styles, savings, and investments, and bank accounts."

So, we used the tables inside *Forever Together Faithfully* and created a working budget including our monthly net pay and all our bills. I know his credit score. He knows mine. I prayed for him after he nearly went into shock finding out how much I spend at Shades of Beauty salon each month. Based on our calculations, and without considering how much John makes driving ride share, it'll take a little over two years before we try home ownership. If I'd fought harder for a dream wedding with my kind of sparkle in it, it would've meant keeping the bank loan and increasing what we owe. I'm disappointed, but there's nothing I can do that won't make things worse.

This morning during devotions, I spent an extra twenty minutes meditating on the word. I highlighted Psalm 3:5-6 three times in the YouVersion app. *Trust in the Lord with all your heart and lean not on your own understanding; in all your ways submit to him and he will make your paths straight.* Then I kneeled to pray.

Afterward, I stood up and all I saw was Ms. Pat with a smirk on her face.

Common chick.
Common wedding.
Could have used those extra funds, huh?

Lunch hour at my desk involves me devouring a Pizza Hut meat lover's pizza, which I wash down with Dr. Pepper. Luna's voice reaches me through speakerphone. Even though she's sweet as Hawaiian Punch, I don't want to chat nuptial plans for long.

As of today, our wedding includes mostly John's ideas, down to the suspended greenery decorations. It's not his fault intimate and romantic means *economical*. We eventually settled on an 6K budget. John will keep his two thousand and apply it to his student loans. Luna and Lorenzo worked their magic and the big day breaks down to:

Traditional ceremony at Rise Community Church, of course.

Four formally dressed men will stand with John: Nate, Terry, Travis and Dr. Jones. Black tuxedo rentals from The BLK Tux.

Four women to stand with me: Nikki, Stacey, Mariah and Binky. Each lady picked a different style coral-colored Alfred Sung dress and the kaleidoscope of choices started when Stacey announced she's pregnant and she'll have a big round belly in October and she needs the sleeveless satin twill maternity dress, and Binky asked for the V-neck high low cocktail style because she wants to slay, then Mariah begged for the elegant V-neck halter satin trumpet, which left Nikki the only one with the tie-back trumpet but I'm fine with all their choices if everything matches and they're paying for their dresses, anyway.

Flower girls: Terry's daughters, Rashida and Rae-Ann. They took part in a wedding back in April so we'll accessorize their ivory lace tulle dresses with wide coral-colored satin sashes.

No ring bearer because neither John nor I want to worry about a small clumsy kid and expensive rings on a flimsy pillow.

The food and entertainment reception package at the non-dazzling Babblebrook Banquet Hall will cost $3000.00. While the place doesn't have room for a hot-air balloon lift-off, we toured the garden area, and it *is* lovely.

Limousine service and fall-themed wedding flower package and engagement and wedding photo package and invitations and jewelry and a bunch of other minor nuptial accouterments and the Luxurious Events fee take a chunk of money.

Oh, and my wedding gown budget is set at $700.00.

We'll have eighty reception guests. John and I have a ton of friends and favorite church members we love, but with forty invites for his side and forty for mine, it means we can only feed our family and closest friends.

We had fun dressing up and taking engagement and save the date photos beneath the Ben Franklin bridge—and that was nice. Invitations go out after Memorial Day.

From the food to the flowers to the coral and gold decorative touches, Luxurious Events coordinates the plan expertly.

Everything covered and elegant and *standard*.

There is not *one* pop of super-exclusive/never before seen/Instaglamorous in this bride's day.

And Luna knows how a purple-flared Jesus chick feels about that, so she calls on the regular.

"Chablis, we want you to love your event too," Luna says. "How do you feel about the plans we emailed you for the reception?"

"They're really nice." I fold up my paper plate and chuck it in the metal trash can by my feet. "Tell me where to stand and how to hold the coral rose bouquet."

"That's nonsense," she says, sounding like a southern-fried Gabrielle Union. "What about our bride?"

"What about her?"

"We care about you. It's our job at Luxurious Events to make sure you're pleased. Tell me what special touch you want, and we'll incorporate it."

"Really?" I grab a napkin and wipe flecks of tomato sauce from my nails.

"Yes."

"Are Sean C. Johnson, Erica Campbell, or Tamela Mann available to sing at our reception?"

"I'm sure if they were, and you had the budget to hire them, we could fly one of them in for you. But for now, think of something sentimental that represents your union."

I kick my heels off and think. What represents us? Well, when I first started crushing on John, we used to run behind the art museum every other Saturday, sitting on benches to rest and talk. He has that detail covered already. He flew back from Germany to ask me to be his lady, though I don't think we can do a Philly International motif.

But maybe?

"We've taken pictures from our first date up through today," I say. "We have a ton of photos and videos. Can you show those before the reception?"

"We can absolutely arrange a slide show presentation with music. Do you have a song that's special to you both?"

One song comes to mind. "'Your Precious Love' by Marvin Gaye and Tammi Terrell."

I leave out the part about the guardian angels.

I doubt they can be summoned on-demand.

Tonight, Ariana guides John and me through a lesson on communication and connection. This should be a serious time when we face each other, knee to knee, gazing in each other's eyes. We're supposed to try this for at least two minutes. We're allowed to blink, but we can't look away.

Other couples probably do this just fine. John and I keep cracking up.

"John and Chablis, you *can* do this. Start again," Ariana says after we laugh for the third time.

I straighten up and try to stop giggling. I take a deep breath before I hold John's hands again.

"Hold up." John looks away and clears his throat. "All right. I'm ready."

Ariana leans against her desk and taps her phone. "I set the timer again. Now focus on each other's eyes."

Like the excellent students we are, we stare each other in the face. He smiles at me. I grin back.

Seconds tick away and we grow serious.

He's a beautiful man, but he's not all brawn, no brain. This man truly loves God. And he has this serious nerdy/techie side that comes out when he's dealing with work. I love seeing him relax reading his favorite Walter Mosley mysteries. The type of guy who calls his grandparents once a day just to tell them he loves them. He visits his father's grave whenever he can to ensure no weeds grow around it. And our best date ever happened when we served at CityTeam a week before Christmas, packing up toys and putting bows on bikes for the kids in Chester. Smart. Compassionate. Loving. My God I'm glad he's mine.

And when we kiss? *Lord have mercy!*

"Done," Ariana says as the timer buzzes. She taps her phone and lays it on her desk. "What did you see? Tell each other."

John raises his hand. "Can I go first?"

"Go ahead," Ariana says.

His eyes twinkle. "At first, all I thought about was your beauty and those kissable dimples. But then my mind went back to those deep conversations we had years ago. How can you smile so much after everything you've survived? I mean, you're like a Navy SEAL wrapped in a gorgeous package. Oh, and I thought about the gospel song, "You Brought the Sunshine," because that's how I chose your nickname. And I thought about... when the police stopped us coming back from Cape May and made me get out of the car and frisked me." Pause. "After... I couldn't talk, I was so mad. You put your arms around me and held me for I don't know — an hour I think. God blessed me with sweetness and sunshine, with a touch of steel for a wife. I won't rest well until you're by my side forever. I love you to life."

Wow.

This is just.

Wow.

"Chablis? Your turn," Ariana says.

"Wait, a minute." I take a few cleansing breaths. "That's not fair John. Don't make me cry in front of the counselor."

Ariana waves away my words. "Cry all you want. I can get you tissues."

"I think I can do this." I meet his eyes. "You're so much more than a face and a body. I have to admit, when Nikki told me you tried out for *American Ninja Warrior*, I thought that was corny. Having the chance to get to know you personally, though? Your discipline is such a gift. I love the way you care for me. And I gotta take your words because they're my words too — I won't rest well until I'm by your side forever."

Ariana gives us two thumbs up. "Communication goes beyond simple words. Your daily communication should include more than who, what, when, where, and why. Share with your partner how you are affected by an issue. And like you just illustrated, express love through exceptional communication meant only for your partner." Ariana says. "The gazing exercise is a moment of connection. Truly seeing your partner. Connection moments can become intimate when you go to your favorite places and do the things you love together. In your homework, you'll outline what makes you feel connected and loved. However, you'll also write about hot-button, sensitive issues, things you should avoid talking about whenever you're tired, hungry, sad, or upset. Discuss those as well."

We're walking past the coffeehouse and laundromat on our way to our cars. John rubs his face and messes with his beard. Tiredness shows in the slump of his shoulders. It's nice that we do our class homework on Sunday nights. I wouldn't think of reading or answering questions with him tonight.

"Exhausted?" I ask.

"Yeah."

"Sure you want two jobs?"

"If Jacob worked seven years for Rachel, I can do Uber and Syner-Cloud," he says. "Plus this job gives me other opportunities. Got to witness to this young bol this morning, 'cause I had Trip Lee's "I'm Good" playing, and he liked it. Kid told me he'd never heard Christian hip-hop before, so I passed him a tract and told him to check out Rise some time. He said he would."

"That's what's up!"

"Yeah, I know."

"Still want to keep Sundays clear from driving?"

He yawns. "Listen, the only thing I want to do on Sunday is listen to Pastor Downes in the morning and rest my head on your lap in the afternoon."

"Sundays for worship and rest. We gotta keep that going. After we become husband and wife, I expect Sunday afternoons to include something more than naps on the couch."

"You know it will."

He kisses me goodbye before helping me into my car, but once he closes the door, I don't turn the key in the ignition. I gaze in the rearview mirror and watch him walk away slowly, four cars down to his Jeep.

"Lord," I pray, "cover John and help him make it home safe tonight. Give him a restful sleep and fill him with energy in the morning."

I open my eyes when he pulls up to my Focus, honking. After I wave, he drives away.

"Lord, please help me push aside all feelings of disappointment." I pray with my eyes open. "I have nothing to prove, so please help me stop thinking about the wedding. John's holding up his end of the commitment. I need to hold up mine. Amen."

The loan application? I canceled it. The credit union offered me a $2,000 personal line of credit to use any time. I don't plan to use it, but it *is* available.

Just in case.

gray space

"WHAT'S ALL THIS?" I scan what used to be empty wall space in Nikki's apartment.

I haven't visited here since mid-January. In my defense, that was around the time when my relationship with John deepened. We went from dating to basically doing life, but without living together. Nikki never complained about the dwindling BFF face-to-face moments, but I know I've missed some things when I see all the colorful acrylic paintings on her living room's far wall.

"It's art." Monster-sized bunny slippers cover her feet, and over-sized red plaid lounging pants dress her thin legs. She pads from the kitchen, a bowl of granola and strawberries in her hand. She holds the bowl out to me. "Want somethin' to eat?"

"No, thanks. Why so many?"

"I got tired of stacking them up in the dining room and had Felicia help me hang them," she says with a shrug. "They're from all the singles painting events. You went to one before."

"Yeah? I can't remember it. Did I even paint?" I move closer to the wall, studying a canvas square of a violet vase with pastel flowers spilling out of it.

"Uh-huh. It's there toward the bottom. That giant sunset with the blackbirds on the horizon."

"You kept it and hung it?" I peer at the brown, orange, and yellow hues blend into a skyline. Those ebony birds are anorexic. I squint, and there's my scribble at the bottom. C. Shields. "Why can't I remember this?"

She curls up at the end of the sofa and crunches. "Because it was BJ."

"BJ?"

"Before John."

"It couldn't be. Was I still chubby?"

"What does that have to do with it?"

"A lot. I mark time now based on pre-fitness or post-fitness. So, was I still chubby?"

"I think you were in between. He'd left the states."

I straighten up and gaze around. With her eclectic decorating style, the colorful paintings definitely work in here. Beautiful African carvings grace her bookshelves, along with weavings she brought back from missions trips to Central and South America. It's awesome how she makes the time to serve. I still use the multi-colored, hand-sewn scarves she brought me from Guatemala.

"Where are you going next?" I plop down next to her.

"Didn't you see the announcement for short-term missions trips for August? I signed up for five days in South Africa."

South Africa. Hmm? "Are they still accepting volunteers?"

"You aren't going anywhere with a wedding coming up. And wouldn't you have to ask John?"

"Yeah. I guess I have a lot more time on my hands now than I thought I would." I stretch my arms over my head.

"You're good with him doing all that Uber driving?"

"Why wouldn't I be?"

"Three words. Single. Thirsty. Women."

"If I was gonna worry about that, I'd be paranoid the rest of my life."

"You're better than me." Her phone buzzes and she grabs it from the table. "Hey, lady... yeah... I saw the message in the group. I'm good. I'm bringing the water and the iced tea... call you back later? Chablis stopped through. Yeah... bye."

She ends the call, and I stare at her until she gets the hint.

"Felicia's sister Jayda invited me to a baking fellowship at six. Something her women's group does once a month. They missed last month, though." She glances down at her lap, then back to me. "I would have asked you to come with me, but most times you're with John on Saturday, and it's for singles only."

"Did I miss my own wedding?"

"You know what I mean. Unattached singles. They invited a speaker to talk about living successfully. It's being held at a big house out in Willingboro."

And I nod at her because I get it. I'm floating in an undefined gray space. With a committed partner, I can't identify with Christian women who are trying to find romantic love or learn to live without it. But I'm not married *yet* so I don't get marital privileges either.

Dang.

Nikki's life resembles my old one. Back when I first joined Rise, she taught me how to present my fears to the Lord through prayer. She bought me my first devotional Bible to use during young adult's Bible Study. Without her being a real sister to me, I doubt I'd feel so whole again. And since we still have this Saturday morning together, I'll enjoy annoying her.

I spring from the couch to stretch my legs. "Hey, go put on your workout gear."

"What?"

"You have time, so let's get out in the sunshine. We can power walk and pray."

"You know, you sound so churchy right now."

"Whatever. Get your kicks."

Nikki shakes her head when she heads to her bedroom. We may walk different paths, but some things transcend life and the specifics of the roads we follow. Like sisterhood that won't give up no matter what. I am not losing a best friend.

I'm nurturing a future godmother.

My phone buzzes, and I glance at it. A text from Daisy:

> Ms. Purple Hair! I need ya in a few weeks for Saturday morning babysitting. I'm speaking at a prayer breakfast in Trenton. Can you sit with the kids?

I don't even have to think about it. Thanks to John, *all* of my Saturdays are free.

> I got you. I'll fill them full of Cap'n Crunch and let them bounce off the walls.

> If u do, I'm sending them home with you! 😊 😊😊 I'll send you more info soon.

Hmm? Daisy? The Worthingtons have plenty of money. I'll have to ask her about her financial adviser. John and I should network with someone who can help us get rid of the debt faster, and free John from working multiple gigs.

Nikki sounds like she's tearing up her bedroom searching for sneakers. I'll stop standing around and go help her.

A best friend's job is never done.

⌒

And tonight is all about Nikki. For her 28th birthday, twelve women, including myself, want to make her feel like a queen. Stacey does her best to help me, but seeing how she's pregnant, I lug cardboard boxes full of yummy goodies into *Paint N' Celebrate* myself.

"Let me help with something else." She shifts her growing little belly out of the way. "I can do more than hold the door."

Sharp edges on a box of Martinelli's Sparkling Apple Cider pinch my hand. I set it down fast. "No, my sister, keep it up while I make another run."

"Okay. I'll stay here if you want to act like Wonder Woman."

One more trip out to my trunk to grab a case of water, and I'm done.

Dominique, the older Italian woman who runs the place, directs us to the party room in the back. "Store anything in the refrigerator. And you can arrange the chairs and tables however you like, as well. I'll be in the main room getting the paints and canvases ready for your group if you need me."

"One more thing." I turn to her. "We have water and apple cider, but I can't guess what Nikki's older cousins might bring in their bags."

Dominique nods knowingly. "Wine is fine here. Bottle opener and glasses are in the blue cabinet."

"Cool. Thanks."

Stacey and I arrived a full hour before the rest of the women to ensure plenty of time to glam this room out for my bestie.

"Great place for a paint party. Nice and clean too." Stacey rips open a box of fancy napkins.

A strong smell of acrylic paint floats past my nose. I ignore it as I put my hands to work, placing the cake, fruit, veggies, and cheese and cracker trays on the long white buffet table. Small purple and white flowering plants get placed in different spots around the room. We add gold tablecloths, printed placemats, and high-heel-shaped party favors to every setting.

"Hey, Stacey." I hold up the birthday crown I bought. Fake diamonds decorate the gold plastic.

"You know she won't wear that. It'll mess up her hair."

"Oh, watch me force her."

Stacey laughs and snaps a pic of the crown set in front of Nikki's chair. The bestie is artsy and she'll love this event, so she'll humor me and put it on. But even if she didn't, she's still a queen.

�❀

Nikki walks in and everyone yells, "Surprise!"

She's wordless as tears spill from her eyes.

Stacey circles around taking a video of the birthday girl hugging and kissing everyone while I climb onto a chair and wave a Kleenex box.

"Attention!" I call out. "Just so you know, Nikki wears Makeup Forever foundation and Smashbox lipstick. Enjoy loving on her but be aware it can come off on your clothes. You've been warned!"

"You!" She releases Stacey from a hug and points at me.

I jump down and step toward her. "What? What'd I do?"

"How'd you get this past me? When did you do this?"

She wraps her thin arms around my shoulders and squeezes and I'm transported to a moment after my baptism, when she helped the deacons drape a white towel around my wet body. I can't remember if she said it, but it was like her gesture told me, *welcome to the family.*

"Happy birthday, girl!" Seeing her so joyful, in a room full of beautiful ladies, my vision grows blurry.

I whip around to survey the crowd. Who should I serve after the birthday girl? Her mother and sisters will settle next to her. I'll dash to the party room and grab bottles of water for them.

In the two minutes that pass before I get back to the painting room, Felicia Taylor and her closest buddy, Krista Bless, have arrived. They've known Nikki since Girls High, and they also attend Rise. That's why I invited them. Some women from Rise Church are my sisters, and some, like Nikki and Stacey, are my sister-friends. Felicia and Krista? They're my Christian sisters. They know the Lord, and we're friendly to one another, but currently that's all I can say about them.

I force a toothy smile as I pass water bottles to Nikki and her family. I'd actually love it if the vibes were better between Felicia, Krista, and me. Three years ago, these same women included me in every girl's outing they organized, but that was before John and I started our relationship. It's amazing how the invites stopped after that. So yeah, I'm feeling some kind of way inside since they started treating me cold because of a bachelor they used to crave. But he picked a wife, and it wasn't either of them.

I *sooo* want to tell them: *God did not make you a tree, ladies. Stop throwing shade.*

Felicia and Krista nod and mumble hellos when I approach them. It's Nikki's birthday, so I step close and smile even wider. "May I serve you some water or apple cider?"

Felicia lifts her nose like she smells something. "Um, water's fine. Thanks."

"Same for me." Krista sniffs.

Nikki yells out, "If you love this place, you have my BFF Chablis to thank!"

I beam, even though Felicia and Krista settle together at the back of the room, whispering and glancing. Maybe they caught wind of my understated wedding and are gossiping about that. Who cares? I return with my head held high.

"You can also use these to water your leaves." I whisper, passing them bottles of water.

They look at me like I'm nuts.

"Everyone." Dominique's voice carries over the crowd. "In another five minutes, I'll show you what we're painting and how to mix your colors. Don't worry about whether you have artistic skills. We'll take it step-by-step, and you'll end up with a unique masterpiece."

And that's exactly what I want because God has taken me step-by-step into a life I never dreamed of.

I'm following Dominique's instructions for mixing a light shade of pink when my phone buzzes inside my skirt pocket. I wipe my hands and pull out my device. It's John.

> How's the party? Nik surprised?

> Oh yeah. She cried and everything.

> You feeling good?

I think about that. I just organized a grand birthday celebration for my bestie, Luna and Lorenzo are hard at work on the garden wedding plans, and John's been erasing his debts.

> I'm better than good. I'm AMAZING. ☺

> Keep that smile going. Grammy and Poppy want us over tomorrow for Sunday dinner with the fam. They won't take no for an answer.

Grammy and Poppy? Can't wait to see them.
But the "fam" also means Ms. Pat.
Yay.

something blue

GRAMMY AND POPPY'S three-story red brick home rests on a sycamore-lined street in East Oak Lane. Today the grandfolks cooked enough for a mini family reunion. It's like a scene from *Soul Food* up in this jawn. Grammy. Poppy. John and I. Nate. Ms. Pat, also known as the woman who will not let me call her mother. Her younger sister, Geri. Aunt Geri's husband, Ronald, and all three of their kids. Everyone relaxing comfortably in the dining room. Steaming food. Air conditioner humming in the background. It's nice.

John and I are the weirdos at the table. We eat little more than baked cod and sliced cucumber and tomatoes. The rest of the fam chows down on fried chicken, fried fish, baked sweet potatoes, sautéed collard greens, mac and cheese, and honey-butter biscuits. John *is* their grandson, so it's okay for me to follow his lead. Otherwise, I'd have a full plate of fried deliciousness. How I was brought up, you eat whatever is put in front of you if you have any home training.

I'm filling our almost-antique blue glasses full of iced tea when Grammy waves to get my attention.

"Yes, ma'am," I say.

"The wedding invitations? My brother Carl didn't get one."

"It turned out it was best for us to have something smaller."

"Oh? How many people are invited?" Poppy asks.

I glance at John. "Eighty. Forty invites for each side."

Iced tea cools my throat when I swallow my drink and look around. John's family members murmur.

"Just forty for John's side. That's all?"

"So our cousins from Detroit won't be there?"

"You can't be serious? Only forty from our side?"

Nate stays silent as he scoops greens onto his plate. His eyes say, *You know this wedding ain't no thing. Don't even worry about it, sis.* I nod to him and send up a quick prayer for his success finding love again. That he has so much faith in me and John after dealing with his own divorce — that says so much about him. He deserves a loving partner to help turn his fly townhouse into a warm home.

Ms. Pat walks in from the kitchen, a full pitcher of lemonade in her hands. "Mama, John knows we have a big family, and we have obligations. They should go on ahead and invite more people."

"What obligations, Mom?" John spears a cucumber slice with his fork.

"Your uncle and his family from Ohio. And your cousins from Raleigh. When Uncle Walty hosted Trenzia's wedding, he invited all of us."

"That doesn't mean I have to invite all of them."

"And what about your cousin Greg and his wife from Newark?"

"We're not that close."

Aunt Geri elbows me. "What about on your side? You don't have more people you want to invite?"

I hold back a snort. "Oh, with the number of people I know, the sanctuary would bust wide open."

Grammy splits open a biscuit. "See there. Go on and make the wedding bigger. It'll be festive."

I put my fork down. "We can't do that because we'd have to feed everyone, and that's thousands more dollars even with a buffet and a limited bar and—"

"Hey, everybody, look. This is how we're doing it." John announces in a loud voice. "It's what we can handle, and it's going to be beautiful. It's easy to invite more people when you aren't paying the bill."

Nate serves himself more fried swai. "It's going to be better than beautiful. It's gonna be fantastic. My baby brother's marrying Chablis, and I'm proud she's gonna be my sister. All that's in my toast speech."

"Ain't nobody asked me anything, but you should have what you want." Poppy chimes in. "Just let me sit up front so I can see it all."

I lean over and whisper in John's ear. "I've officially adopted every man in your family. Thank you for shutting all that down."

"You're welcome, Sunshine, and we're in this together." He whispers back.

I eat my meal and rest my leg against John's under the table while the guys argue about how they all wanted to go to a Sixers game before the end of last season and no one communicated about it, somebody dropped the ball on tickets, and three people still owe Nate after last year's outing.

My plate's almost empty when Ms. Pat leaves the table to take the empty collard greens bowl to the kitchen. Maybe it's me, but I swear she glances back with an ever-so-slight smirk before she steps away.

I pray silently. *Lord, you've placed me here with this beautiful family. Give me the strength I need to be the daughter-in-law you want me to be, no matter how I'm treated. Or give me the wisdom to consider any adverse repercussions that might occur if I try to put this woman in her place before the wedding. I know you've got this. Amen.*

Grammy catches my attention again. "Chablis, have you got your something blue yet?"

"No, ma'am. Not yet."

She reveals her beautiful smile. "I have a silver and blue bracelet I want you to have. It used to be my mother's. Was part of a set. Patty and Geri have the other two and I think you should have the last one."

"No way! Really?"

"Yes, it's yours." She turns toward the kitchen. "Patty! Patty, get in here."

Ms. Pat brings her exclamation point body to the doorway. "Mama?"

"Patty, I want to give Chablis that bracelet from my old set. The little clasp is broken on it and it needs a good cleaning. Can you take it to a jewelry store and get it fixed?"

Ms. Pat purses her thin lips and nods slowly. "Okay, Mama."

Across the table from me, Poppy pushes his chair back to help Grammy out of hers. Before she stands, he tugs her arm. "Where's my sugar?"

She kisses him on the cheek, and he flashes a big happy grin.

Under the table, John squeezes my thigh. A warm feeling washes over me. I place my hand on top of his and we communicate without words.

They're the type of couple we want to become.

"Was he always like this?" I ask Poppy.

"Pretty much. I can't remember all the times I came home from work and Hattie had me searchin' 'round the block trying to find that boy. Always on his bike or runnin' up and down the street with the other kids. Couldn't keep himself still for nothin'."

"You realize he's the same way now?"

"Yeah, I know." Poppy chuckles.

On the front stoop, Poppy rests in a creaky lawn chair while I sit beside him on the concrete step. Both of us watch John race up and down the block, challenging the little boys from next door to beat him to the stop sign at the end of the block and back again. Sometimes he lets them win.

"Granddaughter? Can you grab my sunglasses from the front room? Left them on the side table there, but I need 'em 'cause the afternoon sun 'bout to blind me."

"Sure." I jump up and do what he asks and the whole time I'm line dancing for joy inside because he called me his granddaughter.

I get Poppy's shades, pass them to him, and settle on the step again. John's still in the street, making the neighborhood kids tired for no reason.

"Poppy? You remember your wedding day?"

He slides his sunglasses on. "Coming up on fifty years and I remember two things vividly. My mama and daddy being there, 'cause they passed on a while now, and Hattie. Hattie smiled so big when she took my arm and I knew nobody would ever love me like she did. Yeah, uh-uh, that's what I remember the most."

"Her smile?"

"Her smile. That and the minister called her by her full name. Henrietta Geraldine Jackson. She stopped grinning after that, but she started again after I kissed her." He laughs and slaps his knee. "You know, all the years we've shared, all the trials, she greets me with that same smile every morning. I don't know how I'd get through a day without it. Like oxygen for me. You'll be like that for my grandson."

"You think so?"

"Oh, yeah. It might not seem that way today but pay attention when you keep house together. You'll see. He won't just live with you, he'll rely on you and you'll rely on him. When you look back, you'll need pictures to remind you what happened on your wedding day, because all you'll remember is how you felt when you took his arm. That's all."

I use my hand to shield my eyes from the afternoon sun rays. Family. Smiles. Love. Being united with John on life's journey.

If that's all I remember forty-nine years later, well, that's fine with me.

what the what?

I'VE NEVER READ a single *Brides* article explaining how annoying it is to prepare to live with a man. It's nowhere close to romantic. Not even in the ballpark. But if coffee shop confessions showed me and John anything, it taught us to work through the life essentials early. It's mid-June. Our plan is to merge households in September, a few weeks before the wedding. Today we're taking personal inventory.

I stand in Nate's darkened garage, pulling cobwebs off my calves and surveying boxes. John owns more than half of them.

"Bae, what the what?" I blink at plastic tubs and cardboard boxes stacked from floor to ceiling.

"Why are you tripping? You saw this stuff when I moved before."

"Are you sure? How'd I miss so much?"

"Because you stared at me the whole time I packed."

"You saw that?"

"Oh, yeah."

I jump away from a black spider crawling across the concrete. "Dang."

"I'm not complaining. Hey, watch where you're stepping."

I catch myself before I tumble over a box marked *Kitchen*. "With

117

all the gifts we registered for at Macy's and Target, you could probably donate all your household items."

"Perhaps. I kind of think we need to wait to see what people buy actually buy us."

"You're the positive thinker. Think positive."

John pushes a heavy tote across the garage floor. "I am positive," he says with a grunt, "that we need to hang on to some stuff in case people aren't generous."

My left baby toe grazes the tire of a blue bicycle. And I stand corrected because I thought he only owned one expensive-as-heck Cervelo bike. He owns two. Samantha and I don't even what to know what he named the blue one. Who needs two bikes? Cleats. Basketball. Soccer ball. About ten helmets. Chin-up bar. Yoga mat. It all looks like the top-of-the-line stuff, so I can't exactly ask him to pack it up for Goodwill.

I can't fuss because I've got a lot of junk too. John has already seen most of my apartment.

There's only one thing he hasn't seen.

At my place, he takes one step into my bedroom walk-in closet and his eyes pop. "Aye, yo! Chablis!"

The black trunk. Yep, he strolled into my personal Bermuda Triangle of all things Sephora/MAC/Bath & Body Works. Makeup palettes. Facial packets. Bath bombs. My treasure trove of self-care magnificence.

I snicker. "Don't you dare say anything. I just witnessed the abundance of your fitness obsession."

"But I'm saying, though, you don't need all this. You're beautiful without it."

I stand behind him and pat his shoulder. "Nice try. I'm bringing it all with me."

He points. "Even that?"

That is my humongous silver box of hair tools, extension cords, and hip-height stack of professional makeup books. He's still stunned as I smile and back away. Love me. Love my Sephora addiction.

"Whatcha think?" I ask.

"Yeah, we're getting a two-bedroom. I'm not sleeping anywhere near that trunk."

"Thought so."

A two-bedroom apartment in suburban Philly isn't what I'd dreamed of, but it'll be fine. We can rent a decent space and still pay off debts. Twenty-four months later, I'll have Pinterest boards full of home decor ideas. Williams Sonoma? Not erased. On hiatus.

John's body makes the room seem smaller. He gives me a goofy grin and shuffles toward the bed. "Can I rest here for a second?"

"Knock yourself out."

He eases down and lays back on my comforter, his legs hanging off the edge. "How do I look?"

"Like you dove onto a blanket of Pepto-Bismol."

He rolls off and bounces to his feet beside me. "I'd like to ask can we please avoid decorating our primary bedroom with frilly stuff or anything pink?"

"How about we do a Call of Duty: Black Ops theme?"

"You like gaming. If I surprise you with a bedroom decked out like that, I'll remind you it was your suggestion."

"Ha, ha, ha."

Any other engaged couple would rip off their jeans and t-shirts and toss undergarments to the floor the minute they were alone in a bedroom.

John just walks out, and I follow him to the living room. He calls it discipline and self-control.

I call it crazy because I have this ring on that I don't even take off to shower and we're months away from our ceremony and I'd love some affection until the cops come knocking.

But anyway.

He pulls me to living room couch and sits close like my soul fits with his. Snuggled next to him. Contentment flows to my bones. We're up in here getting ready for the future. Grammy's antique bracelet will soon be mine to treasure until I gift it to my daughter or daughter-in-love and I'm feeling all the feels for everything good God plans for us.

Time to try something Ariana taught us. She said we should get into the habit of affirming our partner—noticing times when we have admiration for them.

I massage his shoulders. "Baby?"

"Um-hmm."

"I appreciate the support you showed for us at Grammy and Poppy's. I admire all that you are, even your disciplined side. And I love you more every single day."

"You got that from premarital counseling, didn't you?"

"Yes sir. Yes, I did."

"That's all right. I receive that. Move a little closer to me."

And I do, and he wraps me tight in his arms and our kisses are delectable enough to make me forget he has a mother.

Ms. Pat?

Who's she?

"Stop fussing about the wedding gown change," I tell Nikki over the phone. "Since the event has gone enchanted fall garden romantic, I wanted a dress suitable to the theme and Elegance Bridal Shoppe is making it happen."

"But a strapless, jewel-bodice, tulle, full-skirted ballgown with sparkling crystals? All right, my urban Cinderella."

It's almost eleven, and I'm lounging on my bed. My iPhone's on speaker mode and I talk and scroll Instagram at the same time. Pic after pic from local wedding artists. Luna already booked us a

ENGAGED

wedding photo package, but that doesn't mean I can't find someone who can turn a picture into a work of art for us to hang in our living room.

"Anyway, don't worry about my dress, you'll love it when you come with me to the fitting," I say. "What's going on with you and Terry?"

"Nothing. What did you think was going on?"

"No special dates lately?"

"We're friends, and we're taking it slow, and I want to keep it that way."

"For how long?"

"Girl, I don't know."

"Wait a minute, uh-uh, didn't he send you... WHAT THE DEVIL?" I stop harassing my BFF and stare at a direct message.

"Chablis?"

Clutching my phone, I read the lines again and again. The DM? From VSweetBoss, aka, Veronica Sweets. I sit straight up and my blood turns icy.

"Chablis? Are you okay? Answer me!"

"I... yeah... I." My stomach knots. "I'm not panicking. Call you back."

I don't wait for her answer before ending the call.

I slide off my bed and four steps lead me into the bathroom where I think I might throw up on the tile. I scan the message again.

Congrats to you and your wonderful man! He blocked me from all his socials, so I'll message you. I know. I know. John probably didn't tell you that much about me. Let me set the record straight. We were so tight he practically lived with me for a summer. Think I'm lying? He likes his eggs scrambled with pepper jack cheese. He always drinks his coffee black. And during the hot months he sleeps on top of the covers. Three months in and he had the nerve to tell me I wasn't right for him after all we did together. And

I mean we did EVERYTHING. I hope you enjoy your wedding. I'm sure you already know you're in for a real treat during the honeymoon. My nickname for him was Mr. Incredible and you can assume whatever you want for why I called him that, princess bride. When you get a chance, tell him Ronnie said hello.

My heart thumps against my ribcage. Satan took the time to have that heffa message me intimate details about the future hubs, which hurts six times worse than a panic attack. I haven't bitten anything, but the inside of my mouth tastes like blood—salty and warm. I slide to the floor and sit cross-legged until my feet fall asleep.

Who's upsetting me, though? Veronica? The woman who enjoyed a hot summer with him? Or John? Who's *sooo* dedicated to sexual purity that he shut me down cold on engagement night. Our physical activity includes handholding, hugs, kisses, and some massages here and there. That's it. Everything else is for our wedding night and honeymoon. He wants that time to be spectacular, and okay, I do too, even if I got weak in March. But still. This is the same man who had no problem getting it in with Veronica all summer long?

How can I drop from treasured to undesirable so fast? And why is John always mixed up in it? I promised to practice self-control with him. Practically pinky-swore it on engagement night. But he had no issue with other chicks. None.

Now what do I do with that?

choices and chill

"NO CHATTER?" John steers the Jeep toward Rise on Sunday morning.

"No."

"I like your chatter."

"Yeah, well, I'm thinking about things right now."

"Heavy stuff?"

I fix my eyes on the road ahead. "Yeah."

"Something you wanna discuss? I'm here for ya."

"No."

He cranks up the sound system. Anthony Brown & group therAPy singing "Trust In You."

Right.

Truth is, I don't want to squawk about that DM. Before last night, each time something bad happened, I tattled to John. Trusted whatever he told me like some crushing fifteen-year-old. *Okay, John. Whatever you say, John. I know you want the best for us, John.*

I'm done with that.

Last night I sat cross-legged on that bathroom floor for nearly an hour, asking God for peace and guidance. Either the Lord or my conscience told me not to clap back at Veronica. The chick delivered a PG-13 description of her summer with my man. If I had made a chess move with a nasty rebuttal, she might have countered with something worse—triple X details, or maybe pictures. So I blocked her Instagram and went to bed.

I slept in anger and woke up feeling defeated.

Thank the Lord for the opportunity to serve. Ministry work with the Help Squad fills my agenda at Rise. I'm scheduled on the Information Desk, while John serves upstairs. We'll be separated for two-and-a-half hours, and that's fine with me because I'm so deep in my feelings John would need scuba gear to dive in and find me.

We park in the overflow lot behind Rise and when John helps me out of the Jeep and tries to hold my hand, I act like my Michael Kors bag needs me to hold it with both arms.

He stops me when we reach the sidewalk. "What's up with you?"

"Nothing." I study those looming clouds.

"Fine. I'll stop asking. You'll talk when you're ready."

"Thank you."

Inside, we man our stations. Sunday morning bustles with visitors, who drift over to my desk when they have questions for where to find bathrooms, the nursery, or RiseUP Youth service. I guide them to the right places. Upstairs, I'm sure John is doing the same.

After church ends, he drives me, still wordless, back to my apartment. I say I need time alone. He respects my decision and tells me he's going back to Nate's for a nap—like some old man.

The bathtub calls to me. Inside my tiled sanctuary, I run water and undress, dropping my *"Need Help? Ask Me!"* t-shirt, black jeans, and undergarments by my feet. I kick them across the bathroom to the wicker hamper. Warm, lavender Epsom-salted water soothes me as I ease into the tub. Minutes tick away and I cleanse my skin. Soaking and breathing. Breathing and soaking. Trying to calm down while heating up.

I want to call my mom, but if I share with her about that DM, she might stress about me and John's relationship. My parents stay calling John their son. The idea of us breaking up would hurt them. I won't worry them unless I have an actual reason to.

The sensible area of my mind says I should nap after bathing. I can wake up hours later, eat a healthy meal, and meditate on 2 Corinthians 5:17: *Therefore, if anyone is in Christ, the new creation has come: The old has gone, the new is here.*

Trouble is, the stupid DM aroused another piece of my brain.

The part called *I'm not a punk.*

See, Veronica didn't just send me an Instagram message. The chick remembered how to make his eggs in the morning—she bragged about being with my man in a way I haven't.

Soap. Bubbles. Rinse.

Soap. Bubbles. *Doggone it!*

If John's desire for me is weaker than it is for other women, that's something I have to know today, not after we jump the broom. If he tells me some trash like he's praying for deeper feelings to arrive, I'll give him the ring back. Call the wedding off. Quit my job and move to Kansas. Start a lavender farm while writing the book, *God Kept Me: How I Gave Back the Bachelor and Reclaimed My Life.*

I sit up and use my toe to depress the silver stopper. Water drains, but I'm still steaming.

"Lord, I'm your child, and I know I should wait," I whisper to steam-filled air. "I'm sorry... I gotta know."

The first red light I reach after driving away from my apartment, I call Nate. "Hey big brother. Are you traveling this week?"

The signal switches to green and I push the gas pedal of my Focus, flying down the street.

"Yep, just reached Scranton," he tells me. "I'll be here until Wednesday. What's going on?"

"I wanted to go by your place to give something to John. He's supposed to be napping. Can I use my key to get in?"

"That's what you have it for. If I have any Amazon packages at the side porch, bring 'em in for me, and put them in the dining room, please."

"You got it."

"Thanks, sis."

"No, thank you." I tap to end the call.

Nate won't be in the townhouse, and he won't turn up suddenly.

Time for John's sunshine to brighten his life in more ways than one.

My phone plays Maxwell, and I hum along to "This Lifetime" while walking around the Gerald kitchen. Warm vanilla sugar candle scent lingers in the air. My sheer red sundress flows light and airy around my body. Perfect for a day like this. I open the window to let the summer breeze fill the room. All those morning clouds have blown away. Sunlight fades against the skyline, and I study it and heat dinner for us. Lasagna. Chopped veggie salad. Garlic bread sticks. San Pellegrino sparkling water to drink. It all came from GIANT. I'm not trying to burn down this kitchen. That would definitely ruin the mood.

My hands tremble a teensy bit while I wait for the microwave to ping. I fan my face, willing myself to stop sweating. Dinner on a warm summer evening. That's all it is—some delectable food on a pleasant night. Future hubby will love seeing me wearing his favorite color, my curls soft and refreshed, and my skin smelling like minty lavender. We'll eat. Get close. I can't predict what will happen after that. I'll go with the flow.

Floorboards creak above my head and send a jolt through me, and I almost drop the plastic container of salad. Heavy footsteps sound from the upstairs hallway.

"Sunshine? You down there? I see your car from the window."

"Yeah, baby, I'm here. Sorry about my attitude this morning. I brought a peace offering. Go to the dining room and I'll serve you."

"You cooked for me?"

"I warmed for you," I yell and spoon warmed lasagna into a serving bowl.

His deep laughter rings out, and I smile, listening to him walk downstairs and turn into the dining room.

But my hands still tremble, and I set the bowl down fast. A small wave of dizziness hits me. *This will pass. This will pass. This will pass.*

What I'm not gonna do is dwell on the fact that the last time I did anything like this, I woke up in the hospital with my head bandaged a week later.

Slowly, I pour sparkling water into goblets. My pinky knocks one over. It clatters to the counter but doesn't break.

This might be too much for me.

"Smells delicious in here, and you look gorgeous. Sunshine?"

John towers over me, watching with wide eyes as I grip the granite countertop, trying to steady myself.

Breathe in. Hold it. Breathe out.

"Oh, my God!" He lifts me into his arms and carries me to the living room couch.

Inhale. Hold. Exhale.

John's arms rest around me, secure and warm, as he whispers prayers, cradling me against his chest. "Let me know when you're okay."

I nod and breathe, clinging to him. We stay that way long enough for me to relax and return to normal. And he's so close to me.

So close.

He rubs my back.

Uh-uh. Not good enough. Not tonight.

My arms snake up and around his neck, my lips nestle against his, then settle in deep. I pour all my attraction into those fleeting seconds. His fingers trail down my back and inch toward my hips, and when he circles his touch lower, I don't stop him. I wouldn't dare. I press closer, loving connecting with him this way. So warm. So good. Flowing together so natural and free. I can tell he's liking this. Heck, he's *loving* this.

"Time out." He breaks the kiss and gently pulls my arms from his neck. "Come on now, I'm getting too excited and I won't want to stop."

"John, you know I'm yours for life." I kiss his ears. His neck. "It's okay."

Breath still coming heavy, he grasps my hands in his and traps them against his chest. "Let me hold you for a while, all right. We have to settle down. Then we can go eat and talk."

Here he goes, telling me no.

Again.

I pull my body to the far end of the couch. Now I'm shaking for a different reason. I cross my arms and draw my legs up, tucking my feet beneath me. I close my eyes for a moment. When I open them, John sits, arms folded across his chest.

I push a wild purple curl out of my face. "What if I say I don't want to wait anymore?"

"I'll remind you we agreed to wait, and I'm not defending myself when I remember the conversation we had talking about how intimacy without boundaries is dangerous. All this time we've been cool, honoring God with our bodies. What's up tonight?"

I snort. "Cool? Oh, yeah. I was real cool until I found out how you misrepresented yourself."

"Misrepresented?" His eyes narrow.

"Stop looking at me all shocked, okay. You had me thinking you're treating me special and then I found out you practically lived with Veronica. She still remembers how you like your eggs the morning after."

"Veronica?" He slides to the edge of the couch, chuckling low. "That's what this is about?"

"You were with Veronica and you were with Trina, and I've heard rumors about other chicks from Rise. I just don't talk about it."

"Wait a minute, hold up! We had this conversation last year. You're not a virgin, either."

"I'm not talking virginity, John. I'm over here trying to figure out how you have so much self-control, but you couldn't keep your hands off the others? How come you're so controlled with me?"

"You really want to know?"

"I asked, didn't I?"

"Because I matured. I know better now. I shouldn't have been with Veronica at all past getting to know her. I got caught up enjoying the sex, and I'm not doing that anymore."

I snort again. "Oh, anymore. I see." I really don't. But whatever.

"Listen, it took me a couple of years to learn, but I learned. A mature man makes clear life choices. My choice was to put that diamond on your finger, and to choose all of you, not just the part between your legs. I chose you to be my partner for life. I chose you to make a home with me. I chose you to give birth to my kids. No, you won't be my first, but there's no doubt in my mind you *will* be my last. So, calm yourself and let it go."

"I'm not letting it go."

He looks me dead in the eye. "All right, then. My body doesn't belong to you yet—"

"For real, John? That sounds so—"

"I'm telling you how I feel, so let me finish. Any sex I had before, you gotta understand why I repented, and I don't plan on ditching my commitment to God. Other women I've been with? I don't want you to be like them!"

"Sounds like you have two sets of criteria for women."

"Which one do you want me to use for you? Check this out, I

truly believe God gave me you to treasure. When we make love, it's gonna be a special blessing and I wouldn't change that for anything in the world."

"So, we can't have a special evening tonight?"

"We can talk and I'll listen to what you have to say, but please understand, I'm not changing my mind."

"And I have to accept that? Even if I feel rejected by my man?"

"Yeah, well, think about the fact that you're living with panic attacks for life. I have to accept that, don't I?"

My cheeks burn. "What's that supposed to mean?"

He whistles. "That was low. Look, I didn't expect any of this at all, and I'm still kind of tired and... just... please forget I said that." He wipes a hand over his face, then stands and extends a hand to me. "Dinner smells wonderful, so we should eat and relax and stop talking crazy to each other. We don't need all this drama."

He's making sense, but I don't want to hear it. What I want is for him to speak the words that'll erase that DM from my mind or somehow satisfy the part of me that feels off for wanting to experience a side of future hubby other women can describe but I can only imagine.

We eat dinner together and watch *A Quiet Place* on Netflix, but with no chill afterward. When John walks me to my Focus, he hugs me extra tight and reminds me about the Garden of Eden honeymoon he's planning for October. He waves when I back out of the driveway.

On the way home, I count stop lights one by one. Twisting curls between my fingertips, stopping, then twisting again.

Strong feelings of peace and righteousness—or whatever— should flow through me because we're walking out God's plan for our intimacy through this engagement. And I know I have to repent because tonight makes me a card-carrying member of the bad girl's club and I don't need to text Daisy or anyone really to confirm everything I know about willful acts of disobedience to God and improper stewardship of my love and relationship with John. All of that double's down on how I really feel in this moment.

Right now?

I just feel stupid.

save the date

THANK God for the opportunity to babysit for Daisy while she speaks at the women's prayer breakfast.

Nothing like three small rug rats to take my mind off my still-unsatisfied-but-soon-to-be-married issues.

Me and the kiddies are all in the kitchen. I'm throwing out empty Honest Kids Organic Juice boxes and clearing plastic lunch plates away when Daisy walks in the back door.

The two oldest Worthington children rush over and tackle Daisy's knees, and then calamity breaks loose. Tucker chases his sister, Caroline, with a green toy dinosaur. She squeals and they circle the kitchen island and exit the room. Baby Brooks sleeps, sucking his little thumb as the swing rocks him back and forth.

In the middle of all this, Daisy remains the picture of calm. She kisses the baby's forehead, flashes me a smile, then pours me an aqua-colored mug of hot tea.

This kicks an uncomfortable truth into my brain.

Sex leads to babies.

Being in my feelings last Sunday could have had me pregnant by sunrise Monday.

I spoon Splenda into my drink. "Daisy, when Caroline grows up, she'll panic whenever she sees a green lizard. Want me to separate them?"

She perches on a wooden stool. "I only intervene if I see blood or tears."

"I love your calm and your house." My eyes rest on her distressed farmhouse table and the mismatched but charming wooden chairs surrounding it. Metal milk cans filled with fresh flowers decorate each corner. "How do you keep this place so clean with three kids underfoot?"

"Clean?" She huffs. "Sometimes all I see are broken toys and baby clothes scattered all over."

"You have a cleaning service, don't you?"

"How did you guess?"

"I used to babysit for this couple at my church, Brian and Tracey Jones. I'd come to their house Friday night, and all the rooms smelled like Lysol. Nothing was out of place. Tracey told me a cleaning team came through every Friday morning."

Daisy pushes a lock of sandy brown hair away from her face. "A big house is nice until you have to scrub rooms every day. After Caroline, I told Tripp either get me some help, or this is our last kid."

"No, you didn't."

"You see Brooks, right?" She takes a sip of tea. "You missed SPRINT this week. Too many wedding and work items on your agenda?"

"More like too much sin in my brain. I've struggled for months, but I actually tried to get John last week."

"Whaaaat?" She asks, wide-eyed.

I lower my voice. "Dinner and candles and soft music and me in a sheer sundress at his brother's house with no one else around."

She holds up a hand. "But you said tried? How'd you fail?"

"John's a lot more disciplined than me, and he wasn't having it. Our timing was off and I was just reacting to a message from his ex." I stir my drink. "So we had dinner and a movie and then I packed up and went home."

"Hold that thought." She stands up and walks over to the family room doorway. "Tucker, you turn that television off before Mommy goes to get the paddle!"

Tucker whines. Caroline mimics him. Daisy goes after both of them. Five minutes of yelling later, she sits her slim body down like nothing happened. The baby never stirs.

"Go on," she says.

"What if John doesn't desire me all that much?" I lean closer to her. "Like, what if he's only marrying me because I'm his friend and I can be that nice Christian chick who can push out the kids he wants? What if this is all a setup and—"

She rests her hand on mine. "Satan is doing a job on you, and you're falling for it. Believe me, you're marrying a decent guy."

I rock myself on the stool. "I think I am. But how do I know?"

"Because a man with an agenda would've already started using you for whatever you have. Men with agendas don't have account- ability partners they pray with before starting the day."

She's right, of course. But still.

"If he's fine, what's wrong with me?" I drum my nails on the countertop.

"Hold on one more time." She dashes to the family room, shuts the door, peeks at Brooks, then gets back on her stool. "Go on."

"I know how John acted with his other women. What I have with him is unbelievable, but I don't know, some part of me wants to experience what they had too."

"Have you been watching porn?"

I roll my eyes. "Oh, please."

"Hey, I pray with young ladies all the time, and I've heard more than you can imagine."

I shake my head. "Yeah, that's not me. I'm bugged out because I didn't struggle like this last year."

"It's possible you set your own boundary for what you would do with John before he proposed, but that was your limit. You didn't base it on God's context for sexual relationships. When you took his ring, your boundary disappeared, but John's limit didn't." Daisy sips tea. "Am I hot?"

"Like one hundred degrees in the summer hot."

"From what you told me, John already experienced easy. He hasn't had sacred and precious and he wants that with you. You have to respect him for that."

I give a sigh. "Yeah, if I look at it that way... anyway, I know I have to stop pushing. Trying to get with him was crazy."

"Praise God your body is in healthy working order. It's a glorious thing your desire is for him and nobody else. If you didn't want him at all, you'd have a bigger problem." She nods toward me. "And how's the mother-in-law situation?"

"Don't ask. She's supposed to get her mother's blue bracelet to me, you know, something blue for the wedding ceremony, but I haven't heard anything, and I don't think she'll give it to me without a fight."

"I hate that. Brings back bad memories, you know."

"I know."

Daisy's had her share of stonewalling from Tripp's family. The Worthingtons are a blue blood Boston family, and they were not ready for Tripp to come home from Princeton with Daisy on his arm. The ultra-liberal Worthingtons showed her love. The conservatives ignored her. From what she told me, when the kids were born, her in-laws softened up. But she still prayed for years to manage her feelings about them.

I lock eyes with Daisy. She stares back. A crackle of understanding passes between us. No words needed.

A crash and two loud wails come from the family room and in a flash, Daisy's up and over there.

Kids. I'm looking forward them, but I already told John I want at least a full year alone with him before we try. He agreed. So while I'm thanking God for my healthy desires, I'll shout a couple of hallelujahs because at least I can enjoy the rest of my Saturday with no concerns about pregnancy tests in my near future.

Daisy deals with the kids and I whip out my phone and take a few pics of myself inside her lovely McMansion kitchen. I'll take a selfie with her before I go. Something I can post on the Gram. Pictures can't settle my mixed emotions, but they can let me give the world a dimpled smile in the meantime.

My time is my own for the rest of the day. I might invite some old friends to my apartment later. Two of them, in fact.

Meat lover's pizza and Dr. Pepper.

Tuesday morning and I'm still in bed. Lights off. Body buried under my pink comforter. Zero intention of visiting the gym.

"How come you're avoiding me?" John asks over the phone.

"I'm not."

"Then please get up."

"Nope."

"It's workout time."

"So go to the Y and I'll call you later."

"I'm coming in there to check on you."

Adrenaline shoots through me and I sit bolt upright. "Uh, where are you?"

"I just parked, and I'm coming upstairs."

Oh, Lord! "No! John! Why aren't you driving Uber?"

"I'm worried about you. You said you needed time to yourself, but now I need to see you. And... what's all this?"

I squeeze my eyes shut because I know what's coming.

"Your trash bag is outside your door, and there's a Pizza Hut box in there? Lay's potato chips? Somebody's been partying."

"Um, I can explain." I rush to throw on his Eagles shirt and a pair of black yoga pants.

"I'm hanging up."

The call disconnects and I exit my bedroom hideaway in time to see him walk in wearing his gray HSTL t-shirt, shorts, and black Nikes. He stares me up and down.

My pink satin sleep bonnet hides my hair, and I'm not taking it off because I haven't visited Quinsara in three weeks. My face is devoid of makeup. His castoff XL jersey hides my belly bloat.

I grin.

He frowns.

This is John Gerald, armchair nutritionist and fitness enthusiast. Finding pizza boxes and chip bags in my trash is like him catching me with another man.

Scratch that.

He'd be easier on me if he found a dude in the hallway.

"I can explain." I duck my head like he caught me doing wrong, which he has, but not with a person.

John never budges about practicing good health habits. Just like he knows I need a partner who shows tenderness, I know he needs his life partner to stay healthy. It's not a body size thing—it's a wellness thing.

He drops onto my couch, staring at his phone.

I shift my weight from foot to foot. "The pizza and chips and soda—"

"You had soda too?"

"Dr. Pepper. Would you like some?"

He shoots me a serious look. "I can tell you're still in your feelings, but you're not talking to me about it."

"It's only food—"

"Maybe for somebody else, but not for you. For you, it's a coping habit, and I watched you work too hard to get over that." He wipes a hand over his face. "I can't care for your heart if you don't share it with me."

"I've been trying to hang in here. I have." I push my words out at a snail's pace. "I got that DM from Veronica. And then you rejected me? Every day, I'm missing you more. Even your mom's attitude about us getting married—all that messes with me." I sigh. "I'm just... I'm sinking a little."

He fiddles with his phone, his thumbs tapping the screen fast.

"What are you doing?" I ask.

"Sending a message to my director and my team that I'm out today with an emergency. Can you please call in to work and do the same?"

"Why?"

"Because it is an emergency. You need me? I'm right here." He taps a few more times, and Willie Moore, Jr. singing "Angel," fills the room. "Ms. Chablis Shields? Can you do me the honor of accompanying me to the gym today for a workout?"

"Sure."

"Good." John heads into the kitchenette and pulls out my coffee maker. "I'd love for us to work out together, then I'm staying by your side for the rest of the day. All the way through our counseling session."

"Are you serious? You'd do that for me?"

"Like I said, I'm here for you. But I have to warn you, you won't be smiling after today's workout. Grin now so I can remember it."

John wasn't kidding. The workout is CrossFit-style intense, but I endure it like a champ. Afterward, we hit the locker rooms to shower and change, then head out for omelets at City Diner.

Shofuso Japanese House welcomes us at noon. With lush green landscaping and a bean-shaped pond filled with fish and turtles, Shofuso is, without a doubt, the prettiest Philly spot for meditation and prayer. Sitting beside John on the wide golden porch, I talk through everything bugging me. He listens as we feed the koi and the orange and white fish glide through the large pond. When we run out of food pellets, we stroll around the Japanese botanical garden.

He holds me in his arms when we pray.

And we shine in our evening session with Ariana.

We share our family plans for raising four children to have faith

139

in God. We want them to attend a Christian school. And I don't mind having the babies back-to-back and being a stay at home mother for a while. The kids will have a big yard with lots of trees so they can run, jump, skip, climb, and dance whenever they have a chance. We want to teach them to live life out loud with unapologetic belief in the Lord. We could not care less that some people might think our plans are a little old-fashioned. Whatever. This is our life, doggone it.

Ariana nods when we're finished. "Having the same family beliefs is one of the major markers of a successful marriage."

Holding hands, we grin at one another like she gave us a gold medal.

"I want you to consider this," she continues. "As Christians, you walk according to the Bible, but that's not always the same as walking together on all issues. Beliefs aren't just tied to your faith. Take a subject like child discipline. What if one of you is fine with spanking, and the other one thinks spanking is child abuse? Or you might agree on tithing, but not on how much to give non-church-based organizations. Think about politics. Social justice. How much money and time you'll invest as your family grows. In your home-work this week, be transparent about your values and set up intentions to grow together, even if you disagree now."

John squeezes my fingers. "Even if we disagree, we'll work out everything. I promised that on engagement night, and I'll never go back on it. Never."

Sister Gunning's gravelly, disembodied voice still scares the mess out of me. But I'm line dancing at my desk when I play her voicemail Thursday afternoon.

"Hello, Chablis. This is Mary-Gladys Gunning from Rise Community Church. I'm calling on behalf of Pastor David Downes. We received the message from your counselor that you and John are completing your premarital counseling sessions. Today I added the entry for Gerald Wedding to the church calendar. First Saturday in October. One p.m. Congratulations on your upcoming wedding, and God bless you."

The wedding is on the pastor's calendar.

Team Gerald. We're on our way!

are we having fun yet?

"HI, Ms. Pat. I'm calling to find out if Grammy's bracelet is fixed. I have time to pick it up this weekend, so let me know. Hope you're having a blessed day."

That's the message I left on John's mother's voicemail. My test team meeting ended ten minutes ago, but it's quiet in this conference room, so I stayed. Plus, I wanted to call Ms. Pat while I was still in full professional mode.

Not a word from her since Grammy asked her to get the bracelet clasp fixed. What if she overrides Grammy's desire to include me in the family heirlooms? I might have to locate my *I am not a punk* side.

I gotta stop—I'm hurting myself over fiction.

Grammy, Poppy, and Nate are on my side. Ms. Pat is outnumbered. No way she's going to pull a public stunt like that. And if I can keep my hurt under control long enough to pray and love and connect with her, I might break through her wall yet.

Deep breath in. Good. Out. Release the tension.

Next thing I know the phone is in my hand and I'm dialing John.

"Hey, Sunshine," he answers.

"Can you talk?"

"A client is having security issues." He speaks fast. "Do you need something right away?"

The higher-ups at his company must be making everyone miserable, blaming flaws on the engineers and architects.

"Not really." I shut my laptop. "I called your Mom about the bracelet and left her a voicemail. Can we get together tonight? Maybe watch a movie or have dinner?"

"Not tonight. From what I see in these emails, I'll be here awhile. After that, I'm trying to get some Uber hours in. I'm making progress. I paid off one of my Visas last week."

"That's good news! I'm so—"

"Listen, I have to go. Sanjay sent me a meeting notice and we're going into the war room."

"Okay. Talk to you later."

"Talk to you." He ends the call.

John works pretty much all the time. Other than FaceTime, I see him at premarital counseling and on Sunday. It's like having a fiancé who stops through Philly every three or four days. But he's doing the right thing, so I can't complain.

Nikki? We chat every night, but she's busy too. She's applying for a master's program at Temple and planning her mission trip to South Africa. The next time we hang out will be at the dress fitting.

It's a hot, sunny Friday. In the summer, a lot of my co-workers take the entire Friday off. What am I doing here? I can finish my projects by two.

I launch my beauty salon scheduling app. Quinsara has an open slot available at three. Great! I'll head to Shades of Beauty and spend an hour yakking to her while she conditions my kinky curls.

Under the dryer at Shades, I scroll through Instagram. There's a DM for me from FrontLensLight, these amazing artistic photographers I messaged a few weeks back. They shoot stunning wedding photos. I had asked what they charge for a small package of ten grand artistic shots. Turns out, it's fifteen hundred dollars. That's not so bad. I can manage it with the credit line from my bank and pay it back in three scheduled payments before October. Easy.

My fingers move fast. From Instagram to the FrontLensLight website where I select the artist package and choose the calendar for our event date. Check out at PayPal. Done. I dash off a quick message to Lorenzo, asking him to coordinate with the photographers for the reception.

If we can't have a celebrity wedding, who says we can't look like we did?

"Six pounds? I'm up by six pounds?"

I step off the scale and push back at my disgust. My curves betrayed me! No way we can do another junk food binge. I need to look glamaliciously svelte in my wedding gown.

Time to search Facebook.

Social dance groups have FB pages, and I follow most of the urban dance pages in the tri-state area. Scrolling. Scrolling. Nothing tonight in Philly. Nothing for South Jersey or Delaware.

A Baltimore group hosts an event near Inner Harbor called the Summer Explosion Dance Jam. It starts at seven and three of the Grandstand dancers will attend. I tap out a question on the event post, asking if tickets are still available.

I'm on my carpet, stretching, when I hear a notification ping. Yes!

A response from the event organizer. Tickets are available at the door for twenty dollars, or fifteen in advance through Cash App.

I tap away, sending money via Cash App, then I'm up on my feet to my bedroom, pulling together a bag to take to Baltimore. I'll run into people I've met from other events, and if I get too tired to drive back, I'll crash somewhere. The Kayak app posts last-minute hotel deals.

Toiletries. Underwear. T-shirts. Jeans. All of it goes into my Nike bag. Dancing in another city is stress-free and calorie-free activity for me. I'll FaceTime John when I get there. He'll be happy I'm not doing anything involving Pizza Hut or Dr. Pepper.

The Summer Explosion Dance Jam is lit! Folks stand shoulder to shoulder on the dance floor. People moving and grooving with smiles and laughter. Showcase performances from dance groups who look like they've studied with Alvin Ailey. Older people getting their steps in and younger dancers right beside them.

Funky rhythms flow all around me on the dance floor. Beat. Beat. Slide. My spine melds to its tempo, swaying like an S with the ebb and flow of notes. I'm sweaty and energy lights up every square inch of me. Dip. Spin. Slide. Here I'm in control with my moves tight and fluid. No one else's decisions boxing me in. Here it's just me, and it feels so darn good to be alive. Sweet adrenaline. Not a sugar or carb high. Not sex. Not terror. Just pure joy pumping through every part of my body.

I live.

By the time I look at my watch, it's midnight, and I'm still hyped. I follow three other cars to an after party in Towson, where we dance until two. The Kayak app helps me book a cheap hotel, and that's where I rest after I'm danced out.

Night gives way to morning and I get a text from Sheila. She's one of the Baltimore dancers. She asks if I want a free ticket to a line dance brunch today. I message back, *Oh yeah*, and she sends me the address. Back to Baltimore to dance my Saturday away. Somehow, in my haste, I forgot to pack my iPhone charger, so my phone goes dead on the drive to B-more. At the event, I borrow Sheila's charger and plug my phone into the wall to charge.

After the last step of *Be Thankful*, I make my way back to my phone. It's all charged. Notifications fill the screen. John called seven times in the past hour. What the what? I gotta call him back.

The side hallway isn't too crowded, so I push through the double doors and tap to return John's call.

The phone doesn't even ring before I hear his voice. "Chablis!"

"How's your Saturday? Getting lots of ride share customers?" I use my Sunday school voice, knowing he'll talk to me about spreading myself too thin and blah, blah, blah.

"You didn't come home last night?"

"No, I went to that after party and—"

"Where are you now?"

"Baltimore." I walk a few feet from the ballroom door to hear him better.

"B-more to Towson to B-more again?"

"Yeah."

"You slept in your car?"

"No, I found a cheap hotel on Kayak, and Sheila told me about the event today and gave me a ticket, so I came over. This is my last dance event though because I want to be ready for church on Sunday."

"And you didn't bother to call me this morning?"

"John, I would have called a few hours ago, but my phone—"

"Chablis, first, I'm relieved you're okay. I was losing my mind until you called back." His tone drops. "Don't you ever do anything like that again!"

I pull my phone away, blink at it, then put it back to my ear. "I found something fun to do and it's something I love and *now* you have an issue?"

"What I have an issue with is... look, I have a few things I need to say, and it has to be face-to-face. You danced, and you had fun, now bring yourself back to Philly."

"You want me to stop what I'm doing and rush home just because you say so?"

"No, I want you home because I'm your man and we need to talk."

"What if I don't want to leave?"

"Then we'll have a problem."

"Tell me, please, what kind of problem?"

"Whoo! Chablis! I am not playing! I'll be in your apartment in two hours. You can decide what you want to do but that's where I'll be."

I open my mouth, but I can't say anything because he ends the call. I clutch my phone and blink at the screen.

So dumb. John acts like he never spends time with Terry or his other buddies. He does, and I'm always cool with it. Have I ever mumbled a word about him biking those trails with Travis, or hanging out for hours after ManUp men's group? No. I always give him his space.

People mill around the hall outside the ballroom, chatting with friends, and buying nachos and fried wings from the food stand. I go pee, then take myself back inside the ballroom where a crowd fills the floor doing *Cali Jam*.

Sheila from Baltimore watches me pack my hand towel and water bottles in my bag. "You're leaving?"

"Yeah."

"They haven't even announced the door prizes for the raffle yet."

"I know, but I have stuff going on at home."

"Everything all right?"

"You know what? I don't even know." I shrug and pull my backpack strap over my shoulder. "My man wants me back there, so I guess I have to go. Thanks for the ticket. You all are awesome." I give her a quick hug.

She passes me glossy flyers for the next Baltimore event. "Here, share these with the Philly dancers. And whatever it is, God's got you, girl. You be safe."

"Thanks."

Nothing registers in my brain on the drive back. On I-95 North, I don't enjoy the warm sunshine or sing along with Jor'dan Armstrong or Sstedi or do anything I'd normally love on a long ride back to Philly.

I clutch my steering wheel. Body stiff. Eyes on the road. Flying down the straight areas and leaning into the curves.

April. May. June. July will end soon. All I've done since John's ring touched my finger is smash into issues that drive me nuts. Now he's directing me home because I went dancing? I've been doing this since before he asked me to be his lady. My blowing off steam going to dance events doesn't happen all the time and I'm not married to him yet, which he clearly pointed out the night I tried to make love to him.

Is this what I'm signing up for? I have heard some eyebrow-raising marriage stories at Rise Church. Like Shanta Jamison's husband, Rick, who forbid her to wear ripped jeans. And Eve Carter's husband who told her she's not allowed to weave her hair. And it's a known fact Dr. Jones made his wife Tracey formally agree to take care of everything home and child-related so he could pour his full attention into building his private practice.

That's just Rise. I have three college girlfriends who aren't interested in ever marrying because they've never seen a marriage work and they don't want the trouble of coordinating life with a demanding adult. One floods her Instagram with pictures showing her happily raising her toddler daughter alone.

And none of that is any of my business in this moment. The only people who matter right now are me and John, so I'm heading home to see how this all goes down.

I'm wearing the man's ring.

What choice do I have?

And none of that is any of my business in this moment. The only

Morally, I've done nothing wrong, but that's not how I feel when I step into my apartment.

John leans against the living room wall with his arms crossed. Sweat stains darken his *Pray Train Conquer Repeat* t-shirt. His black cycling shoes rest on my kitchen floor with pebbles and dirt caking the bottoms. He makes my apartment smell like sweat and wet grass.

"Nice hair. Nice nails." He stares me up and down. "You look relaxed. Your cheeks are glowing."

"I've been dancing since last night."

"Dancing? That's all?"

"John, you know that. Last night, I turned the phone around to let you see me on the dance floor."

"Since when do you decide to crash in a hotel room without telling me?"

"John—"

"Don't, okay. I knew you wanted to be with me, and I keep making us wait and I thought you could handle that. I mean, love always trusts and assumes the best."

The inside of my mouth becomes a furnace. "What are you saying?"

"I can't believe I'm asking this, but I'd rather know. Were you with somebody else last night?" He closes his eyes. "Did you cheat on me?"

A chill runs through me, and even though the answer is no, I can't speak. My heart hurts.

This is what he thinks of me?

"Chablis?"

I find my voice. "No, I didn't—"

"A last-minute hookup before the wedding? Some brother down in B-more willing to take care of your needs because I'm not?"

I'd never.

I'm not.

No.

I spin around so fast I almost tumble over my own feet.

My vision blurs and I can't see the knob when I reach for it and his voice fills my ears but I don't care that he's calling calling calling my name when I rush out the door and slam it behind me.

past tense

ARIANA DOES all the talking Tuesday night in our session on work and life balance. It must be tough. John and I stay tight-lipped most of the time.

She needs a chainsaw to obliterate the tension in this jawn.

"You'll grow closer whenever you share all the aspects of your work experiences with each other," she drones on. "Also, be transparent about your career aspirations. Agree to talk openly if either of you needs to pursue a degree or special certification. Work/life balance doesn't happen automatically. You must set agreements and boundaries..."

Thirty minutes into this ridiculousness and our friendly counselor comes for us.

She tosses her notebook on her desk. "All right. Both of you. What's the problem?"

"We had a rough weekend," I say.

Her eyes take in my clenched fists. "I think it's time we set this lesson aside and deal with the current issue. Can we do that?"

"Fine." I shrug.

John nods and leans forward. "Why not?"

She sits back in her cushioned chair. "Tell me about this weekend. What happened?"

John glances sidelong at me, then looks at Ariana. "Chablis drove to another state to go line dancing with people she hardly knows, but she didn't tell me about it until after she started partying. She has no concern for her own safety, and she spreads herself too thin. She slept over without telling me about it. I don't know all those people, and I don't like all those dances."

My mouth drops open.

Are we in the first grade?

Did he just tell the teacher I stole his lunch money?

"Besides her not communicating plans beforehand, what didn't you like?" Ariana asks. "I thought she danced before you got together?"

"She did. I mean, she loves staying active, and she loves people. That's the Chablis I fell for. When she substitutes teaching for the senior citizens at Overbrook Rec, and her Thursday lessons at The Grandstand, that's all good. But some of those line dance events? And the sexy dancing? This weekend, it bothered me."

"Sexy dancing?" Ariana's eyebrows raise.

"They're only line dances," I say. "Ariana, I'm not doing stripper moves out there. Choreographers create those dances for ages eight through eighty."

John turns to me. "Really? *Sensual Sensei*?"

"That's one dance."

"Yeah, all right. Just one? *Sex In the City*, *Subtle*, *Body Language*. I mean, I could go on if you'd like."

"I do a few routines to slow songs, but no one's touching me because I don't do any close dancing because the guys are all sweaty or gay or old enough to be my daddy or married and—"

Ariana stops me. "Chablis, I want you to listen to your partner. John, how do you feel about her performing those dances in public?"

He chews his gum so hard a vein pulses on his jaw. "I want her to think about exercising a little more modesty because it's hard to hear dudes saying stuff in the background when she dances."

I roll my eyes. "No one talks about me. That's not true."

He keeps grinding his gum. "Last time I visited The Grandstand, when you danced *All Snap Freak*, two dudes passed by my table and pointed at you. One of them said, 'Yeah, shawty right 'dere with them curves, I'mma hit that one day.'"

"Someone could say that when I'm walking on the street or while I'm shopping."

"True, but I heard it at The Grandstand and I had to stop myself from punching a dude in the mouth."

"I think I understand." Ariana's calm tone is as smooth as a shell-free boiled egg. "John, part of being a life partner means you'll have to work out your feelings about how Chablis takes part in the activities she enjoys. She's a whole person who loves life, and she is who you chose."

John slumps in his seat.

"And Chablis?" Ariana directs her gaze to me.

"Yes."

"John will be your spouse. Like it or not, he may say when your activities bother him, even if you don't see a problem with them."

I search my bag for a tissue to blot my runny nose. "Ariana, he's not saying everything on his mind. Please don't get it twisted, he's not worried about me dancing, he's worried about me *cheating*. But that's nonsense because he knows he has my heart. At least no ex-man of mine ever DMed him, telling him how I like *my* eggs in the morning."

John's eyes inches toward the carpet and he stops chewing his gum but says nothing.

Ariana shoots me a look that says she understands I'm talking about more than breakfast food.

We all sit quietly for a moment—long enough for me to feel the weight of what I threw out there.

As far as I know, John has told no one the real reason I have panic attacks. But I get mad at him one time and release all his dirty laundry.

What kind of queen am I?

"Chablis and John, take a time out. I'm sure you don't want to hurt each other." Ariana moves to her desk and pulls two sheets of paper from a pad, handing one to each of us. "It's clear you have differences, and it'll be good for you to discuss your concerns with an open mind." She sits back down. "Use these papers to write your issues, then go over them one at a time."

John folds his sheet in half. "Write and talk, and what else?"

"When you talk, keep your tone neutral. Both of you are seeing things from your own perspective, so use 'I' language when you discuss your views. Also, no hitting below the belt," she adds, glancing at me. "Don't escalate or threaten each other. Review each other's points and search under the surface for the actual issue. You aren't each other's enemies. You're just not seeing eye to eye right now. Does that make sense?"

We nod like two kids pulled apart for scrapping on the playground.

"If anger arises, I want you to remember: underneath all that emotion is an urge to be heard and respected. Listen for that urge so you can address your issues with compassion. If you ever get to a point when you're wounding each other repeatedly, stop and take a break. Always take a pause when you don't want to make things worse." Ariana opens the office door. "Pray about your issues after you talk them through, and if you need some help, call me, please."

My hands get busy shoving my notebook and pen into my bag.

We have issues.

We have debt.

We're weeks away from sharing Colgate.

Everything about this seems like marriage, except we haven't taken any vows and...

Never mind.

Significant moments on Instagram involve fun people and events, or fun people and food, or fun people doing anything fabulous. If you love social media, you scope out those Gram-worthy people, places, and things and take that pic and post it, then sit back and collect the love.

Nate's townhouse presents the perfect Instagram moment. The coffee table holds a green vase with long-stemmed red roses and a white card with *Chablis* scribbled across the envelope. Those fragrant blooms beg me to take post pictures, hashtag them #ThisIsWhy-ILoveFutureHubby.

But I'm still ticked, so I stalk past the rose display without saying a word.

In the kitchen, I grab a bottle of water from the fridge and sit at the table. John sits opposite me and that's fine because I don't want to move closer to him. Don't want him to touch me because nothing inside of me feels loving. Even the sound of his breathing irritates me.

We're supposed to use these stupid sheets of paper to list our grievances, but I'd rather jump back in my car and drive home.

"We should get started." He hands me a black pen.

I keep my eyes on my paper, scribble the three things on my mind and slam the pen down. "I'm done."

"That's it? As much as you talk, I figured you'd have more."

"And as little as I get from you, I'm surprised you wrote anything."

"Well, I did."

He writes for another minute.

The roses smell incredible, but I'm *not* telling him that. "John?"

"I'm finished. You first."

I tap my paper. "Why'd you make me sound like a chickenhead in front of Ariana?"

He shrugs and gives me an empty expression.

"You think I'm a chickenhead?"

Still no answer, and this time the shrug lasts longer. I'm about to marry a man who thinks I'm a pretty chick who makes brainless decisions? Now he's barely talking?

"Say something!"

"Here's my something. Calm. Yourself. Please."

"I'm as calm as I'm going to be, considering. Want to know my second thing? You're too strict about everything from food and exercise to where I am and how I'm spending my time when I'm on my own."

He abandons his pen and places both hands behind his head. "I cover you. I need to know where you are."

"Like Clark Kent just waiting for Lois Lane to get in trouble?"

He tilts his head and his muscular chest rises and falls harder with each breath.

Heat fills me, and I keep talking. "No, wait, I get it now. You really are Superman. Without the glasses." I should cut it out, but all I see is red and words keep flying out of my mouth. "But you know what, I can handle everything except you thinking I stepped out on you. You said you think I cheated? What if I did? Maybe you kept me at arm's length too long? Got you thinking someone else might want your treasure?"

John's mouth goes slack and his eyes bulge like he wants to call me something that begins with B. But just as quickly, calmness reigns.

"Oh, okay, yeah. I'll be cool," he says with a sniff. "I know you only said that to clap back at me from Saturday. Do you even read your Bible?"

I lean close enough for him to smell my breath. "Did you read yours, Mr. Incredible?"

When I ease back into my chair, central air whirrs in the background. The cold hangs between us.

John sits stock still. "You were unsaved when dudes from your high school nicknamed you, Cha-BLISS. At least that's what Aaron told me. Remember Mariah's Labor Day cookout? Aaron was my Spades partner. After dude tipped back a couple beers, he pulled me to the front porch and asked if I knew what really happened the night you got attacked. Told me he was the first in the family to figure out his gorgeous babydoll-looking cousin had cheated on the *wrong* guy."

I squeeze my water bottle and liquid runs down my fingers. It might as well be blood, because that's what I imagine when I close my eyes. When I open them, there's John. Powerful body. Chiseled features. Skin smooth like velvet over sturdy steel.

"Veronica. Leilani. Nisha. Omi. Shanda." He pushes out names and they slip to the floor like dropped ice cubes. "Some of those ladies won't think about men the same way after they trusted me with their hearts and bodies. All because I had a good time with them, but I didn't love them. And yeah, I repented, but repentance and apologies can't fix all the damage I caused."

"John—"

"Hold up, I'm not done." He scoots closer. "Let me tell you about the ladies I won't name. The ones who locked me in the friend zone unless they wanted my company at midnight. I'm talking the type of women who ditched relationships with me because my outward appearance doesn't match what I'm like inside and they didn't want to catch feelings for a nerdy, Bible-focused introvert who could be half-blind in twenty years." His eyes search my face. "I fell for you and you loved me back, I swore to God I'd do His will every step of the way. You know for a fact God guided us past the messy way we treated people and the destructive things people did to us. For years he's been renewing us in his image and every day, I pray and I struggle against my flesh. I pray for both of us."

Pause.

"If you don't get it by now, we're mirror images of one another," he says, sliding his chair back in place. "Us. Me *and* you."

I swallow hard. "You and me."

John clears his throat and picks up his paper, scans it, and tosses it aside. "I only wrote one thing and I'll summarize. I keep bumping up against your impulsiveness and it bothers me. You justify everything—"

"I don't—"

And I stop because his determined expression chills me. Like he approached the Lunatic Ledges obstacle at the *American Ninja Warrior* qualifiers, and he already knows how he's going to get over it.

"What should we do now?"

"Probably a good idea to actually listen to Ariana and give each other a minute to breathe." John stands and stretches his arms toward the ceiling and lets them drop. "There's a flaw in a client's architecture and SynerCloud wants to save face. Me and Sanjay are flying to Palo Alto. We'll be there until we can figure out how to fix the flaw."

"I didn't know SynerCloud wanted you out there."

"I found out this afternoon, but at least I'm saying something before I go." He barely glances at me when he heads out of the kitchen.

I call after him. "Do you want to pray?"

"Yeah. Alone."

girl, get your face out of the carpet

RELATIONSHIPS DON'T CREATE ISSUES. They reveal them.

I didn't learn that from Ariana or *Forever Together Faithfully*. I might've heard it on one of those podcasts John listens to when he cooks dinner. Maybe *The Secret To Success* or *The Work in Progress*. Whatever. A wise person spoke it, and it's true.

Last night, John escaped upstairs, and I gathered my roses and stalked out of Nate's townhouse.

I waited until I reached home to read the card.

> Sunshine,
>
> All I want is for you to feel secure and loved. Don't you know my world would crumble if anything bad to happened to you? You're more lovely and precious than the rarest rose money can buy.
>
> All my love,
> John

I woke up this morning and processed those words ten more times, then dropped the card on the nightstand.

So we're taking a break for a few days. That's cool. We don't need to go at each other like we did yesterday. We can chill. He's still my future hubby and nothing will change that.

Friday, after my early morning meeting, I shut my office door and call John.

"Hey, you," I say when he answers.

He yawns. "Hey."

"Work hard last night?"

"Yeah, and the client took us out for a late dinner."

"You had a good time?"

"We solved the architecture flaw, so we earned that celebration meal, but I'd rather be in Philly holding you."

Hearing that gives me a rush. "I wish you were here, too."

Silence.

"I'm sorry."

Our words crash into one another, but we might as well get used to it. We'll be saying it the rest of our lives.

He sighs. "Sunshine, we're supposed to have a good time this season. I don't want to fight with you like that."

"I don't want to fight either."

"I'll be here through tomorrow, making sure the client is satisfied with the solution, but I don't think they'll have any problems. Can you pick me up from Philly International on Sunday? My flight lands at one. Spirit Airlines."

"You got it. I'll be there."

"Listen, I've been thinking and praying the whole time I've been out here. Thinking about you and me and what we have together."

"Same here."

"I have a lot more to say, but it's not a phone conversation."

My stomach ties itself in a bow. "Did you want to do a light work out before we talk?"

"No, but we can have a walk, or do something else. Your choice. Whatever you want, I'll do it." he says. "I have to get moving now. See you Sunday?"

"See you Sunday."

We end the call, and I switch my phone off and slide it into my desk drawer. I stare at the project plan scribbled in black letters on the whiteboard across from me.

Like I expect it to have answers for how I feel.

Saturday, I'm supposed to be at Mariah's house, hanging out with her and her daughter, Binky. Binky's real name is Benita, which means blessed in Spanish. Only her father, Oscar, who's from Puerto Rico, calls her that. Together, graceful Mariah and handsome Oscar produced a daughter so striking she could model for *Teen Vogue*. As my junior bridesmaid, I expect Binky to steal the show at the wedding.

I should have driven to Wynnewood a half-hour ago. Where am I instead? In my apartment on an extended morning prayer vigil. I haven't eaten a thing, and I don't plan to. I don't need food.

I need to hear from the Lord.

My living room resembles the front of a cathedral. Lighted white candles decorate the top of the breakfast bar. My laptop is there too. Open and playing harp music from Pandora. An NIV Bible, my phone, and two boxes of Kleenex rest beside me.

I'm face down on the tufted carpet. Other than reaching over for tissues to wipe my wet face, I don't come out of this posture. Everything that means something to me this season, I pray on it. My relationship with John and his role as my future husband. My role as his future wife. Ms. Pat. Money. Debt. The wedding. Self-control.

Bits of white tissue stick to my eyelashes. I can hardly see, but I'm too nosy to ignore my phone when notifications ping.

From Mom:

> Why aren't you answering my calls? Do you know your daddy was on the phone with John for three hours last night?

From Daisy:

> Ms. Purple Hair, I just got your prayer request. I'm holding you up, my sister.

From Nikki:

> If you answer my texts, we can pray over the phone. Call me!

From Stacey:

> You had one big fight, kid. One. Hubby and I had three last weekend, and we're still a couple.

I should message everyone back, and I will. Later. After I meditate on Psalm 119:28 and 29. *My soul is weary with sorrow; strengthen me according to your word. Keep me from deceitful ways; be gracious to me and teach me your law.*

Make no mistake, I do not want to lose my man. Not to mention my parents would be devastated if we broke up. So I pray and rock and call on the Lord to move.

Another hour passes and snotty tissues fill my wicker wastebasket. I'm all cried out, but stay on the floor, asking for guidance, breathing, and listening.

Someone FaceTimes me. I snatch my phone and swipe fast,

laying it next to me on the carpet. "Unless you're God or John, I'm not talking right now."

"Cousin, where are you?"

It's not God. It's Binky.

"Home." I pull my head up high enough to talk without rug fibers touching my lips. "I'm praying. Meditating with the Lord."

"Well, finish, 'cause you said you were coming through. Bring your flexi-rods with you. I need to borrow them."

"I'm not lending you my hair tools. You never give my stuff back."

"Is that harp music?"

"Yes. Why you all in my business?"

"Get your face out of the carpet. I need those flexi-rods. And can you introduce me to Quinsara? Maybe she can give me a temporary color like yours."

I flip onto my back and open my eyes.

Binky has a horrified look on her pretty face. "Eww! What happened to you?"

"I'm troubled."

"Your mascara—"

"I cried it off, I know."

She rolls her almond-shaped eyes. "You probably smeared some on the carpet. You better treat it with OxiClean."

"Arrgh! What do you want?"

"I want you and some flexi-rods. I want to get my curls popping like yours on top. So come on over."

My harp-infused moments of prayer and peace have ended, so I sit up. "Fine. Give me time to clean my face. I'll bring the rods, but you better give them back. Which ones do you want? Orange or purple?"

"Orange. What's wrong with you, anyway?"

I blow my nose. "Luna called me yesterday. More guests are sending in RSVPs."

"That's what's supposed to happen. You're getting married."

"You don't understand. We're having some issues and I think he might ask for some space or postpone the wedding or something."

"Issues? I cannot imagine that. You two are relationship goals all the way."

"What do you know about relationship goals?"

She shuffles from her kitchen, through the screen door, to their outdoor deck. "Practically all RiseUP Youth follows you two on Instagram. We see you working out together and reading the word at Bible Study and holding hands wherever you go. You're all love and John only has eyes for you. I know, because I've seen women try to talk to him at church, but he never gets close to anyone."

"Really now?" Specks of tissue dot my eyelashes. I use my fingernail to pluck them out.

"Y'all give us hope. Like we can look forward to being in love and following God and looking strong while we're doing it."

"Yeah, well, Mr. and Mrs. Strong are having a weak moment." I pick more tissue bits. "Somehow those pics missed Instagram."

"I want to meet somebody like Mr. John when I go to college. Somebody who follows the Lord and loves me. Then if we fight, we fight for each other and let God do His work." She slides red-tinted heart-shaped sunglasses on her face. "Can you bring the Kat Von D eyeliner? Can I borrow that too?"

Fight for each other. "Binky?"

"Uh-huh."

"Thanks."

"Sure." She shrugs. "You don't use that Kat Von D much, right? So can I keep it when you bring it? And the makeup setting powder?"

"I love you, and no!"

"That's fine. As your junior bridesmaid, I'll still wear some on your wedding day."

This young lady? I swear. "See you in a few. Bye, girl!"

Time to get up from this floor. I reach for the sky, stretching my arms as I pull myself up. I scoop up the empty Kleenex box and fling it into the recycling bin.

There's more to this relationship than John and I. Young people watch us. If we don't walk this time out in a way that glorifies God, what will they remember when they look for mates? This goes beyond dating life and the wedding.

I adore my man when he calls me Sunshine, shops, cooks for me, and rubs my back when he prays. But can I appreciate him when he's strict? Can I understand when he's overworked and tired?

When we disagree? Can I settle down instead of getting in his face?

Can I really live with him as his wife?

lights out

FOR ALL INTENTS AND PURPOSES, John *is* my life partner. He's the person I think about most on the daily, and the only man I've ever wanted to marry or have children with. And for more than a year, our lives have changed for the better because we're together.

That's what I feel *and* what I know.

So I'm calm when I park my car beneath the Spirit Airlines sign and wait for him to walk out of Philly International. Last night, after more prayer, the spirit nudged me to settle down and listen close to what John has to say today. Not because I want to rush and get to the part where we're enjoying life again, but because I need to hear his concerns and see where his heart lies.

It's every bit of a hundred degrees and sweltering this Sunday, and I have the urge to drive home and take three cold showers. A mocha-brown woman in a thin tangerine sundress stands at the curb and fans herself with a magazine. She holds the hand of a little girl with long braids and a tear-stained face.

I turn the air up full blast, and when I glance over again, John approaches my car. Wrinkled white t-shirt and dark jeans. Laptop satchel slung over one shoulder and black leather travel bag on the other. His face shows exhaustion, but his smile lights up when I wave.

A sweaty-faced airport security guy looks to pounce on me when I leave the car, but I don't care.

"Hey!" I open my arms wide and ignore rushing traffic. "Hug me good."

John's bags slide to his feet when he gathers me in his arms. "Mmm. I missed you." He runs a hand across my curls. "Did you miss me?"

"Umm-hmm." I close my eyes and rub my cheek against his beard, floating in warmth. "You asked me to pick a spot for a walk and my choice is the Art Museum. Put your bags in and let's ride."

"Drive me to Nate's first? I need a shower bad, plus we can switch over to the Jeep."

I hug John's shoulders once more and dash to the driver's seat. He'll clean up and we'll head to our favorite place and talk. Cool. Fine.

We're together. We're good.

The elegant museum lobby becomes a marble refrigerator I step into with much gratitude. *Thank you, Lord, for precious relief!*

"Ready to tour?" John points to the ticket counter.

I nod yes and we buy tickets and stroll through the arched hallway to the wood-paneled elevator a museum curator must have imported straight from an Edgar Allan Poe story. Upstairs we're wordless when we move from room to room, studying works of art. I separate from John and enter a smaller area with classic Christian works. Alone, I stand before a painting of a potter's wheel and the curves and lines and muted colors move me to pray.

Lord, you've created such great beauty in this world. Help me appreciate the beauty in this journey you allowed for John and me. Thank you for the time when I had larger curves and weaved hair and Nikki pushed me to ask an athletic mumble-mouthed guy in our ministry to help me get healthy. Thank you he said no, and then he said yes, and we connected. You guided us to friendship and then attraction. We started from the bottom now we're here with our lives about to intertwine. You provided some clay called Chablis, and some water called John and your fingers hover, ready to remix us on the potter's wheel, recombining those resources into a useful vessel. Lord, please let us become that new creation.

Outside the West Terrace is where we take a break to rest our legs. The great stair hall stretches through the middle of the museum. Halfway down, John grasps my hand and guides me to the side of the staircase. I sit with him on the step.

An older couple passes us, and they lead a thin, red-haired boy by the hand. He struggles to climb the stairs. When the kid glances over, I offer him a smile because I understand. The stairs are hard and it's tough to keep holding on, even with someone else leading.

Others walk up and down the staircase and to me, they resemble moving artwork.

Artwork. Yes! That's it! What a gorgeous place to take before and after wedding pictures. If our wedding party posed here, we'd be the talk of the Instagram universe.

I turn toward John. "Wouldn't this be a good place to pose the wedding party? Think we can do that? I can ask the museum about it. Or no, I'll call Luna and Lorenzo first. Or you know what, I'll ask Daisy because she and Tripp might know who—"

"Pictures, huh?" He pulls his phone from his pocket and scoots closer. "More pictures?"

"Well, yeah."

He shakes his head and blows out air that sounds like frustration. "I need you to pick one for me, please. Engagement night, coffee shop night, or the night of our first session with Ariana."

Okay? Zero idea of the connection. "I don't get it. What am I choosing?"

"No, never mind. Don't pick one. Forget I said that." He taps his phone screen. "Do me a favor? Take your phone out and look at it please."

I dig in my bag to find my phone, and once it's in my hand, I swipe the screen fast and see a CashApp notification. I tap to open the app, and there's an entry from $JLGerald. Fifteen hundred dollars.

"What's this?" I ask.

He puts his phone back and faces me. "That is the money you paid FrontLensLight to show up at our reception. You thought Lorenzo wouldn't tell me?"

My skin grows hotter than it did when I picked John up from PHL. "Bae, don't get upset. I only wanted to bring something special to our day. We had a ridiculous weekend after I hired them and I forgot to say anything about it, that's all."

"Here's what I don't get, so help me out. We already calculated my paychecks, and yours and reviewed the budget and set our personal spending. The wedding day plans are done. You don't have that kind of money to spare. Did you figure out a way to pay for extra photographers?"

"Kind of, but not right away." I wince. "It's not a big deal."

His shoulders sag. "See, the fact that you think it's not a big deal, that's what concerns me. Three times already, you agreed we would stick to a budget. The last time, I looked you in the eyes and asked you to cancel that loan application. Did you do that?"

"Yes."

"All of it?"

"Yes."

"What then? The credit union offered you something else?"

I shift my gaze to the concrete stairs beside us. Solid steps leading to a hard landing. "A personal credit line."

"I can't believe—" He leans back on his hands. "Uh-uh, it's more like I don't want to believe what I've been experiencing with you this year. It's like I'm sitting in the audience at a Broadway musical watching something I hate."

I hug my purse tight. *Listen. To. My. Partner.*

"Chablis, what happened? It seems like your motivation shifted about twenty-four hours after that ring landed on your finger. You changed."

I changed?

This from the man who bushwhacked me with a 90-thousand-dollar debt bomb?

If I was a different woman, I'd punch him right in his chiseled chest.

"For real, John?" I keep clutching my bag like it's a life preserver. "If I changed, then change happened when you told me about your money situation. Change could have started when your mom started her micro-aggressions—and she's still holding onto Grammy's bracelet. And I don't even want to flash you back to that scandalous message from your ex-girlfriend."

"I apologized about my finances—it wasn't right I didn't share it with you before I asked you to marry me. With my Mom, I know she hurt you and I'm sorry about that too, but I believe God will answer my prayers about you and her. And Veronica was ridiculous. That was a hater move and you know that." His baritone voice dips low. "For the first time, I'm having doubts about our relationship. Am I marrying the woman I fell in love with?"

I scoot away to increase the space between us. "If you can say something like that, you're not thinking right about me."

"Maybe not." He follows and erases the space I just created. "But with everything we've done these last few months, are we growing closer to God or further away?"

Closer to God? Further away? I know I should have an answer for that, but I can't think of one in this moment when my sundress itches me and I scratch my calves and hope he'll take back that statement about *doubts*.

"John, I don't know, all right. But you know I love you and you know we have a great relationship."

"I just confronted you about using borrowed money without telling me!"

"Oh, please! Miss me with that mess, Mr. Gerald! You told me about your debt after I took your ring, and I forgave you instantly. You can't do the same for me?"

"This isn't about forgiveness. I forgave you right after I found out, but that doesn't mean I don't wonder why you have to keep pushing for more. So now I'm thinking, what's next after this wedding." He throws up his hands. "We say I do and you press me for a brand new house before we're ready? A Mercedes? A bigger and better anything?"

"You know I wouldn't do that."

"So then how come what I can provide today isn't good enough? Or, don't even think about me. How come with all God provided, you still need more?"

My underarms grow wet, even though my skin has goosebumps and all those premarital counseling lessons about communications and unconditional love and who knows what else jostle around my mind and I still can't think past John saying *doubts*.

"Chablis?"

His shoulders slump like he carries a sack of bricks on his back and he can't figure out how to get it off. Eyes still dark. Hands slack as he rests his elbows on his knees.

Looking heavy? Because of me?

I squeeze my eyelids shut. "I want to outshine every woman who's been with you, especially the ones who can't stand I'm marrying you, *and* I want to stand at that altar shining in front of your mom because she wants Trina instead of me. And... I want a new image of myself so spectacular I can't see that bloody discarded teenager ever again."

I open my eyes and John's golden-brown ones stare back at me.

He takes my hands in his and rubs them softly. "I can't change how you feel, but honestly, if you can't accept and cherish how much God sacrificed for you for eternity, you might never get it. And... I have to weigh how that might play out in the future."

Hearing that chills me more than the word *doubts*.

"All you want is for us to glorify God?" I ask.

"Please."

I grab a tissue from my purse and wipe wetness from my nose. "No more wedding shenanigans. I love God, and I love you and... that's where my attention will be. You told me your version of unapologetically dope is having *all* the people we love surround us? That's still true?"

"I mean, yeah."

"All right. Then I'll talk to Luna and Lorenzo and they'll make that happen. Simple."

"What are you thinking of?"

I don't answer because security staff walk past the landing and one of them waves and points toward the exit.

The museum's closing. Lights shut down all around us.

John stands and extends his hand to me. "Time to go."

Outside, the humidity becomes a hot, heavy blanket. Still, I dab my face like I'm recovering from a winter cold. When John tries to wrap his arm around my shoulders, I shrug it off.

I move further down the sidewalk. "I'll get a Lyft or something. I wanna be alone tonight."

Once again, he erases space between us, but this time he faces me and crouches lower so we're eye-to-eye. So close his beard balm's lemon and aloe scent fills my nose.

His words are a loud whisper. "If you have a panic attack or something else happens to you, I have to answer to God and your father because I failed to cover you. Whether or not you want to be protected, that's my job and I take it seriously. But it's your call. Do you submit to me having that role? 'Cause if you're having a hard time today... you really have to think about doing it for life."

In the heat and stillness, I think about that word. *Life.* And three other substantial words tied to my decision to be with John: *Consideration. Sacrifice. Submission.*

I look at him.

I look at my ring.

I look back at him.

But all I see are the backs of his Vans when I follow him to the Jeep.

battlefield

A SIMPLE WEDDING with no further stress on the future hubby? No need for financed money or extra anything, with the bonus of inviting as many people as the Rise Community Church sanctuary can hold?

Not. A. Problem.

To: Luna St. James, Lorenzo St. James
   From: Chablis Shields
   CC: John L. Gerald
   Subject: Final Shields/Gerald Wedding Changes

Dear Luna and Lorenzo,

Thank you for hanging in here with us. I know we usually talk on the phone, but I wanted to send the following in writing.

Our event will have one last change.

We will have the same wedding party, officiant, and order of service, but the entire ceremony will now occur at Rise Community Church. Instead of a full buffet and entertainment, we request only light refreshments served in the Rise Hall following the wedding

ceremony. Please cancel the Babblebrook Banquet Hall. We understand they will keep the $300.00 holding fee.

I spoke with Mary-Gladys Gunning and she said the Rise Hall is
available for us on our wedding date. Please contact her to confirm.
Light refreshments should comprise appetizers, vegetable and fruit
trays, and non-alcoholic drinks. Please arrange this for three
hundred and fifty people.

All other wedding day details such as the decorations, photo
package, videographer, and flower package should remain
unchanged.

Thank you,

Chablis C. Shields

I click *Send*, then hide my phone in my desk drawer and bury
myself in software test plans.

And how do I *feel*?

No comment.

I wasn't expecting John to invade my apartment after work, so I
jump a little when he walks in, frowning and tugging his beard. Who
knows why? He sounded fine when we talked about wedding
changes this morning.

He drops onto my couch and I step past his legs and plant myself
at the opposite end. No kiss. No hug. His presence usually makes me
feel like melted marshmallows inside, but I'm not exactly joyous so I
keep my distance.

He tries to tug my feet to his lap. "Are you all right? I mean, you
didn't say anything else after that email. Luna and Lorenzo asked me
about you."

I pull my legs back and tuck my tootsies beneath me. "My dimples aren't on display, but I'm fine. None of you need to worry about me."

"Seriously? You don't sound good."

"Anyway." I hug a throw pillow. "Our wedding day is as simple as it can be, and we can invite everyone we missed before. Send some invites to your college buddies, and I already started my list of line dance people. Call my dad, please? He probably wants to hear from you."

John pulls out his phone and dials. "Hey, Dad." He shifts his body forward with the phone to his ear. "How're you doing tonight? Yeah. We're good. She's right beside me. Yeah."

A pillow becomes my comforter. I hug it to my body while John tells Daddy we're still a couple, that he treasures me, and all we're doing is shifting our attention away from the wedding so we can focus on each other and God. Words that are light and positive and brief.

He ends the call with pain in his golden-brown eyes. "Your dad... I mean, I love him like he's my own father."

"I know."

"He said not to worry about the banquet hall changes. That even if we lose money, we can work it out later. Can you believe that?"

"I can."

"He said he loves me like the son he never had."

"Because he does."

Future hubby slides his phone onto the coffee table and keeps leaning forward.

I take out my phone. "Grammy and Poppy?"

He waves a hand like, *go on, you got it*, so I make that call and leave them a message.

We phone John's mother on both her numbers. Relief floods me when she doesn't answer. I'm not in the mood to detect any joy she might have because our relationship hit a snag. We leave her a voicemail.

All the other calls and texts happen in a blur. Our wedding party receives a group text—we're focusing on our relationship and won't be talking much about the wedding day, but their roles are the same except the full wedding and refreshments will occur at Rise Community Church.

I text a few supportive friends and family members.

John calls Dr. Jones.

I call Daisy.

We leave a message with Pastor Downes and ask for prayer.

Then we're done.

Rain falls softly outside—it gives me the sense the sky is crying. John stays quiet after the last call. I study his slouched body. It says, *Lord, I'm tired.*

He's tired?

I can't figure out how I feel, but I know I need to move.

I push my body to the couch's edge and reach for my black and white Nikes.

"Stay," I tell John. "Let yourself out when you're ready but eat something before you drive. You can take my Wawa chicken and spinach salad in the fridge. I'm going to the Y."

John slides over and puts a hand on my arm. "I love you. You gotta know that."

I shake him off. "Doubts though? Remember when you slid this ring on me?" I flick one finger in the air and hold the others down. "You told me we'd always work things out. Did you lie?"

"We *are* working things out."

"Welp, we worked out the wedding day. You wanted simple? You got simple." I stand and shove my feet into my sneakers. "Now I gotta get to the gym."

No saved, single, and waiting-for-her-Boaz woman would leave a man who reads his Bible daily, has a degree from Drexel, looks like he should be on the birds roster, works a tech job with full benefits, and would rather drink spinach smoothies than sip a Coors. John has never seen the inside of a jail and there aren't any kiddies in the world yet with his contributing DNA. He reps romance and commitment and plans to raise a God-fearing family. My parents call him son. My buddies adore him. He's in love with me and treats me like a black diamond.

Those kinds of cars don't pass by every day.

He spent more than a year learning about me, but where's his heart now that he knows I'm more wrecked internally than he thought?

And what was I thinking when I promised to follow him before I considered the fullness of lifetime sacrifice?

Doubts?

I'm mentally exhausted thinking about that word, which is why I'm running at the Y after eight PM. This fitness space smells like sanitizer and day-old sweat. The workers clean each hour but the aroma lingers like the funky ghosts of trained bodies past.

My feet pound the treadmill and I stare at the mirrored wall in front of me. My glistening self gazes back and speaks facts: *You're not that unconscious teenager. You're a champion... but you're still a mess.*

Years ago, body blows nearly knocked the life out of me, but even that pain can't compare to the hurt of disappointing my man during the best time of our lives.

I don't want to think about a glamalicious wedding.

I don't even care about it anymore.

My legs and feet burn. I should stop this machine before the pony-tailed gym worker jogs over here and drags me away for excessive sweating.

My phone stays propped on the console and I read banner notifications as they pop up. The texts from my family members are interesting.

From Aaron:

> What up, cuz? Need me to talk to your man?
> I got a glock and a pit bull.

From Mariah:

> You'll be okay, beautiful. Don't you worry,
> sugar pie. Praying for you darling lady.

From Binky:

> What!?! I need to be seen at that dope
> garden reception! Get it back!

Second message from Aaron:

> Y'all can hold the party at Uncle Sonny's.
> No, wait, where he gonna hide all his guns?
> 😂😂😂

That makes me stop the treadmill and crack a smile. God bless Aaron for trying to make me laugh during all this craziness. Gotta message him later and thank him.

The console clocked me at seven miles inside one hour. My personal best. At least I can do the happy dance for that new achievement.

And maybe somewhere, sometime, God will take my tears and the best and worst of me and transform it all for his glory.

♪

There's no crying on the dance floor, at least not at The Grandstand Dance Hall & Social Club. In here, the polished wood boasts permanent grooves in places where happy feet beat the floor into submission. Air conditioning stays on full blast to keep the DJ cool while he plays our favorites. Every month the Grandstand hosts one all-request party—the crowd controls the playlist. This Thursday is it.

I'm the fifth person through the door and the third to request a dance. My choice is *STL Battlefield*. I scribble the name on the Requests board and sit at the stage edge until the song plays. Maysa's soulful voice carries through the speakers, and I perform the movements on the floor. Only two other women join me, but I don't care. My footwork moves in rhythm to the lyrics, and I let dance express my emotions.

Even if love isn't a battlefield, life sure the heck is.

Song over, I go to the table where I left my dance bag. I peek at my phone screen and there's a picture message from John. He flashes the peace sign alongside his goofy grin.

His message:

> You can only pick one. Roses, lilies, or tulips.

I plop down on a rickety wooden chair.

> Roses, of course.

> Cool. There's a guy selling some for five dollars here at the Exxon.

This brother? I swear.

> Roses that smell like ethanol?

> Do these make you smile?

He sends a picture of a beautiful bouquet.

Hmm. Pretty. They could make me feel better if I could stop seeing us on those hard museum stairs with John saying *doubts*. Flowers can't erase that scene.

After I do a few more dances, who knows. I might smile again.

I want to see that. Message me in an hour?

Ok.

I stand to stretch, and a smile indeed becomes my reality when Stacey and Nikki push through the double doors.

I sprint over and wrap them in a group hug, careful not to bump into Stacey's round belly. "Bridesmaids! What are you doing here?"

Nikki wears a thin white Adidas sweatshirt and matching leggings. "Girl, stop. You're always trying to get me to visit. I thought you could use some company."

"Yeah, I do. Thanks for coming through."

Stacey eyes the dance floor. "Always wanted to try it. When do lessons start?"

"Tonight is mostly requests, but Jamie'll teach one dance each hour. I'll ask her to teach something easy for you." I lead them to my corner table and pull out a chair for Stacey. "So much going on, I keep forgetting to ask. Did you find out what you're having?"

"A girl, and the little diva is growing fast." She sinks into her seat with a glowing grin. "I'm so glad morning sickness is over. It was killing me in the beginning. At least we have everything we need for her nursery now."

"Do you have a name?"

"We're going to wait until we see her face since we couldn't think of something. First, Hector talked about naming her Jubilee. I know he meant well, but I told him she has to go to school and the kids will think she's named after an X-Men character."

"Jubilee might not be so bad. Kanye West named his kid North. Beyonce named hers Blue Ivy."

Stacey rolls her eyes. "We're an unknown brown couple living

Germantown. She needs a name that won't get her beat up in gym class."

I scoot my chair over and make space for Nikki to hang her leather bag beside hers. "Think you might remember what you dance tonight?"

"I hope so," Nikki says. "I could take it to South Africa next month. Teach the kids something fun."

"They do AfroDance over there."

"Never heard of it."

"YouTube has videos of it. You should check it out because it's something to see. Really lively."

Stacey does a double take when the dancers flow into *Intensity*. "How long does it take to learn something like that?"

"Advanced level line dances can take an hour or more to learn."

"You ever think about praise dancing at Rise?" Stacey asks. "If you can dance this way every week, you'd be a great praise dancer."

"I don't know. Praise dance is about giving glory to the Lord—it's all for Him. This right here is how I have fun and relax. Line dancing is all for me."

For me. For me. For me. The words echo in my mind and scenes from the last few months flash before me. The debt I was sooo quick to take on without telling John. Keeping the credit line a secret. Trying to seduce my man and snatch away our precious chance to discover one another within the covenant of marriage.

My heart beats fast and I push myself from the table. "I'm gonna ask for another dance. Jamie'll start teaching soon."

"They have water at the snack bar, right?" Nikki unzips her bag.

"Yeah, they cost a dollar, but put your wallet away." I pull a ten from my pocket and push it towards her. "Your waters are all on me tonight."

Stage side, the Requests board has four more dances added. I scribble *She's The One* beneath them because that fun dance will drag me out from beneath my feelings where I don't want to stay.

My bridesmaids seem to have a good time when they get the

chance to dance. I'm resting by the stage while they learn and repeat new movements. They're all smiles watching Jamie teach *Get Right Back.*

Step. Shuffle. Kick ball.

Change.

I close my eyes. *Help me, please Lord. What are you saying in this circumstance? Am I too quick to do things without considering my partner? Idolatrous? Kill that in me, Father. Lord, I'm done with all that. Let your example of sacrifice be the vision for our marriage. I submit myself to you. Show me how to glorify you during this engagement time and beyond. Amen.*

Stacey and Nikki finish their dance and walk off to the restroom, and I pull my phone out again. I send John a silly picture of me grinning.

He texts back,

> That's my Sunshine. Have you eaten? Are you hungry?

I grip my phone and stare at the ceiling when tears fill my eyes. Have I eaten? A question from a man who cares about my well-being. And that's good because I'm all about caring for him, too.

> I haven't eaten yet, but I'll call out for a chicken caesar salad. What about you? Did you get all your protein today?

> I'm about to. Can you pull a chair over?

I look up, and John walks in with the rose bouquet, two takeout containers, and a plastic bag. I direct him to the table, and he sets the food down and pulls cutlery and napkins out.

What else can I do but grab an extra chair so he can enjoy dinner with me?

He waves at our friends when they head back to the dance floor.

His fingers smooth Purell into my hands and his, then he blesses our food.

"I hope you like your meal." He opens his container. Blackened salmon salad.

I open mine. Two slices of meat lover's pizza.

I punch his bicep. "You know what? I don't believe you!"

"What? I know that's your favorite."

My stomach grumbles, but I'm so touched, the pizza can wait.

I close the lid. "John?"

He chews and swallows. "Uh-huh."

"Me and you?"

"You and me." He wipes his mouth and leans over for a quick cheek kiss. "I didn't lie to you when I proposed. We're in this until the end, no matter what. I'm never bailing on you. I'm fully committed."

"But—"

"I know I said doubts, but I was frustrated by what I found out, and I didn't use the right word. I should have said that we have more to work through than I thought when I proposed. But our commitment is a commitment to be there for one another as we work through the hard stuff." His eyes meet mine. "I don't care how long it takes. I promise you, you and me, we're going to sit down and talk about everything. We're going back through our counseling notes and *Forever Together Faithfully* lessons."

"You think we haven't been following all the teaching?"

He raises his eyebrows like, *are you serious?*

"Okay, maybe we haven't," I say with a sigh. "We need to be Team Gerald before we're legally Team Gerald."

"What you said? Now that's everything."

"If we can be great with one another, who cares what we post on the Gram. We don't have to impress anybody. We're not celebrities."

"Did that just come out of your mouth?"

"Whatever, man."

He wipes his hands and reaches under the table to squeeze my thigh. "Love you, Sunshine."

"Love you right on back. Drink some coffee when you drive tonight because we'll be talking after you get home."

Center floor, seven old head guys do *Breakwater*. A Philly classic. Two middle-aged ladies join them, and my mind grinds while I watch.

What if I try again with John's mother? I can at least attempt to show genuine love. She still has Grammy's bracelet, but I can let that go in favor of bringing even more positivity into our lives.

"We're not on the ministry schedule this Sunday, are we?" I ask.

"No."

"Okay, I think we should make a change. What do you think about us worshipping with Grammy and Poppy at their church?"

"You know my mom will be there."

"And if Nate's in town, it'll be a real family affair, won't it?"

stupid church hat

SUNDAY MORNING ARRIVES and I dress in my only "churchy" outfit: a peach-colored matching skirt and jacket, silk blouse, white stilettos and hat, and conservative fake pearl earrings and bracelet. I carry a white leather purse in one hand, and an NIV Bible in the other.

I fling open my apartment door and John scans my attire and bursts out laughing.

"You must be my fiancée's older sanctified sister." He snickers. "Are you auditioning for *Sunday Best*? Can you go get Chablis?"

I'm thinking he's so funny I forget to laugh.

"You can go on and take your comedy act on the road." I step into the hall and lock the door behind me. "I'm ready, so let's go."

A little after nine, we park down the street from Vine Street Baptist. A traditional-style church, Vine Street boasts large stained-glass windows, plush wine red carpet, wooden pews, and golden crosses on each wall. Inside the sanctuary, my sense of nostalgia rises. My parents weren't churchgoers when I was little, but Memaw dragged me to worship service every summer Sunday. Her church looked like this. Thinking of it now, I can almost taste the graham crackers and apple juice the kind-hearted Sunday School teachers

189

gave us little kids. Vine Street even smells like that old church: aging wood with a hint of lemon Pledge. I'd bet money the women's bathroom holds the scent of Estee' Lauder and talcum powder.

John and I slide into the fifth row next to Grammy and Poppy. So cozy, it makes me grin. With my fiancé's arm around me, in a pew beside my future family members, and a red hymnal and complimentary Bible in the holder in front of me, I'm at home. I don't even flinch when Ms. Pat saunters over dressed in her white usher outfit, complete with the nurse gloves and the orthopedic shoes. She raises her eyebrows and moves to the side of the aisle closest to her parents.

"This is a surprise. Good morning," Ms. Pat stares me in the face.

I tug my man-made pearls while John and I parrot, "Good morning."

"I didn't realize you all were coming," she says, her eyes still riveted to mine.

John speaks up with his voice full of respect. "We wanted to worship with you, Mom."

"Did you know?" She rears back. "This is the first time you've brought her here, I think. Am I correct, John?"

Poppy raises a wrinkled hand and flashes a big smile. "I'm here every Sunday, daughter. Same place. Same pew. Aren't you glad to see me?"

Ms. Pat doesn't so much as giggle. Instead, she straightens her posture, pats Grammy on the shoulder, lifts her chin, and moves toward some octogenarians near the back of the sanctuary.

No worries. I came prepared for this. My purse holds a package of peppermint Trident. After I watch Ms. Pat saunter back away, saying nothing further to John or me, I pull out the gum, pass one stick to him, open one for myself, and sit here chewing.

Poppy leans close. "Got one of those for me?"

I pass him a stick, and all three of us are chewing.

Grammy frowns and leans across her husband's lap. "You all know you not supposed to chew gum in church."

Poppy wraps his arm around her. "Baby, leave us alone. We won't drop gum and papers on the floor. Our grandson and his fiancée are trying to stay calm, and I think they're doing a fine job, 'cause our beloved daughter can be a piece of work."

"Norris, now you hush." Grammy swats his knee with her fan. The one with *Vine Street Baptist Church* printed on one side, and *Cakin Family Funeral Home* on the other.

"Naw, Hattie, I'm telling the truth now," Poppy says. "She supposed to hug this pretty lady and take pictures and show each one of her church friends her smart son chose a wonderful woman. What's she do? Rolls her eyes and acts all hincty, instead of being glad he loves her enough to come here. So what if he doesn't let her run his life? He ain't seven years old. He's his own man."

And if it wasn't for the robed choir starting their march to the altar, I'd leap out and start hollering and testifying. Praise the Lord! Someone gave voice to my reality.

When we all stand and grab our hymnals so we can join in with "To God Be the Glory," I tug Poppy's arm. He leans down, and I get a whiff of his Old Spice.

"I wanna love Ms. Pat, but she's making it hard on me. She still has Grammy's bracelet." I let out a sigh. "Other than pray about her. What else can I do?"

He puts down his hymnal and hugs my shoulders tight. "All you need to do is love her son and live to please God," he says. "My daughter will come around. She wasn't always like this. Nate and John weren't but seven and ten years old when her husband passed. She spent years working and arranging everything for those boys. She raised them well. Got one winning sales awards, the other in technology. Both college graduates, but they so independent, they don't need her much anymore. It broke her heart when John didn't make it to the altar the first time. Then, both of 'em chose wives without asking her blessing, and that mighta hurt her again. Now, Nate's wife didn't work out 'cause she was kind of wild. But you?" he steps back and displays that radiant smile. "I know you're here to stay."

Poppy's white beard scratched my cheek. But I don't care. "How do you know?"

"Because you're already family." He takes my hand in his. I place my hymnal in the holder so I can grasp John's hand, and we sing together. Gospel music fills the room, instruments, and voices in tune with one another and praising the King. Vibrant and lovely.

We are all in God's family.

And no matter how Ms. Pat treats me, she can't change that.

Not even on her worst day.

"We can talk to her together. Come on." John says after the pastor ends service with the benediction.

I stop him. Ms. Pat will treasure her baby boy forever. She has issues accepting me. This is my battle. Not John's.

"No." I push my purse and Bible into John's hands. "I'll talk to her on my own."

"Okay, Sunshine. I'll support you. But I have to stay here holding your bag?"

"Yeah, big guy. And while you're at it, take my hat too."

That stupid hat squeezed my scalp and gave me a headache. I yank off my head covering and pass it to him. It smashed my curls, so I must look a hot mess when I approach Ms. Pat. She stands at the sanctuary's back, talking with two other female ushers when I approach her.

I use my professional office voice. "Pardon me, ladies. Ms. Pat? May I speak with you?"

The women stop talking and Ms. Pat turns to me. I know they've gotta wonder what jacked up my hair.

Ms. Pat steps over without introducing me. "Yes, can I help you?" She asks in her own keeping-it-neutral tone.

I take a deep, cleansing breath. "I know we started off on the wrong foot, but I'd love a chance to start over." I lock my legs to steel myself from moving. "I never explained myself after I turned down your help for the wedding. I've always been uncomfortable with you bringing up Trina, since she's John's ex. I have nothing against her because I don't know her. You might be friends with her, but John has moved on. I'm here and I'd love for you and I to form our own friendship."

"That's what you want?"

"Yes, I do." I keep my eyes riveted to her serious face.

She stares me down with eyes the same color as her son's. "Let me tell you, I expected something bad to happen with that wedding. You're just as flighty and empty-headed as I thought, with your purple hair and your ripped-up jeans. John almost married a graceful, refined woman with a flourishing law career. Why he came back home and pursued you, I'll never know."

And just like in a science fiction film where the giant lizard monster pops out, and the girl can't do anything except stand there and shrink smaller and smaller, I stay pasted in place in front of my future mother-in-law.

Years of doubt fill my ears. The worthlessness of my broken places. For all that I've learned and grown and changed, it's still not enough, and Ms. Pat's words make me want to fold in on myself and disappear.

Still.

In the middle of all my darkness, Jesus calls me to forgive, reminding me He loves me, and nothing's going to change that.

"Ms. Pat, I love John and I'm marrying him, even if we have to go to City Hall." Gratitude wells up inside my heart, making it pound its own joyful rhythm. "Nate, Poppy, Grammy, I love all of 'em. I'm honored to call them family soon, and you know what, not one of them needed to earn that love and affection."

She blinks like she wants to find the best possible response phrase, but she never does.

"You have a blessed day," I say and move on down the aisle. I run my fingers through my purple curls and fluff them out bigger and badder than they were before I stuck that stupid church hat on my head.

Why did I wear this outfit? I can't pretend to be someone I'm not to meet with someone else's approval.

I reach John and slide out of my suit jacket.

He stands up. "Done talking to Mom?"

"Yup." I lean against him and yank off one white heel, then the other.

John passes me my purse. "You worked everything out?"

"We worked out about as much as we're going to today." My earrings come off, and I stuff those in the purse along with the fake pearl bracelet. "It's gotta be past eleven. Can we get some breakfast, please? I'm starving."

"Hold up."

"What?"

"Why are you taking your clothes off?" With a gentle touch, he places my jacket back around my shoulders. "Did she say something about your suit?"

I plop down in the pew and stare at him instead of running my mouth about the dumb comments his mother made. I *am* bold hair *and* colorful makeup *and* fashion that zig-zags. I'm still going to be her daughter-in-law.

"I'm taking this off because it isn't me." I fluff my curls more. "Shoulda wore my *Can't Nobody Love You Like Jesus* t-shirt."

"You can't keep stripping in church. I'll take you home to change. We can make some omelets."

"We can't stop past Sabrina's Café for brunch?"

"No." He pulls me to my feet and lands a moist kiss on my forehead. "I can't afford it because I'm broke. I'm doing well knocking out debt, though, so I'm not using my driving money for food."

We hug his grandparents goodbye and head on out. The minute fresh air hits my face, all thoughts of Ms. Pat's tirade fade away. She might never understand why John chose me.

And that's cool, as long as *I* know why.

○

"Please don't burn up that skillet," John leans over my shoulder, peering at the stove. "Isn't that heat too high?"

I humor him and turn the burner down. "You think I'm gonna start a fire because I'm cooking for a change?"

"I'm saying, don't burn up the pan. Just because we're registered for new pots doesn't mean people will buy 'em for us."

I wave him away. "Whatever, man. I can make us a great brunch meal. I'm doing this."

"Sunshine?"

"Yeah." I flip the omelet and it doesn't break. Yay!

"Look at me."

I turn and he kisses me until I don't have breath left. Then he releases me and winks like, *yeah, I'm counting the minutes until fireworks time.* He walks backward and snatches his buzzing phone off the bar.

"I have no idea who this is," he mutters. "John Gerald."

That kiss sent sparkles to the base of my brain. Now I can't think. Um, where are my plates?

"Who gave you my number?" John says with fire in his voice.

I turn around and his face resembles an angry question mark. He can't be talking to a telemarketer because he'd end that call. My stomach dips when I study his eyes. It's like he's seen a ghost.

I step toward him and he holds up a hand.

"Yeah, I am." He still looks heated. "Thank you for your kind words, but I'm here with my fiancée right now and she..."

And my mind blanks because his body language communicates *oh what the heck no* and I don't wanna guess because I don't wanna be right and after he talks thirty more seconds my gut feeling launches into overdrive.

"It's Trina. I'm sorry." He mouths and moves to the middle of the living room, phone in hand.

A few minutes later, he returns to the kitchen as the omelet turns to scorched yellow rubber. I push the spatula under it, anyway.

"You want to tell me what that was about?" I ask.

"Trina told us congratulations. My mom gave her my new number." He leans against the kitchen counter. "She wanted to share something else privately, but I can tell you she didn't say anything disrespectful." He rakes his fingers through his beard. "I would've shut that down in an instant."

Some days, when it rains, it pours.

First John's mother, now Trina.

I hold this oily red plastic spatula and stare at my future hubby. I have a choice. Inside this burned egg-smelling kitchen, I can fuss and worry and start a fight about John's level of honesty, or I can trust him.

We've come this far. God *is* the God of my relationships. I gotta let him be that.

"Fine." And that's all I say before I dump rubbery egg mess into the garbage can beneath the sink. "Reach in the fridge and hand me more eggs."

I need to start over.

tell me mama

IT'S cloudy today but I don't care. After work, I couldn't wait to drive to Fairmount Park and move my body beside this beautiful landscaping, so I called Nik and here we are. Sweat runs through our natural curls and we race-walk through nature.

Automatic. Natural. Stress. Reliever.

Twenty minutes of exercise and I'm dying to talk about the elephant on the trail.

"Penn State?" I point at Nikki's fashion choice. "Excuse me, ma'am, but isn't that Terry's hat on your head?"

She rolls her eyes at me. "He left it in my car the other day."

"Guess that means you're close enough to wear his clothes."

"It's a hat, not an intimacy statement."

"Mm-hm. I didn't feel comfortable putting on anything belonging to John until we defined the relationship. That hat says you're either there or getting close."

She slows down, still not looking at me. "We're closer now, I'll say that."

"Dang, you ain't giving me nothing."

Nikki stops, and I halt my legs and turn toward her. Gravel

crunches beneath my Nikes. The Japanese House rests around the bend, so maybe she wants to go there.

"What's up?" I ask.

Her eyes search the hazy sky. "Terry and I were on our way back from Deptford Mall on Saturday, and he said some weird stuff. Said he wouldn't mind starting a brand-new family with me."

"Pardon? And what did you tell him?"

"What do you think I said? I told him he shouldn't think about starting new nothing until he talks to the girls every day. The girls love him. They wouldn't give him a moment to himself when we went to Ms. Clarice's pool party. Even Ms. Clarice mentioned it. Terry needs more quality time with Rashida and Rae-Ann, not less."

"And you think you're keeping him from doing that?" I flick a blood-sucking mosquito off my arm.

"No, it's not me. It's him. He needs to do more than just take them places on the weekend. He's a decent brother, and he's respectful and all that, but if he turns out to be just a Facebook father, he's not for me and I'm bouncing from his life. And you better believe I told him that too."

Facebook father. Also known as a guy who never makes breakfast, checks homework, or helps his precious angels brush their teeth, but he absolutely must fill his Facebook feed with pics of him "loving" his darling babies during extravagant outings.

"Aw, Nik. What did he say to that?" A blue Volvo veers in our direction and I guide Nikki to walk closer to the grass.

"He mumbled something about making sure he takes them to their next doctor visit," she says. "But I called Ms. Clarice yesterday, and we're going out soon—me and her and her grand babies."

"Oh, so you have Ma Duke's approval, huh?"

Nikki flashes a grin. "She's like a really fun auntie and I love her sense of humor. She likes to tell her sisters that I'm in the church and I go on mission trips and all that stuff. I think I'm the last of the old-fashioned girls in her eyes."

I study the road beneath my feet as we walk again. "That's... really great."

"Sorry."

"No, it's all right. Ms. Clarice is good people. I just wish she could teach Ms. Pat a thing or two."

"You don't have that many weeks left. She'll be the one looking like a nut at the wedding if her relationship with you doesn't get any better."

We climb the small hill toward the wooden gazebo, and I roll my eyes. "How can it when Ms. Pat was the one who gave that heifer John's new cell number?"

"No, she didn't!"

"Yes, she did."

"She's coming for you hard, but something good came from it."

"What could be good about a seventh-level of hell demon whispering in Trina's ear and telling her the lie that I'm okay with her calling my man?"

"At least you know she didn't have his new number before."

"True. But still."

We reach the top of the hill, and I walk around in circles instead of stretching.

"Where do you want to go after this?" Nikki arches her long arms toward the sky. "What about going to eatLARGE for some of Chef Gabriel's food?"

"No." I plant myself on a dusty bench and the sun-warmed seat makes my behind hot.

Nikki reaches for my hands. "I want you to pray with me. Let's pray."

"No, thank you, Sarah Jakes Roberts, I don't wanna pray." I get up and pace again. Every time I think about John taking that call, negative energy churns through my body so much I want to punch a bag or a person. "Ms. Pat prefers Trina. I knew that before. But now she's taking action and trying to bust up my relationship. That's too much."

199

Nikki glances at me like she understands more words won't help.

A breeze blows through the area, bringing a cooling break. I close my eyes and receive it like an embrace and a whisper from the Holy Spirit saying *shh, honey, honey, honey. I know, I know, I know.*

"Nik, I think I'll stay here with the bushes and flowers a little while longer."

"Enjoy your nature moment." She does a few runner's stretches and blows me a kiss. Then she unzips the side pocket of her running pants and pulls out her key fob. "Behave yourself!"

"Didn't I earn the *God's Woman Achievement Award* from Rise?"

"That was three years ago."

"I'm the same person."

"Okay, lovely, you confirmed it. Just remember it." She jogs down the grassy hill to the parking lot.

⌀

I remember just fine.

What I remember most is *I'm not a punk.*

At home, I shower and lotion and apply Smashbox photo finish primer, face powder, lip gloss, and mascara before I slip into a soft white t-shirt and my True Religion super T curvy skinny jeans. The curls get a quick refresh then I trot to the kitchen.

My mini tripod holds my phone on the breakfast bar. I set the phone to video mode and step back.

I look good.

I hope I sound good.

I press the red record button. "What up, though? Hey friends and family! God is good. I am in love and so ready to get married. I'm counting the days. These past few weeks have been a roller coaster ride like none other. It's hard out here on a Jesus chick! So I want to ask you all to please keep me in prayer." I lean close to the screen. "Viewers, here's the thing: I love my fiancé John. I truly believe we're meant to be married, especially when I think about how God brought us together. So people, no worries, I am marrying him. It's just that I have to accept his mom. Did I forget to say her name is Patricia? Oh yeah, PATRICIA GERALD, doesn't respect me and has been praying I'd leave ever since we got engaged. I'm starting out my marriage with real mama drama. So please pray for my relationship with Ms. Pat, who by the way told me I may not call her Mom. If you all can do that for me, I'd truly appreciate it. Thank you! Everyone, please walk with the King and be a blessing!"

I replay the video seven times.

Then I erase it.

No need to post that rant to the Gram. I only needed to vent my feelings.

True, Ms. Pat is playing hard ball, but I can't beat her at her own game. It still hurts when I think about what she said at Vine Street Baptist, but if the Lord needs me to forgive her seventy times a day, I'll do that.

I whisper a prayer for her, then give her a call.

"I'm still hoping to get to know you better before the wedding," I say to her voice mail. "If you're free next week, maybe we can have dinner. Call when you can. God bless."

Tuesday night at premarital counseling, I sit back and focus on Ariana's teaching. She has no idea how much her words shape my thoughts.

Parents and family.

"Your connection with your parents will change because their roles are changing," Ariana says. "You'd be surprised how many couples don't consider how the bond between parent and child shifts after the child marries."

Tell me about it.

"Acknowledge these people will always be your partner's parents and show respect for them by avoiding dismissive comments."

For real, did God show this woman my *almost* Instagram story?

"Work with your partner for how you'll handle your parent's expectations after you marry. For example, consider how much they want you to visit and how you'll manage holidays."

John gives a nod. "I hear you. I know for my fam, Christmas is the big one, especially for my grandparents. They helped raise me, so I can't see our new family missing them that day."

"I'm an only child," I say. "But I have a ton of aunts, uncles, and cousins. So with my family, I wouldn't want us to miss the summer barbecues or any of the South Carolina reunions."

Ariana nods. "Sounds like you're already making those family choices. Your homework will guide you toward more decisions. The biggest takeaway — forsaking all others means turn to each other first for your feelings, concerns, advice, and solutions. Partner first. Others second."

Partner first. Others second. I look at John and his expression shows he gets it. I didn't need to post to Instagram. My partner has my back now and always. Whatever stressing family moment happens, we'll handle it like champions.

Yeah that's us.

the village

NIKKI CAN'T KEEP a secret to save her life. She even called to ask which of my favorite colors I like better. Pink or purple. I said purple, and she said good because that would look great on the cupcakes. Minutes later, she called back and begged me not to tell John she asked. Then she told me to keep my schedule open for Saturday afternoon.

Even if she hadn't spilled the tea, I'd have figured it out. There's no reason for me to travel to Tracey and Brian Joneses' house unless I'm visiting Life Group, and that hasn't happened since before premarital counseling. How convenient is it for John to want to take a break from ride share driving to "stop by" and talk with his mentor today? And, of course, he must bring me with him.

So here we are, on our way to the co-ed wedding shower.

Cute. Sweet. I'm going along with it.

When John turns the Jeep into the Joneses Chestnut Hill neighborhood, I examine my nails instead of pointing out the familiar cars lined up blocks before we reach the house, even though my dad's ancient money-green Cadillac blocks the end of somebody's circular driveway.

In the Jeep, I pull out my mirror for a last-minute check. The curls pop. I run my finger over my smooth edges and make sure my *Proverbs 31 Woman* t-shirt and matching pants are wrinkle-free. When I walk in, I'm sure my mom will roll her eyes so hard they might fall out and hit the floor.

John helps me out of his ride and leads me to the back of Castle Jones, and that's when I peep something that does indeed surprise me.

Wedding shower? No. This is better than a shower. This is a huge backyard picnic with all our favorites. Favorite colors. Favorite friends and family. Favorite people from Rise Church. Even Daisy and her husband Tripp are here.

My tastes intertwine with John's for the color scheme: purple for me and red for him. From the tablecloth colors to the mylar balloons, and all the decorations in-between. The Adirondack chairs arranged by the charcoal fire pit are purple and red. Touches of silver bring everything together. I have no idea who paid for all this, but Lord, please give that person a triple load of blessings.

I'm speechless as people walk over and surround us with love and well wishes.

"Surprised?" John hugs me to him, and we stand for pictures.

"A little."

"But you love it?"

"Oh, heck yeah." I squeeze his waist.

Mom saunters over and whispers in my ear. "You're such a diva! Lavender? Matching nails? You knew!"

"I plead the fifth." I let go of her so I can hug my dad, who kisses me on the forehead and moves over to hug John.

Scanning the faces in the crowd makes me dizzy, but I grin and keep touching folk.

"We love you both. Congratulations!" Tracey and Brian Jones kiss me on the cheek. Tracey could be a model, with her perfect-sized body dressed in a gray silk T-shirt, matching pants, and delicate silver sandals on her pretty feet. Her so-scrumptious-I-could-nibble-his-face son, Reginald, rests in a soft sling around her middle. She and her husband appear calm for two people with a baby at their age. After age forty, I plan to hang a retired sign on my ovaries.

I hug them back. "Thank you. I love you too. Thanks for hosting."

"You're welcome." Dr. Jones holds his adorable wife by the hand. "All we had to do was turn over our house and yard. Your friends did everything else. All the hard work? Thank them." He points across the yard to Nikki, Terry, Stacey, and our other buddies, all in constant motion, taking care of food and guests.

My eyes zero in on a table of edible delights so beautiful I almost don't want to eat them. There are trays filled with finger foods and sandwiches, chicken wings, potato salad, cut vegetables and sliced fruit. Glass pitchers hold ice-filled purple drink, which I assume is lemonade because lemon slices float on the top. What knocks me out most are the mini picnic setups. Red checkered blankets and cushions for people to sit on. They even included taller seating and tables for older guests. The scene resembles a grand celebration behind a mansion in Fairmount Park.

"John? Can we get married now? Pastor is right there." I say this as a joke and turn to discover the future hubs missing.

He didn't go far.

A circle of men surrounds him at the edge of the driveway. Nate and Poppy and Travis and other guys from Rise Church and Syner-Cloud and ManUP men's group. Tears come to my eyes when Poppy embraces John. Then Pastor Downes steps in and wraps his arms around him. These men helped John become the husband I'm about to receive. Men strong enough to bless another man who will dedicate his life to protect his treasure.

If I could clone every single one of them, I would.

My family and friends swoop down on me and the faces blur, but I want to take my heart and give each one of them a piece. It's that kind of moment.

Pastor Downes settles everyone down. "Come on family, fall in here." He calls out when he walks toward the yard. "Let me bless the food. We're all hungry and we need to eat. Prayer time y'all."

John returns to me, wrapping his long arms around me from behind. It's amazing that he's the only one who can do that without me feeling an ounce of panic. There's something spiritual to that, I just know it.

"Let's bow." Pastor Downes prays. "Gracious Father, thank you for your love, which we see reflected in John's and Chablis' eyes. We've arrived here from different places and spaces to celebrate them with a meal together. We are thankful for love, which seeks us and finds us. We are grateful for this meal. We pray your blessing upon those who prepared it. Bless Chablis and John and all of us as we celebrate. In the name of Jesus Christ. Amen."

"Amen." I stare up at John.

He locks gazes with me. "Amen."

"All right, y'all, break it up." Pastor Downes rolls his eyes. "Take your happy selves over to the table and get some lunch first."

I'm in the middle of chatting and chewing with my girlfriends when my college buddy Simone walks in and surprises the heck out of me, holding her toddler son Najee on her hip. Together with them and my other friends at a large picnic table, the moment almost feels like a regular ladies-only bridal shower. A full hour passes before I find my way back to John's side.

I squeeze him. "Wow. Good to meet you. Come here often?"

He laughs and grips me tight in his warm arms and I'm full and exhausted and so darn grateful I can barely stand it.

The midday sun has faded by the time Terry leads us to two white tulle-covered chairs. We sit side-by-side and Nikki takes charge.

"Everyone! Time for the best part. Games!" She grins so wide her lips must hurt. She passes an index card to Terry and they're about to read something when they're interrupted by the Joneses back door sliding open.

Footsteps make me turn around.

Ms. Pat.

It didn't register to me she hasn't been here all afternoon. I guess she wanted to be fashionably late. Whatever. I am bigger than this.

I stand and jog to her. "Hold on, everyone! My future mother-in-law is here." I wrap my arms around her and wink as people take pictures of us.

That love bomb must have worked because she smiles when Binky rushes over with a lawn chair for her. Ms. Pat holds tight to a well-wrapped gift box, refusing to give it to Binky for the gift table. Maybe the present is too expensive? Who knows?

I return to my seat and plug back in to all the love in the yard, *thank you Lord.*

Nikki directs our attention to the important stuff. "Our first game is *Who Said That.*"

Time flies and our friends take turns leading the crowd through *Who Said That* and *A Trip Down Memory Lane* and *What Would The Bridegroom Say.* All of its fun, especially while eating buttercream-covered cupcakes with the future hubby.

I'm so blissed out I don't pay any attention to Ms. Pat, other than to pray my mom starts nothing because of course I squawked to her about that Trina call.

I'm out of my seat, trying to get Simone and Najee's attention, when Nikki stops me.

"Chablis, we have one more thing." She looks to Terry, who gives her some sort of hand signal. "All right. I got you." She gives the thumbs-up, then leans close to me. "You need to go sit with John in the chair next to the fire pit."

So far this afternoon has been lighthearted and carefree. I sit beside John in an Adirondack chair; the atmosphere grows quiet. He looks at me and I look at him like we're both thinking *what's going on here.*

People assembles themselves in a circle around us, holding large index cards.

I don't miss that Nikki and Terry are hand-in-hand.

Nikki's face lights up. "Chablis, my girl, you've been a blessing to me since the day you joined Rise. I'm not losing a friend, I'm gaining a big brother. God bless you both."

She steps over and presses her card into my hand. Written in gold ink is a prayer for us. *Dear Lord, bless John and Chablis to live well, love well, and stay together for a lifetime. With love, Nikki.*

Terry takes her place and his lips turn up into a smile as he nods at John. "You're my boy and all, but I can't hold this story any longer."

"Aww, man, no. Don't do me like that." John groans and hides his face.

"Nah, bruh, she's gotta hear it." He clears his throat and looks at me. "So, I came to visit Rise one Sunday. I think after John trained you for a couple of months. He pointed you out and I said to him, she's cute. He was like, we're just friends. A couple months pass and he mentions you again and I tell him, it seems like she's down for you. Then I finally met you at his place and later he told me, she's cool, but I don't have the time. So he goes off to work in Germany, right, and around Christmastime, he calls me talkin' about he lost contact with you and he asks if I think he should try to find you, right? I was like, bruh, who cares what I think, but if you play around and she stays on the market, I'll feel bad for you if you lose her. Three weeks later, he's on my phone saying, Terry, pick me up from the airport. I was like, what are you doing? He's said, that's my lady and I'm coming to get her."

I turn to John. "That happened?"

"Oh, yeah." He takes Terry's prayer card.

"How come you never told me?"

He shakes his finger at Terry. "Someone was supposed to save that story for the wedding."

"What can I say? This seemed like a better moment." Terry smiles and drifts into the crowd.

Dr. Jones and Tracey take Terry's place and Dr. Jones says, "Years ago when John told me about *American Ninja Warrior* and started running down trails and jumping off walls, I prayed, Lord, please give this young man a wife before he kills himself. Chablis is the answer to that prayer. Our prayer is that your hearts remain close to the Lord and close to one another."

We thank the Joneses as they give us their prayer card. Orange rays of fading sunlight stream through the yard and the people parade continues.

Stacey thrusts tissues into my shaking hands so I can wipe away smeared makeup as one by one. Couples give us blessings, advice, and prayer cards.

Pastor Downes' arm wraps around Sister Juanita when she says, "Nothing ranks higher than your relationship, not your careers, your kids or other people. Love each other first."

Pastor Hargrove, who produced seven kids with his wife, Cynthia, says. "Always be ready to be with each other. Take my advice, don't just make love. Make dynamite together!"

Grammy leans on Poppy's arm. She says, "Read your Bibles every day and teach my great grands the value of reading the Word." Then she says, "And that sex advice is true so y'all make it happen."

Stacey and her husband Hector say, "The core of your marriage is friendship, so be best friends at all times."

By the time the couples finish, our hands overflow with prayer cards. Wet mascara has my eyelashes interlocking. When Pastor Downes leads us all with one last prayer, I'm thinking it's not possible for the wedding to surpass all of this yummy loving goodness.

I look at John, and his golden eyes twinkle. Our wedding date? Just a whisper away.

We're almost there. Ready to start our lives together.

Men and women drift away in groups, and only Ms. Pat stands before us.

"Mom? Did they miss you?" John asks. "You have a prayer card for us?"

"No, I have a gift for your new home." She steps to John and places the silver ribboned box on his lap. "I've watched you all your life, son." She's so close, her legs touch his. "You're so determined and you know your own mind. This is your history. Remember it." Wind blows through her hair, moving wavy locks in slow motion against her cheeks. "Chablis, you'll learn more about my son every day. Start with this."

John tugs the ribbon. It slips down his legs, then onto the soft grass. He lifts the top of the box. From beneath gray and white tissue paper, his hands pull out a silver scrapbook. My heart warms at the pictures of my future husband. The first page is a baby picture, and he's newborn with his eyes shut tight. He flips through the pages and we're treated to a retrospective of his childhood. From clutching a plush brown teddy bear while sitting on his father's lap, up through the school years and beyond. I grip his hand as he views the picture of himself with his brother at his dad's funeral. I see the Coke-bottle glasses, then him growing taller and stronger, until the specs no longer appear in pictures. Him at the prom with his date. With friends before and after high school graduation. Endless pictures of him riding bikes, running track, lifting weights. Graduation from Drexel. More pictures with his family. And photos with people from Rise Community Church. From the apartment he used to live in before Germany. Then the Brandenburg Gate. The Berlin Television Tower. The Berlin Wall Memorial.

Another picture of John at the Berlin Wall Memorial.

And another.

Then the memorial becomes the historical background of John standing tall and proud next to a delicate butter-pecan colored woman whose red-glossed lips frame her white teeth in a wide smile. She wears a faded jean jacket, a thin white t-shirt, and happiness.

Trina.

the photograph

MY CHOICE.

I can think about that picture, or I can think about that strange look on John's face after he slammed the scrapbook shut and took off after his mother.

I can think about that picture or I can remember how he stood toe to toe with her, saying he had enough and she must respect our union or leave our lives.

I can think about that soul-crushing picture or I can memorize the historic homes I pass on this beautiful street. Large houses nested by leafy trees show off while I wander down the block.

No one can accuse me of being in my feelings if I drift far enough away so they can't see my face. Because I can't unsee that photograph.

John. Trina. Germany. Happy.

I have no idea where I'm going. The neat yard of the brick home ahead of me has a large weeping willow. I slow down and study how the delicate branches sway in the summer breeze.

Good to meet you willow tree.

I'm Chablis.

The second choice.

"Sunshine?"

The Jeep shows up by the curb, but I don't glance at the driver. I don't have to. When he's around, every cell in my body comes alive. I'm not married to him yet, but I can smell him in my dreams at night.

I stop. "Yeah."

"I'm sorry."

"For what?"

"I never told you Trina came to visit me."

I quit staring at the Jeep's tires to look at John's face. Bloodshot eyes. Drooping mouth. "Why would you? I was only a bubbly church chick crushing on you. You didn't have to tell me anything."

"You were my wife back then, it just wasn't official."

"My life isn't a Nicholas Sparks novel. Don't say something like that to make me feel better."

"It's true."

"It's not."

"Trust me, please."

My tired feet turn me around so I can walk in the opposite direction. John would have to do a U-turn to follow me. A couple of beats after I head back toward the Joneses house, that's exactly what he does.

"Sunshine?"

"Stop following me! You know I have issues."

"Aren't those issues fading daily?"

I stand still.

John keeps speaking from the Jeep. "At the wedding shower. I came up and hugged you when you didn't know I was there. You didn't jump. No cold sweats. No deep breathing. You're healing. God's been healing you a little more each day."

On the pavement, I hear our voices from three years ago. *Do you know why I'm training you? I'm cute? No. I'm not cute? Chablis? I take it this has nothing to do with my cuteness? Now we run. This time I'll run with you.*

With me. "What do you want me to do, John?"

"Please take a ride with me," he asks. "Please."

In the Jeep, we travel past Castle Jones and I wave at the loved ones we pass as they walk to their cars. They can't possibly identify what's on my mind. All they see is the John and Chablis who finished another milestone. A couple heaped with more blessings than a lifetime can hold.

But here in the quiet? All I feel is the jagged devastation of our broken places.

This bench we sit on behind the Art Museum? It's old, but the faded brown wood and paint-peeled black metal still holds us up. The gazebo above us opens to the sky, where color changes show us night will arrive quickly.

We've been here before. From the past, I hear John's words again. *I would love to love you. Do you still want to love me?*

For more than an hour we rest our backs against one another. Curving concrete paths. Walkers and joggers. Families with strollers. Lovers walking hand in hand.

Premarital counseling ends after Labor Day.

September our belongings will live together inside a two-bedroom apartment.

October? We'll share Colgate.

These are facts. Ms. Pat tried to share some with me, but I was too prideful to listen.

No enemy is more chilling than the one who's right.

Trina landed on Planet John first, but they broke up. That makes me his second choice. Period.

Darkness falls, and we're still silent together. Future Geralds trying to let the past pass us by.

A tall man walks toward the middle of the lawn. Khaki shorts. White polo shirt. Phillies cap. His large hands break and snap glow necklaces. Yellow. Red. Blue. Purple. Orange. As soon as one glows, he secures the ends in a plastic circle and lays it at his feet. When they're all done, he calls out. Small children I didn't notice in the growing darkness run to him and surround his knees. One by one he places circular glow lights around their necks. They hug him and run off to play. The man sits down and observes the children at play. No matter where they travel on the grass, he sees them.

"Can we walk?" I ask John.

"Yeah."

We stand and stretch our legs. I put my hand in his hand during the stroll from the park to the gray metal bridge at the edge of the Schuylkill River. Shallow and bug-filled, dark brown sludge slithers slowly beneath our feet. At the end of the bridge, we stop and observe river water flowing away from the city.

Air separates time and memories from where we remain in the present.

"Trina?" I ask.

John pauses, watching dark water flow for a moment before he speaks. "Like I told you before, I broke off our engagement because she didn't really want to be married. A husband and kids? None of that was important to her."

"Why'd she fly to see you in Berlin?"

He studies the mud beneath our feet. "She wanted to get away and talk to someone she knew would listen."

"She stayed with you?"

"For a few days."

"Were you lovers?"

"No. Nothing even close to that."

Ducks sleep in peace on the muddy riverbank. "Trust you?"

"Please."

"When you let Trina visit, you gave your mom the wrong idea. She probably thought both of you were trying again. Then you show up with me on your arm when you move back? No wonder she hates me."

"Trina probably sent those Berlin pics because she thought Mom might like them."

"Ms. Pat got her hopes up and you crushed them."

John turns to me. "I'm only a man, and I need you to forgive how I handled that. Believe me, I was never as happy with Trina as I am with you."

"Keep going."

"What I said back in Chestnut Hill? That was true. One Saturday when you and I were running here, I had to slow down to wait for you, and the Spirit said *be easy on her, she's your future.*"

"Mrs. Gerald in seven weeks?"

"Seems that way."

"You could have told me about Trina visiting you. I would have understood."

"I hate drama and I didn't want to risk bringing any to our thing —we were just getting started. Rest your heart about Trina. She asked me to keep some things in confidence for a while, and I'm a man of my word. I can talk about it now though. She actually changed her mind and opened her heart to the idea of marriage and family life, but it will be with a Brooklyn woman she met through friends at her law firm."

"She's a lesbian?"

"No, she's fluid. Attracted to both men and women. But her parents are against that. I think they thought they could influence Trina to rekindle things with me, but that wasn't happening. Her relationship with her parents went south when they kept pressuring her. When Trina called me, all she did was wish us well."

I look through gray metal squares. Sludge lies beneath. "Messy."

John cups my chin and lifts my face upward so my eyes meet his.

He communicates with only his touch that we're standing on a sturdy bridge, holding us above the mess of life.

And I get it, too, that it doesn't matter which woman came first or last.

Because God placed me first in John's heart.

ⵁ

John's father's name was Nathaniel.

Nathaniel Johnson Gerald.

A tombstone artist etched the name in strong letters in the middle of the slate gray headstone, along with rest in heavenly peace and an ornate cross. A beautiful tribute. It sits in the middle of sun-dried grass between two bold dandelions sporting their fluff.

John moves fast and stoops down to grasp those lawn intruders, ripping them from their roots and tossing them to the side.

Summer sun's rays beat down on us. The odor of aging concrete combined with withered grass and dried leaves fills my nose. Late August in the City of Brotherly Love, and here we stand, after church service, at a gravesite. Warm winds rustle the tree leaves, and John remains close enough to me I can hear the soft swish of gum in his mouth.

My words aren't needed here. This is John's time.

He bows his head. Eyes shut, he whispers his prayers.

A few minutes pass, and the wind sings a lullaby. I imagine verses about a man who worked too hard and died before his time. A guy who loved holding his wife, wrestling with his young sons. A man who worked loads of overtime to buy his beloved family a comfortable home in the Northeast. A hardworking, faith-filled man gone too soon.

My hands are sweaty and I rub them together. I try to step aside and let John continue his moment, but his arm snakes out to draw me close to his side.

"The little black Bible? From engagement day?" His voice sounds hoarse, and his eyes remain shut as he makes a simultaneous question and statement.

"Yes."

"It belonged to him."

"Really?"

"Mom gifted it to me when I graduated from high school. I don't know what she gave Nate, but she gave me that Bible. I read from it once a day." He sniffs. "And... uh... no one's seen it except for me for a long time."

"Not Trina?"

He opens his golden eyes. "No." He sniffs again, turning back to his father's grave. "I got the idea for the Bible when I asked to marry you. Only you. I think Dad would have wanted you to see it. He highlighted 1 Corinthians 13 for my mother."

Another wind whips through and a broken tree limb falls. It smacks the earth with a soft thud.

John takes my hand. "Lord, I have the love of my life by my side, and I treasure her more than I do myself. I loved my Dad, and thank you for the seven years we shared, and for helping me remember all he did to serve his family. I promise to keep that legacy going. Amen."

"Amen."

"I am standing here before God and my father and this is me telling you, you're who I want forever." He faces me. "You're enough just the way you are, not because I chose you... but because God chose you. You are a daughter of the King. Now I want you to say that you're enough."

Is that fire in his eyes? For the broken chick on the sidewalk, who shouldn't have lived? The same unfailing love I found in my Savior. They both see into my soul. And they love me.

"I'm enough?" I say.

"Come on now. You can do better than that. Let me hear you say it louder."

I lick my lips. The wind rustles my purple curls like it's cheering for me, too. "I'm enough."

"One. More. Time." John cups my face with both hands.

"I'm en—"

This kiss sends fireworks to the base of my brain, but I don't see any guardian angels.

This time I see stars.

moving on up

JOHN and I haven't heard from Ms. Pat since the scrapbook incident. But God works good for his children through all situations and now I *finally* understand Ms. Pat's issue. Years ago, her baby boy fell in love with a woman she bonded with and she kept hoping they would marry. I jumped into the picture and massacred her dream. Hence the prayers and stupid insults.

But I'm still here and I'm at peace, flying fast to the next milestone in this engagement journey.

Faithful premarital counselor, Ariana? I'm convinced she'll drag John and me past the finish line despite ourselves. She gave us a two-week break from counseling while she vacationed in Punta Cana.

Tonight, deeply tanned with a wide grin, she starts her last important premarital counseling subject.

The one I've been waiting weeks for.

"There are three levels of intimacy—intellectual, emotional, and physical," she says. "During your relationship, you've been growing your intellectual intimacy whenever you dialogue about life and world events. Emotionally, you've become intimate when you discuss matters of the heart, and when you do things with one another that bring out concern and caring." She clears her throat. "Before I go any further, are you still abstaining?"

"Yes," I say, fluttering my eyelashes. "Yes, we are. Is this when we get our gold medal for being good?"

She continues. "Any who, I understand this is a very special time for you. You should work out your first sexual time with care, but with reality in mind. Let your personalities dictate what to do but understand the honeymoon night is only one night. You'll enjoy a future full of enriching physical encounters, so think of your honeymoon as a start. Sexual intimacy and the bonded feeling that comes out of it will provide your relationship a lasting sense of oneness."

John squeezes my hand and both of us stare at our counselor like two teenagers in tenth grade health class.

"Plan your sex, and I'm not just talking birth control." Ariana glances from me to John. "Exactly what you do and how you do it, that's for you to manage. Your workbook will guide you with questions, but even if you write nothing down, talk through your tastes and expectations. Your physically intimate moments should be frequent and loving—get an idea of how that will work out for you. That's what I want you to do tonight, so I'm ending the session early."

She needs to send us home with a chaperone, but all she does is wave and walk back to her desk.

"Bye. Enjoy your chat!"

I should be calm about this. It's not like we haven't talked about lovemaking before. We have. But we've never discussed specific sexual tastes or fantasies, or body exploration, or any of the wild and wonderfully tantalizing stuff I've been telling myself to chill the heck out about since my man slid the ring on my hand.

I cross my legs while snippets of sexy R&B songs remix themselves inside my brain.

John, quiet, guides the Jeep down the road.

No. No. No. No. No. I am *not* strong enough to hold this conversation next to my bedroom and end the night like we just discussed painting our future kitchen Carolina Blue.

"Bae? Um. Where are we going?" I ask.

"Your place."

"You want to talk great sexpectations in my apartment alone? Just me. And you."

He doesn't answer. Instead, he changes direction and drives to Nate's townhouse. Thankfully he's home, but he is upstairs, so we head to the back of the dining room and sit down for the official future Geralds super confidential sex chat.

"I scanned the back of that chapter." John lays his workbook on the table. "I'm gonna start, and we can go back and forth. Sound good?"

I fold my hands like a good little pupil "Cool. Go for it."

"First, are you anxious about becoming my lover?"

"You're kidding right? No. Are you nervous about being with me?"

"Not at all."

"Have you ever been sexually abused?"

"No, what about you?"

"Well, this one time, at band camp—"

"Stop playing. That's a serious question."

"Bad joke, sorry. My answer is no. Next question... do you understand how the female anatomy works?"

"Seriously?"

"It's one of the suggested questions. Look right there." I point at the workbook page.

He flips to another page. "Let's stick to the questions for our situation, please."

"I'm skipping down to frequency. You want us to get together a couple times a month? Couple times a week?"

"Umm-hmm. A few times a day would be like heaven. Morning. Evening. I can drive to your job at lunchtime. You can close your office door."

"John?"

"Hey, I'm a healthy guy. Got a lot of testosterone."

"See now, and you just told me to be serious."

"I am serious."

"All right, whatever we can handle based on our energy level, that's what we'll do. Do you want me to wear lingerie? Victoria's Secret and all that?"

He rubs his hands together. "Now I love that question. What do I want my wife to wear? You know what, it's up to you. Naked works for me all day every day. If you wear something special for me, I'll love it. If you wear scented body lotion and your wedding ring, I'll love it."

"Duly noted."

"My next question. Is sexy talk okay? Can I say naughty things to you?"

He's teasing me, which is why I flutter my eyelashes and use my raspy voice when I answer.

"Oh, please, yes, Mr. Gerald. And may I do the same with you?"

"Uh... yeah," he stammers. "My next one is... now I know some women don't like to, and I don't want to just put it out there like that, but since we're bringing up what we want—"

I know what he's asking, and it's fine with me. "Relax bae, that's a yes from me. And you?"

"Why do you think I asked?"

"Let's get back on track. Any sensitive body areas to avoid?"

"I'm ticklish on the bottom of my feet, but you found that out the first time we gave each other foot massages. What about you?"

"You can run your fingers through my hair, but never grab the back of my head. If you do, it could trigger a panic attack and that's the end of our night."

"Thanks for telling me. I needed to know that. I wouldn't want to hurt you at all." He rocks back in his chair. "How do you feel about shower and bathtub sex? Different positions?"

"Oh, I hope we do everything. Now is my satisfaction important to you?"

"Listen, I pledge to do *whatever* it takes to get you there. Every time." He looks me up and down. "Is it getting hot in here, or is it me?"

"It's you and me. And I'm here for you too. One hundred percent." I give him a fist bump. "What about after a hard day at work?"

"Let's check in with each other and maybe try to get some sleep first. No pressure on the other person?"

"Agreed. And can we be adventurous?"

"Adventurous how?"

"Do we have to do it in the bedroom all the time?"

He leans over and whispers in my ear. "I'll go anywhere you want to go. Back seat of the Jeep. On the beach. At the park. I'm your man."

"What about sexting and naked videos of each other?"

"No, not into it, and I don't want you to start either."

"You don't trust me?"

"I'm a cloud architect. I trust you. I don't trust hackers."

"Understood," I say. "Now how should we deal with times when one of us wants to make love, but the other doesn't?"

"I asked a couple married guys this question and got some good advice. Like be respectful about declining it and have a real reason. And finishing watching *Law & Order: SVU* isn't a good reason. If you turn me down because you're not with it, I have to respect that. But you have to be the next person to initiate it."

I roll that around inside my brain. "So the next time, it would be my responsibility to approach you and get the ball rolling."

"Yeah, so one of us isn't always the person who starts it or always the person who rejects it. Keeps us from getting resentful."

"Well, I'm out of questions. You have anything else?"

"Only one thing, but it's not a question." He slides over and holds my hands. "Listen, it's been a while for both of us. Our first few times together might not last that long. If I don't get it right with you the first time, please don't be disappointed. I can't read your mind so teach me what you like and how to love you."

"As soon as we start, class is in session. We'll teach each other."

"That's what I'm talking about. And we just had one dope conversation. Wife of my dreams right here."

"See, we communicated our expectations and everything. You know Ariana would give us a thumbs up."

He releases my hands and stands up. "Let me get you back to your place and I'll call you for prayer."

"You're taking me home now?"

He grabs his keys from the tabletop. "I have to or we might teach some lessons tonight."

On the ride back to my place, I'm not frustrated about the fact that we're waiting for the wedding night. We flew through those questions so easily, like we're getting our minds set for the big day. When we make love, it'll feel like a graduation.

Or no.

More like homecoming.

Our first place together won't be the house I'd imagined in March. But even though the apartment we chose doesn't appear like what I'd pictured as our starter home, it *is* classy and upscale. Granite countertops. Crown molding. Modern colors. The kitchen's only a few feet bigger than the one in my current place, but it includes all stainless-steel appliances. The complex also boasts a fitness center, pool, and a lounge room with two fireplaces.

This evening we're in the management office at the Glenshire Hills Apartments, reviewing details with Francisco, the rental agent. Since John and I are responsible full-time job-holding folk with no kids or pets, this should go well.

"Everything looks fine." Francisco scans our lease application. "I need to run a credit check for both of you as part of the tenant screening process. After that, we should be all set. There's a fee of fifty dollars. How would you like to pay?"

I knew this before we came in. "I have the check with me. Should I give it to you now?"

"No. You can give it to me when we're done, that's fine."

John says nothing. He sits bolt upright in his chair. He also chews his gum so hard I see that vein popping out in his jaw.

Oh no! I tap his arm. "What's up with you?"

"My phone keeps going off and I know it's work," he says. "Same client from before...there's an architecture flaw."

I relax. "So step out for a minute."

"Excuse me." He pulls his phone from his pocket and leaves, but he's back in only a few minutes.

When John sits down, Francisco says to us, "Mr. Gerald, your credit check was fine."

John grins like he knows he's been blasting through debt like a champ.

Francisco looks at me. "Ms. Shields. In your history, I found a hard credit check in the last six months."

Oh Lord! That stupid loan application! "Is that a problem?" I ask.

Francisco turns to his computer and clicks his mouse. "Not really. Just something I wanted to mention to you, because today is the second credit check. Repeated checks can impact your credit history. Neither of you have bankruptcies or foreclosures. Those were the red flags I was looking for." He pulls papers from his printer, straightens them, then pushes them in front of John and me.

We scribble our signatures and initials on a twelve-month lease. Key pickup happens September 1st.

We're not shacking up, so we work out a strategy.

John will move his stuff from Nate's townhouse to the new apartment. He wants to "prepare" the space for his new bride. I don't know what that means exactly, but he's a romantic, so I'm looking forward to it.

John and Nate will take my belongings from my current abode to the new place.

I will move out of my rabbit hole and stay with Mariah and her family until wedding day. I lived with them back when I went to Temple. Their Wynnewood house has plenty of room, and it's only minutes away from Glenshire Hills.

Our brand-new apartment will have lots of space too. Especially since I plan to tell the guys to dismantle my tired IKEA furniture and leave it for trash.

I do have standards.

pinterest dreams

I STAND in the doorway of my soon-to-be-former bedroom while two men survey the only furniture remaining in my white-walled cubbyhole of an apartment.

John wears a faded Eagles shirt and gray jersey shorts. He's on his knees next to the sofa.

"Sure you don't want this?" He asks. "We can fit it in the U-Haul."

"It's old, and it's IKEA. Trash it," I say.

A blue and white sweatband rests on Nate's bald head. "The bookshelf and coffee table too?"

"Brothers Gerald, please, I'm done with all of it. Make the dumpster the final resting place."

"Okay, on two." John holds the edge of the sofa and nods at Nate. "One. Two."

They hoist the sofa like it weighs nothing. A few minutes later they return and do the same thing with my tall white bookshelf, wooden coffee table, short white bookshelf, and my bed frame, dresser, and mattresses. The only thing I'm taking from that old bed is my pink body pillow. Gotta cuddle up to something while I crash at Mariah's.

Nate appears again at the entrance to the kitchen. "Any more moving boxes? Did we get them all?"

I scoot to the kitchen and twirl around the space. "No, big brother, I'm good. Want water?"

"Got some in the U-Haul."

"Bless you for helping."

"You'll get my bill." He swaggers to the hallway.

John slides past his brother and straight to the kitchen where he scoops me up and seats me on the counter.

"Ewwhh! No! Stop!" I push at his sweat-covered arms. "You're glistening and you smell like hot dumpster."

He presses his lips against my cheek and gives me two sloppy kisses. "I'll shower at our place after we stack your things inside."

I grin. "Our place?"

"Our place." He grins back.

"You ready?"

"Let's do this."

"I need to clean and do a once around before I drive over."

"See you there." He kisses me twice on the forehead, then he's out.

The guys spent less than an hour putting my black trunk of all things hair and makeup, books, clothing boxes, keepsakes, appliances, and my rolling suitcases into the U-Haul. Cushions, knick-knacks, and anything I didn't have a deep connection to, I gave away. I even donated my TV to Goodwill because it isn't a flat screen.

All furniture gone, I sweep, mop, and wipe out all the cabinets and drawers. I finish fast and survey my work.

After, with my hand on the front door, I blow goodbye kisses to the empty rooms.

"Bye, Chablis Charmaine Shields."

. . .

John and Nate mounted the Smart TV on the living room wall. They also installed curtain rods and sheers above the patio doors. John's large dark walnut bookshelf stands in one corner. The top shelf holds his favorite books. Bibles. Study guides. A concordance. Walter Mosley novels. Books by James McBride, Dr. Myles Munroe, and Ta-Nehisi Coates.

Our college degrees rest in gold frames above the middle shelf. And that middle shelf? Fresh red roses in a metal vase beside the little black Bible and two silver-framed pictures: one of our first date, and the other from engagement night at eatLARGE. I snap a pic and post it to the Gram with the hashtags #ThisisWhyILoveFutureHubby and #TheWordBeforeUs.

He left the bottom shelf empty for my favorites.

That's funny.

Our reading material will live together before we do.

I travel down the hall, calling out to John before I turn into the guest room. "The curtains are nice and you outdid yourself with that bookshelf."

His bed is made up with a forest green comforter. A standing work desk against the far wall holds his charging laptop. I don't even have to ask if the Wi-Fi works. It's probably the first thing he connected this morning.

John stands up from stacking my moving boxes in the corner. "Come on," he says and leads me into the hall again. "Christmas came early for us, Sunshine."

He opens the primary bedroom door. Sitting in our empty room is a beautiful, brand-new, four-piece dark gray queen-sized bedroom set. Bed. Dresser. Mirror. Nightstands. Matching lamps. Luxurious silver quilted bedding and pillows plumped up like a Raymour & Flanagan display.

I cover my mouth. "When?"

"Nate asked what we wanted for our wedding present. I told him the TV was enough, but he said it's a used TV and he wanted to give us something new. I told him we need bedroom furniture. I picked it out, and he paid and delivery happened yesterday. Put it together last night."

"When were you going to tell me?"

"Today. But, listen, I'm locking this bedroom until we get back from the honeymoon. After that, I want to sprinkle rose petals across the bed and we can christen it together."

"Ooh! Romantic."

He winks. "You know your man always has a plan."

An empty crystal picture frame rests on one nightstand. "What's that for?"

"The first picture taken of us after we say I do."

My eyes dart from the frame to the cushy pillows, to the cut-glass vase I'm sure he plans to fill with fresh flowers for his new bride. That silkened dream of a bed? We'll probably make our kids on it.

I kiss his handsome face, then wave him out and slam the door shut. "Get back in the guest room before I drag you to City Hall so we can have fun on that bed."

My phone vibrates with a text message. I pull out my device and smile. "Oh! Cute! Check this out."

John's already back to arranging boxes. "Whatcha got?"

"Nikki and the twins! The face paint makes them all look like kittens. Look at those smiles."

"Where's Terry? Don't tell me he has face paint too."

"Ha ha ha. He probably took the picture. They're doing Dorney Park today."

"Nice day for it. Hope they have fun and get back."

"Why?"

"Storm coming later."

I text Nikki back a bunch of smiley faces and hearts. So good to see Nikki and Terry growing close. I think Rae-Ann and Rashida help bond them. Last week Nik told me Terry's plans to buy a house with a third floor to make into their personal bedroom/living area. He's working with their mother to keep them several nights a week.

John's body odor hits my nose when he crosses to close the window.

"Whew! You need to shower, like now. Mom and Daddy are stopping through soon."

John moves his eyebrows up and down. "Wanna join me?"

"Stop teasing."

"Who's teasing?"

"You. Faking me out to see if I'll go for it."

"Can't trick you for nothing, huh?"

"That's right."

He reaches inside a blue plastic tote and pulls out a fluffy black towel and a bottle of body wash. He calls to me when he walks out, "Next month you *will* join me."

I smash my hands against my ears and sing. "La la la la! Don't need to hear that or think about it. I'm still being good."

I skip to the balcony and tackle my future brother-in-law even though he's sweaty too. "Love you big brother! That bedroom set! Blessings on blessings on blessings. You are your brother's keeper."

"Welcome, sis. Been looking out for baby brother all these years. He told me what was needed and there you go."

"Well, thanks." I let Nate go and glance at his phone screen. Glossy-lipped women smile back at me. "You're trying a dating service? That's not Tinder is it?"

He switches his phone out of sight. "Just like a sister to be nosy. I have too much class for Tinder. I'm trying eHarmony."

"Oh, for real?"

"I have to open up sometime. Can't be around all this relationship happiness and keep a closed heart."

"No, you can't. We wouldn't let you."

. . .

Mom wants to talk furniture. Or rather, our lack of it.

"Chablis, what are you all going to sit on?" She asks.

"We have a table and kitchen chairs. Grab one of those." I sit cross-legged on the rug with my phone and pin home decor graphics to my Engagement Pinterest board. With one full month and two more paychecks coming, I can take my time turning white walls and sparse rooms into the inviting and lovely Chalet Gerald.

Nate stands on the balcony drinking Aquafina. My dad finishes his quick tour of our new place and moves toward the sliding doors for icy refreshments. John's still getting dressed and I wait for GrubHub to deliver lunch for my moving men from Golden Wok.

Mom scans the inside of our double-doored walk-in closet. "Not even a cushion? Something?"

"Mom?"

"Chablis, at some point you'll have company. You can't have only an area rug and a flat screen TV in this room."

"Hey, but it's a Smart TV though. It's nice, right? Nate let us have it. He's getting a new one. We don't watch a lot of TV, but we can watch Netflix movies on it."

She makes a beeline to the balcony. Calling for my dad. "Honey! Finish that water! We're running to the Target and get Chablis and John stuff for the living room."

After Dad swallows down his drink, they go to Target.

John smells like body wash when he strolls in. He wears his *Grind Hard, Pray Harder* t-shirt and shorts. The beard looks soft and touchable.

He joins me on the floor. "Where's Mom?"

"She grabbed Daddy to go to Target. They'll be back." I'm still messing with Pinterest.

"Call her. Guess what we just ran out of?"

"What?"

"Toilet paper."

I dial Mom. "Mom! We need Charmin. Pick some up."

"And dishwashing liquid," John says.

"John said get us some Ajax too."

I hold my phone away when she yells. "Will you two please grow up and create a real household! I hope you cleaned that place good!"

"We did. Two days ago. Thank you, Mom! Love you, Mom!"

I tap to end the call, and John slides down and lays his head on my thigh. I abandon my phone and run my fingers through his beard. He closes his eyes.

"Hard moving everything this morning?" I ask.

"Moving was a breeze. Making sure the TV didn't break was the hardest thing we did. Hungry now, though. Food coming?"

"It's on the way."

In the quiet, I listen to him breathe.

John rubs my knee. "I'm still praying."

I move my fingers through his beard, touching his chin. He stops me but says nothing else. He doesn't have to.

His mother should be here fussing with us about empty rooms and missing toilet paper. Asking us if we've eaten yet. Telling us our kitchen shelves need contact paper. Wondering if we'll have enough room if a baby arrives sooner rather than later.

Ms. Pat.

John's marriage to me shouldn't mean he has to lose her but having her in our lives means I have to develop the strength to treat her well, regardless of how many stabs she makes at me. I've already forgiven her for the scrapbook stunt, now I gotta forget it. I have to forget about her close friendship with Trina as well. And to do that, I need less of myself.

More of God.

Stacey told me mommies-to-be go through this thing called nesting, when the new mother gets a burst of energy and wants to organize, clean, set up, and otherwise finish tasks related to their bundle of joy.

I don't think that applies to wives-to-be, but this Monday after work I'm in the new apartment. Organizing. Cleaning. Fixing. Throwing dirty clothes in the washer. John didn't ask or expect me to do any of this. I don't have to act like Merry Maids *just* for him, but tonight I want to. We both work and we can make a chore schedule later. In the meantime, I'm gliding around our new space and loving it. I don't sleep here yet, but this *is* my home, and this kind of activity makes me feel like more of a resident.

I'm also cooking, or at least I'm trying.

Some women have relationship goals.

I have culinary goals.

John whistles when I serve him eggplant parmigiana, roasted peppers and Caesar salad. "You *made* all this?"

"Yes, sir, I did, sir. Followed the recipe from Pinterest."

"This is *niiiice*."

I bring us glasses of orange San Pellegrino and sit beside him. "Bless our food?"

His hand covers mine. "Heavenly Father, thank you for this food we are about to receive. Bless it and bless the hands that prepared it. In Jesus' name. Amen."

"Amen." I pick up my fork. "Let me know if it's too salty."

He tastes his meal. "No, this is delicious. It's great."

"Thank you." I flutter my eyelashes. "Thank you very much."

We eat in silence for a while. John hasn't changed yet, so he still resembles a *Men's Wearhouse* poster. I'm barefoot, wearing his old cotton Phillies shirt and black short-shorts, but I touched up my hair and makeup before he arrived. Cute and comfy wifey mode.

"This afternoon I scheduled a spa day at Tranquil Streams," I say. "Day before the wedding, but I'll be done with everything before rehearsal."

"They're styling your hair too?"

"No, Quinsara and Raven are doing our hair and makeup the morning of."

"Oh, I was wondering how Quinsara lost her best client."

"You know better. She has me for life. And Luna called to do one last check about the rehearsal at Rise. I told her there're no changes." I take a sip of sparkling water. "But, uh, when she mentioned changes, it had me wondering."

He stops his fork in mid-air and glances sidelong at me. "Wondering? About what?"

"I know its last minute, but what do you think about throwing an after party? Like at an Air BNB? With just our friends and the wedding party? It could be wonderful."

"When did you dream this up?"

"Today."

"A last-minute party rental? Food for everybody? Drinks?"

"I know what you're thinking, but we could keep it small."

John rubs his forehead. "No, okay. It's too late for anything like that. And I thought you were done scheming on the wedding."

"I am."

My eyelashes don't flutter because I told him the truth. Honestly, I've been done with the wedding. Now an after party, that's a whole different celebration.

"You sure about that?" He asks.

"I'm positive—"

"Listen, I know your heart is in the right place, but let's please keep things simple." Weariness weighs down his voice. "Just... less of a chance for anything else to go wrong."

He swallows the rest of his dinner and leaves the table. Long steps carry him out of the kitchen and down the hall where the guest room door clicks shut.

What did I say?

John's out driving Uber while I finish our laundry.

Mom's voice blares from speakerphone. "What did you do?"

"Nothing." I pull wet towels from the washer and move them to the dryer I just emptied. The air smells like Gain. "Mom, I did nothing. All I asked is if we could have an after party for our friends."

"I wondered if you were ready for this. He's still upset after his mom's scrapbook and the pictures?"

"I guess. I tried to put that out of my mind."

"If you could name his emotions, how do you think he feels?"

I pull John's button-down shirts from the wicker hamper. "I'd say he's grieving."

"Oh, then he wants to rest his mind awhile."

"What are you telling me?" The t-shirts are dry and ready to fold. I grab them and take a walk to the kitchen table.

"You can't gloss over his feelings. He needs you to comfort him."

"Mom, I'm right here."

"And are you making life bearable for him? Or are you busy running your mouth about the next thing you want?"

"Right now, I'm shaking out his clean gym shirts. How's that?"

"That's a start."

"And I cooked dinner tonight."

"When you finish throwing away all that burned food, find something else constructive to do. And don't you ask that man for anything else tonight."

I sigh, folding t-shirts. "I won't."

"Love you, baby girl."

"I love you, too."

The call ends and I tap my Pandora app. I'll sing along with Charlene Nash or Koryn Hawthorne or Kierra Sheard. Music can keep me company. That's another thing John and I have in common, we listen to our phones more than we watch TV. Our primary bedroom doesn't even have a television, and we don't want one in there. By the time we christen the bed, TV will be the last thing on our minds.

My arms are full of folded workout shirts when I pad to the guest room. John is a neat freak. He made his bed and the clutter-free desktop holds his Dell laptop. He placed his old dresser inside the long closet, so I search for the drawer that holds workout clothes and stack his fresh shirts inside. Takes about five seconds.

I sit on the edge of his bed. The nightstand holds a metal lamp, glowing alarm clock, and a navy-blue journal with a pen beside it.

I probably shouldn't peek, but it would be nice to know what he writes. I grab the journal and hold it.

Wait. His private thoughts and prayers are in this. It's not for me to see.

I reach to put the journal back and a picture slides to the side. I snatch it fast.

It's me. Laughing. Dancing. Short cap of pink curly hair and bedazzled t-shirt. Line dancers surround me at The Grandstand. He must have taken this with his phone, then went to one of those drug store kiosks and printed it. I flip it over. Scripture references scrawled across the back. *Isaiah 41:10. Deuteronomy 31:8. Isaiah 41:13. 1 Peter 5:7. Psalm 34:4.* Under those, he wrote, *Father, keep watch over my wife, keep her safe, renew her strength, guide her footsteps, bless her with peace and happiness. Continue to heal her mind, body, and soul.*

This photo came from the weekend he arrived from Germany to find me. We weren't even dating yet, and we were nowhere close to being engaged. And this is the picture he uses to pray scripture over me? This is how he likes to remember me? Illustrating joy?

I slide the picture and journal back on the nightstand.

He'll pray for me tonight. I know he will.

Because that's the type of man he is.

I walk to the empty balcony. I'm surprised Samantha and John's other road bike aren't out there. He must have put them in storage.

It's dusk, but I can make out an elderly couple across the way.

They walk side by side. Thin white hair. Wrinkled skin. The man uses a cane. They make their way toward Trader Joe's near the end of the block. The woman walks a little faster than her partner, but she stops and waits for him. He leans and lets her support his weight. They move slowly, but they make it to their destination together. I rest against the metal railing. "Father, please keep transforming my heart. You brought us together to serve you as a unit. Make me the companion you most want me to be for John. Not the woman I think I should look like in a wedding dress or on Instagram, but the partner he needs. I don't care about anyone's impression of us, I only care about yours. I love you, Lord. Amen."

The sun sets and darkness settles around me.

John doesn't see well in the dark without his lenses.

Target sells night lights. I can dash over there and buy some. Position them throughout the apartment and help future hubby out by spreading more light through our place. And while I'm shopping, I can buy my own special prayer journal and I'll put a picture of my beloved in it and pray scriptures over him.

Cause I'm not content just to sprinkle light across our apartment. I want to light up the heavens with blessings for my man.

Like stars in a midnight blue sky.

off the market

RINGING. Ringing. Ringing.

At work, I rush into my office after my mid-day team meeting. I'm feeling kind of vulnerable and not sure I should do this, but I still push the door shut when Ms. Pat answers my call.

"Hello," she says.

"Did I catch you at a bad time?" I drop into my office chair.

"No."

God. Please. More of you. Less of me.

"I don't know if John or Nate told you, but we moved into Glenshire Hills Apartment. It's nice. We can walk to the Trader Joe's and the Farmer's Market. We're right by those fancy dress boutiques. Free People. SoulCycle is down the block. Close to Ardmore."

"You're living there already? With John?"

"John lives there with our things. I'm staying with my cousin for the next few weeks. She's close to the apartment complex."

"Oh. I was about to say. That doesn't sound like my son. Unless he bumped his head working out."

Feels good to laugh. A small giggle on her end and it feels even better.

"Ms. Pat." I close my eyes and block out visions of our time in her living room. And at church. And at the wedding shower. "John loves you a lot, and I know what he said but he needs you in our lives."

"Did he tell you to call me today?"

"No. I'm calling on my own."

"And you're fine with that picture of John and Trina?"

My stomach dips a little, but steadies when I touch my engagement ring. "I'd say I've moved on from seeing it. She's a part of his past and it helps me understand she was a really special friend of yours."

"Still is."

"Yes, well, I'm calling to say you are welcome in our home. We have nothing but love and respect for you."

The seconds hand on my gray metal desk clock ticks away. I watch it, clutching the phone in my hand.

"I see. Thank you for calling."

"No problem."

"Goodbye."

I place my phone on the desk. "Lord, please intervene. I can't make her love me, but I'm praying you'll allow her to remain in our lives for the sake of my husband. He loves her. He doesn't want to see her go. Be it your will, provide your healing. Only love from our side, Father. Please, allow us to only show love. John and I together as a team. Amen."

Seven premarital counseling sessions over and training ends with dinner in Olde City hosted by Ariana, Pastor Downes, and first lady Juanita. Sister Gunning left one of those scary voice mail messages two weeks ago to remind us.

At the Downes' home, Ariana opens the door and laughs. "That's one way to say it!"

The future hubby and I dressed in the matching black and white OFF THE MARKET t-shirts Terry bought us as a wedding shower present.

John whips out his phone, and we pose with Ariana for pictures. Then we step inside and Sister Juanita calls us to the kitchen.

"John. Chablis. Get in here!" She pulls a big aluminum pan of stuffed shells out of the oven, placing it on the counter before coming over to envelope us with a hug. "Congratulations, my darlings!"

The Rise Church grapevine says Juanita Downes' food rivals any gourmet kitchen in Philly. The chatter must be true because I step into a cloud of rich smelling oregano, basil, and warm ripe tomatoes which makes me shoot John a look like *yeah, buddy, don't even think about turning down anything she cooked.*

"Family!" Pastor Downes appears from a side staircase. In three smooth steps, he glides to his wife and takes her hand. "Let me pray right now because it's time to eat this good food right here."

We bow our heads, Pastor blesses the meal, then we each pick up a serving dish and head into the Downes' dining room.

Pastor Downes waits until we're in the middle of devouring spinach salad to drop a bomb. "John and Chablis, I want you to transition away from your work with Help Squad."

I gulp down a half-chewed leaf and glance at future hubby.

John leans toward me for a split second before turning his attention back to our Pastor.

The Help Squad began as an experiment out of singles ministry. We won't be singles much longer, but I didn't think pastor would kick us out of our roles so soon.

John speaks for both of us. "You want us to step up for marriage and family ministry?"

"No, I'd like you both to pray about volunteering with RiseUP YOUTH."

I double-blink. "Youth ministry? You mean Teen Club and youth retreat and all that stuff?"

"Again, pray about it first. But, yes, I think you'd both be wonderful with that ministry." He rests his back against the chair. "I've been studying the church landscape. Each year we have fewer young people interested in following the Lord for their lives. Some of that has to do with who our young people want to identify with. These kids can't relate to aging pastors in church robes, but they can see themselves being young and fly. They need ladies with sharp purple haircuts and software engineers with tattooed arms who still represent Jesus in their walk. I think the Lord wants to use you. You're millennial Christians working out your salvation daily."

I think about that. We've both matured, but I don't know if anyone should pattern us.

Still, John's already nudging me like he's ready to say yes.

I nudge him back. "Don't we need special training to do youth ministry?"

"Dr. Wilma Blackshear is the RiseUP Youth director. Once you pass the Pennsylvania background checks, she'll guide you. All you need to do is follow her instructions." Pastor Downes fills his glass with more lemonade.

"We'll pray about it and let you know," John says.

I exhale relief and dig into scrumptious stuffed shells. Ministry work? That's not a problem. But am I a role model? I don't know.

Thankfully, for the rest of dinner, we talk marriage related stuff. Sister Juanita serves dessert in the Downes living room, and we eat strawberry shortcake and chat about the wedding ceremony.

Sister Juanita sits on the love seat next to Pastor. "I've heard of Christian couples who only exchange Bibles at the altar. But, uh, how can I put this—"

Pastor Downes puts up a hand. "Naw, naw, forget putting it gently. Look here family, wedding rings need to be on your hands at all times. I don't want anybody walking into Rise thinking either of you are single. Because you will not do what, family?"

"Mess up your record," John and I say together.

"That's right." He moves his bushy eyebrows up and down. "I have a thirty-year record of not losing a couple. Y'all will not be the first to trip me up. I want your t-shirts to say married on them. I want your cars with married bumper stickers—"

Sister Juanita places a hand on his shoulder, halting him mid-rant. "What your pastor is trying to tell you is to be prepared. It's not if temptation comes for you, it's when. Some people will respect your married status, but others won't. Guard your hearts. Calculating men and women might consider it a challenge to take you away from your spouse."

Ariana gives us a caring look. "If either of you feels drawn to someone else, talk to your partner as soon as possible. You have to use moments like that to evaluate if needs are not being met in your relationship. Admitting to your spouse that you're attracted to another person-I can't sugar-coat it; that's going to be a tough conversation, but it's worth it. Definitely think about couples therapy before you have an affair. Illicit love affairs can spell marriage disaster, but you can prevent them with communication and counseling."

"Yeah, so y'all get those bumper stickers." Pastor gives a nod. "Seriously, John, cover your wife. But remember to give her room to be herself. Chablis, cover your husband with prayer, and know that he always thinks of you first. The beautiful thing about covenant is that you're held together by God. God walks right with you and helps with your commitment to one another."

Since the Downes' home is only minutes away from Penn's Landing, when we leave, we stroll to Spruce Street Harbor Park. We walk along in silence beneath pastel-colored lights, following the walkway that leads through the urban beach overlooking the river. I'd love to lie in a hammock with John and stare up at the night sky, but Nikki told me street people nap in those during the day so I'll pass.

Tonight we've switched places.

John reads messages on his phone. After fifteen minutes of being ignored, I bump into him on purpose.

"Hey!" I bounce off his bicep and land three steps away. "You got a side chick you wanna tell me about?"

He looks at me like I'm crazy, which I might be, but whatever. "Huh?"

"Those can't be work messages."

"Actually, they're not. Not this time." He taps his phone screen again. "What do you think about California?"

"It's fine, I guess."

"I need to know. Seriously."

A warm wind wraps around us, and I move closer to him. "All I know about Cali is what I've read or seen in movies and music videos. Its expensive to stay in Silicon Valley, and Apple headquarters is there and so is Saddleback Church and—"

"It's not cheap, but if a company pays for you to live there..."

I stop walking and tug his arm so he stands still. "I'm not a dummy. Are you trying to say you need to live there?"

"Maybe. And it's *we*."

"We?"

"I'm not going anywhere without you that takes longer than a month. We're a package deal." He takes his phone out again. "Another Palo Alto tech company heard about my work for Syner-Cloud—and they're trying to recruit me. Seems like an opportunity I shouldn't pass up. Here, take a look."

I push the device back at him. "I don't need to see it."

And for real, I don't. It's another change. Life circumstances in remix mode.

That's what I *know*.

That's not how I *feel*.

How I feel is shocked because we just moved into our apartment and I haven't even lived in it yet because I can't stay with him because we're not married and I gotta quit my job and head to Cali if John wants to work there and that means leaving my family and my friends and my church and line dancing and everything I love about Philly.

Deep breaths. Slow breaths.

John gathers me into his powerful arms and presses me close to his heart. We're beside the dark river, breathing in the lukewarm air of a tired city, giving its last gasps of life for the day. And as suddenly as it came on, pressure in my chest subsides.

In the end, wherever he goes is home.

"So, yeah, we'll use FaceTime with our family and we'll find an awesome church." I whisper. "Anywhere you need me, I'm gonna be right there. You can only pick one. Apartment, condo, or studio by the ocean."

I release his shoulders and try to come back down to earth, but he won't let me go. A few beats later, he sets me free.

He gazes in my eyes. "A studio by the ocean for me and you?"

"For you and me."

When his phone buzzes again, he glances at the screen, but this time his eyes turn dark and his mouth droops. He sighs and pushes his device toward me. "I don't even know what to say about this."

I study his downcast face again before I peek at the screen.

A message from the woman who gave birth to him. The one who insists she hates texts.

> Marry who you want. Have a great wedding.
> Have a good life. I won't be there for either.

ditched

CLASSIC. Drama. Queen. Move.

Ms. Pat's attempt to shake us up worked. John tried to visit her, but she locked him outside. I called her. Even Nate called her. She actually talked to him, but then he called us back and told us the same thing she texted: she's done with us.

An hour ago, I prayed after leaving her yet another voice mail because tonight is the wedding rehearsal. Ms. Pat will pull a no show, I know she will. From here on out, she'll be a missing person for every celebration. Our official housewarming. Baby showers. Birthday parties. Baptisms. Anniversaries. School graduations. All the family life milestone markers. Ms. Pat may be the woman who keeps repping Trina for the wife role, but what will I tell the kiddies on Goodies with Grandparents day? Grandma Patty doesn't love you because she hates me?

Lord, please don't let that be our future.

My luggage lays open on the Rodriguez' home guest bed. The fuchsia bag is for tomorrow night. The slick silver pilot case rolls with me to the honeymoon. I've tucked away everything else I brought here inside a black storage tote John will pick up after we return from wherever we're flying to.

"Chardonnay! Leaving so soon?" Oscar stands in the hall outside the guest room, probably thinking he's being clever. He's been calling me Chardonnay for seventeen years now.

"Same old joke. When you gonna get a new one?" I wave him in. "And yeah, for the second time in life, I'm about to mosey on out of this place. Bless you for housing me at Casa de Rodriguez."

"You're a good houseguest." Oscar raises his coffee cup to me. "Hang out here anytime."

"Thanks. Mariah's gone early?"

"Yeah, she's down to eatLARGE already. They've been doing good business with breakfast on Thursdays and Fridays. Personally, I can't see eating smoked salmon, baby spinach, and mushroom breakfast bowls, but the foodie crowd wants it."

"That's Chef Gabriel. He crushes it with his entrees."

"Thought you were staying here tonight?"

"I am. But in a couple hours I'll be at Tranquil Streams for my spa treatments. And you know Mariah and Binky will be with me at the rehearsal tonight. We get back and I'll have to crash; I need to pack my stuff now."

"That reminds me. I should schedule a spa day for Mariah soon. She deserves it. Well, I need to get to work, so enjoy your last spa day as a single woman, Chardonnay."

"Hey!"

Oscar puts his cup down on the dresser and moves in for a hug. "I'm never going to quit saying that, so stop complaining. See you tomorrow."

I hug him back. "See you tomorrow."

He picks up his coffee and leaves, and I turn back to the bed. Seven-thirty in the morning, but I'm paranoid. I don't want to forget anything. My phone alarm will buzz at ten so I can get my behind out of here and drive to the spa. With the family and friends all busy today, and Luna and Lorenzo handling everything else, I can turn my phone off and soak in fragrant relaxation all afternoon till time for the rehearsal.

Precious. Luxurious. Me time.

Back to the honeymoon case. All right. Sundresses and bras and undies are packed. Swimsuit. I have my leather sandals. My *give-John-a-heart-attack* lingerie is in there, along with travel bottles of scented lotion. Toiletries zipped up in my waterproof case. I should load my makeup in the Ziploc bags now. If I leave any of it here while I'm traveling, the good stuff will migrate to Binky's messy room, never to be seen again.

I spin around. What else? I feel like I'm missing something. I'll finish with the makeup. Whatever I can't remember, it'll come to me.

I grab a Wet One to clean sticky residue off a foundation bottle when my phone lights up on the dresser. The caller ID picture makes me grin when I swipe the screen and answer. "Yes, I will marry you. I haven't changed my mind."

"Chablis?"

This isn't my beloved's voice.

"Travis?" I put down my foundation. "John told you to call me?"

"John had an accident. We biked Schuylkill River Trail this morning. We were doing fine all the way through to Manayunk Towpath, but the Towpath is a mix of gravel and pavement and wood boards. John rode over a rough transition and dumped off the bike."

I freeze. "Is he okay? Broken bones? His head?"

"The EMTs are lifting him into the ambulance. He was disoriented when I pulled him up, and he's got a bloody cut across his forehead. He smashed his arms and legs bad, and I don't know about his back, but I think that's okay because he crashed onto his left side."

My stomach churns. "His head! Was he wearing his helmet?"

"Yes, and it's intact. It's not bent or cracked."

This calms me a little. "Okay. Um. Okay. Can you get a ride to the hospital?"

"One of the other bikers on the trail is helping me right now. She's got her Suburu here, and she's going to give me a ride."

I spin around and everything looks foreign—and my skin itches.

I scratch my ears, my neck, my forearms. "I'm leaving. Call me as soon as you know what hospital he's going to!"

My brain has shut off, so I end the call. My mini backpack hangs on the bedroom door with my car keys inside. I grab it, clutch my phone, and sprint down the stairs and out of the house, slamming the front door behind me.

I'm merging with traffic when Travis phones me with the name of the hospital. I keep the radio off inside my car and sit straight up, driving without blinking. If a cop sees me and tries to pull me over, we will start a high-speed chase because I'm not stopping. My nose runs and I wipe away snot with the back of my hand. Breathe and pray. Pray and drive. Breathe and pray and keep on driving.

Lord, please.

Lord, I love this man.

Lord, don't test me like this.

With each step I take from the parking garage to the emergency room, I pray.

Lord, if John has a concussion, I understand why you chose me for him. I know what to do. I don't care what he looks like or what's broken, I'll stick by him. Forget a stupid wedding. If we can't have one, who cares. We have an apartment together—Pastor can marry us there, and I don't care what anyone thinks about that. I'll still be his wife, even if he has a brain injury. If he needs a nurse, I'll hire one. If he needs therapy, I'll take him there. Father, your will be done. Yes, Lord, you picked the right person for him. I'll give him as much sunshine as he can stand. I'll hold him and pray for him every single day. I promise. Lord, you've been here for us through the good and the bad, and you've always taken care of us.

I could give a rip about debts or whatever Ms. Pat thinks about us marrying without her blessing.

I just need future hubby to be okay.

My Nikes thump the floor to the rhythm of my heart.

Rushing, rushing, rushing.

Almost there.

I round a corner and speed through double doors toward the emergency room desk. The redhead nurse's sea-green eyes open wide in surprise.

I lean over the counter, shouting. "A man was brought in here after a bike accident! His name is John Gerald!"

"Are you his wife?"

I don't miss a beat. "Yes, I am."

She checks the board behind her, then turns back to me. "Exam area seven."

Seven. Seven. Seven. My blood runs hot and cold, and I pivot around and count numbers. I'm standing next to number two. Three. Four. Five. Six.

Seven.

I sling the stiff yellow curtain to the side, and my eyes dart to the bed. John sits up with a pillow to his back. He wears a light blue hospital gown, and a thin beige blanket covers his legs. A white bandage stretches from his left temple halfway across his forehead. Angry-looking red scratches mar his left cheek, and his beard looks dusty.

However, his golden-brown eyes are wide open, and he stares at me. "Hey, Sunshine."

Those prayers? Everything I chanted when I zipped into this hospital? All of it disappears.

"You idiot!" I throw my hands in the air. "Who goes on a long trail ride the day before their wedding? By the Schuylkill River? With daredevil CrossFit Travis?"

He winces. "Calm down, okay. I took a tumble, but I'll be all right."

Even though he's talking in a soft tone, tears stream down my cheeks. My stomach aches, and I can't see his face anymore. My sight turns blurry.

What if he got knocked unconscious?

What if he'd died?

John winces again, handing me a tissue from the flat gray box. "I'm okay. Please stop crying."

My tears drop onto the blanket. "Travis told me you dumped off the bike and your body crashed to the ground."

"I did, and my face scraped across a splintered board. Travis helped me up, but I had trouble standing, and the cut over my eye started gushing, so he called an ambulance."

"Your head?"

"I wore my helmet, but when I fell the board still scratched me up good."

"You look busted."

"I'm bruised, not broken."

That sounds like the title of a gospel song. "Where's Travis now?"

"He was here, but I told him he should take his bikes home."

"Really? You're in the hospital worried about bikes! And why weren't you riding yours?"

"That doesn't matter. He let me use his, and I told him to get it home because it cost him three grand."

"What about your head, man? You went out there, not even thinking about..."

I bite my tongue before I say *your own safety*. Those were John's words after the July line dance event.

He's silent as he stares at his lap. This is the first time he's ever scared me like that, but it probably won't be the last, so I need to cut it out and help him.

I have to let him lean on me.

"Don't you have to get x-rays or scans or something?" I ask.

"Someone's coming to take me to Imaging in a few minutes."

"If you don't need observation, I'll take you home after you get the results."

"What about your spa appointment?"

"What about it?"

"You're not going?"

"No." I glance up at the clock on the wall. Nine AM. In twenty-eight hours, this man will be my husband. Today he's bruised, scratched, and cut. Hospital bandages cover his left hand, but I grasp it anyway. "Somebody has to take care of you and keep you out of trouble."

His eyes turn glassy. "I didn't mean to take away your relaxation time."

"It's just a spa day." I give future hubby's hand a light squeeze. "I can schedule another one anytime. I'll take out my nail kit and do my own mani-pedi. I'm more concerned about rehearsal tonight, but we'll figure something out."

"I love you."

"I know." I stroke his rough fingertips. "That's why we're taking vows tomorrow."

sacrifice

FLUORESCENT LIGHTS above and blue-speckled white flooring below. John and I sit in the examination area for about another twenty minutes, and then the medical assistant arrives and transfers John to a wheelchair. I walk alongside. Down the long hallway. Up the elevator. Down another corridor until we reach Imaging.

"Now you can only pick one." I joke when he wheels into the dim room. "Hotel. Honeymoon. Brand new bedroom."

"All three. Aww yeah!" He waves a hand in the air before the door shuts behind him.

A Lysol-smelling hospital hallway is *not* the experience I expected the day before I marry, but it is what it is.

First on the agenda? Take my phone outside and let the fam know about John.

I call Nate first.

He answers right away. "Ready for the big day?"

"Not yet, and before I tell you what happened, first, he's fine. Your brother had a bike accident. This morning John went on the trails with Travis, and he had an accident and we're at the hospital."

"Get outta here. You can't be serious!"

"I am, big brother. I just came downstairs from Imaging. The techs are scanning his body for damage."

"But he's conscious and everything?"

I shift my phone to my other ear and step further away from the building. "He's scratched real bad, and there's a gash across his forehead, but otherwise he seems fine. We were cracking jokes just now."

"That knucklehead, I should pop him when I see him." Nate sighs. "And how are you doing?"

"After I put my heart back in my chest, I'll be fine."

"Is my baby brother really that crazy? Trail riding before his wedding?"

"You know how he is."

"Yeah," Nate chuckles. "You need me to come down?"

"No, but uh, I need you to call your mom. Tell her what happened and to call us, please. She won't answer the phone if I call. And tell Grammy and Poppy because they'd want to know. I'm not sure about the rehearsal tonight, we'll call you about that later on."

"I hear you. I'll keep my phone close. I'll call Mom for you."

"Thanks."

I tell him the hospital and we hang up. That wasn't so bad. I swear if there was a brother-in-law of the year award, I'd nominate Nathaniel Gerald for it.

After the MRI, we have to wait on the results. So it's me and John back in examination area number seven, watching trash TV as Maury Povich announces *you are not the father*.

"You can only pick one," John says during a commercial break. "Tropical garden. Beach. Private blue lagoon?"

Visions of rapture dance in my head. "Private blue lagoon."

"Yes, ma'am. I love the way you think."

And here comes Ms. Pat, rushing her exclamation point body straight past me and over to John. "Son, are you okay?"

"No, Mom, I'm hurt, but I'll be all right."

She smacks him on the shoulder. "Fool! What were you doing

biking today? You don't have the sense God gave a chicken. Don't you have to pick up your suit or check on anything for your wedding?"

"Mom, turn around." He points at me. "See Chablis right there? Tell her hello and hug her or something. She's the one who made sure you found out."

I waggle my fingers. "Hey there, Ms. Pat."

She keeps looking at John. "Hello."

Whether or not she wants to recognize me, in less than a day I'll be her daughter-in-law. She can't change it and I'm done letting her change me.

I will love this woman if it kills me because I'd rather die a thousand embarrassing deaths knowing I did the right thing.

I stand up and push my shoulders back. "Ms. Pat, please come outside with me. A word. Right now."

She whips around. "You can't talk to me here?"

"No! Now come on." The yellow curtain's in my hand and I'm pulling it to the side before I even realize I'm moving. I'm even more surprised when I look back, and she's actually following me.

I stop when I'm outside the revolving glass door. Ms. Pat strolls out and circles me, finally standing on my right, staring at an ambulance as it rushes by, on the way to an emergency.

I face her. "Ms. Pat, John and I? Our family starts tomorrow. Tomorrow. And I don't want to keep playing *Family Feud*. Why are you trying to disown us?"

"That's not even the right question." She stares at the rose bushes across the street. "You should ask why my son is choosing you over me."

"When John supports me, he's not choosing anything. You're always going to be his mother."

"He never listened to me from the moment you came along."

"Look, he didn't want to get with Trina again. He loves me and it shouldn't matter that I'm not a lawyer or a family friend—" I pause. Take a deep breath and blow it out. Start over. "There's no need to go back and forth about this. Here we are today—"

"Yes, here we are, and you still don't feel like a daughter to me."

"Maybe if you treated me like one I'd feel like one!" The sound of my shouting shakes my core. *Please, God, help me settle down.* "Ms. Pat, no matter how you feel about me... do you love John?"

"He's my son."

"Are you proud of him? Do you want to cuddle your grand babies? Congratulate him on his next promotion? See us raising the next generation? Do you want to miss out on everything good coming up? Do you truly love him?"

She shuffles around, moving her purse to her other shoulder. "Of course I love him."

"Then, for his sake, be in his life. Don't be spiteful because he didn't end up with Trina. You can still love her and be a part of her life, just not as her mother-in-law. Because you're *my* mother-in-law."

Ms. Pat blinks like she's still processing that concept.

My phone alert goes off, and I pull the device from my purse. Ten AM. "Are you busy today?"

"Not really."

"Wonderful. I'm booked at the Tranquil Streams Spa to get a facial, massage, pedicure, and manicure. Go enjoy the treatments on my behalf. It's all paid for, but if you want to leave them a tip, they would appreciate it. I'll call to transfer the services to you. Enjoy the spa, then come visit us at our apartment later to check on John."

"Chablis, are you serious?"

"Absolutely. You go on and relax at the spa, my treat. My appointments start at eleven."

"Thank you, but I'm not going anywhere until I know he's all right."

"Then listen to what the medical team says. If you're satisfied, please, go have a spa day."

"What are you going to do?"

I slide my phone back in my bag. "My husband, my responsibility. I'm driving him home to take care of him."

Inside, we all wait another twenty minutes before an attending doctor and nurse step into the examination area. According to his scans, he has no broken bones or internal bleeding. All they need to do is print his discharge papers and pain medication prescription.

Ms. Pat squeezes John's hand, then she pats my shoulder on her way out. "Thank you."

"You're welcome. Enjoy."

"Praise the Lord!" John's eyebrows raise.

I roll my eyes. "Oh, please. You better hush and pray for rapid healing!"

John's mom leaves and I call Tranquil Streams to tell them what happened and to transfer my services to Patricia Gerald. She can show ID when she arrives. They make the change and give me twenty percent off my next service at their spa. Sometime next week I'll write them a five-star Yelp review.

We call Travis to let him know John will be fine and we'll be home soon. Travis tells us his bike isn't damaged other than a few minor scratches.

The hospital discharges John with a prescription for pain medication and typed instructions for caring for his cuts and bruises. I gather the pages and place them in my bag. I'll get my car and drive the future hubby home.

Time to take care of my man.

I'm ready.

steady love

WE REACH our apartment and I'm juggling my bag, John's medication, and his helmet. I stand on our *God Bless This Home* mat and open the door. My foot pushes Dear Resident mailers to the side of the dark brown hardwood floor so John doesn't slide on them when he limps inside.

Home sweet home.

Still no living room chairs or couches, but we bought a second wooden bookshelf, peace lilies and snake plants in white ceramic planters, huge navy blue and white cushions from Target, and framed black and white art photos on the walls. The outlets hold moon-shaped LED automatic night lights, and my essential oil diffuser makes the whole place smell like lavender and eucalyptus.

I've never loved an apartment so much.

John wanders to the kitchen while I put things away. He looks a little dazed when he walks out with a bottle of water. He's banged up, scratched, and dare I say a little funky. Poor thing. Time for wifey to provide some TLC.

I beckon to him. "Bae?"

"Yeah."

"Come on."

"What am I doing?"

"Whatever I tell you." I point him down the hall.

Hours away from taking vows and I launch into full wife mode as I...

Direct future hubby to the bathroom to shower.

Give him fresh lounging pants to change into.

Comb his matted beard and massage *Soft Like Butta* beard balm into it.

Swab his scratched face with peroxide and apply fresh bandages.

Feed him chicken caesar salad for lunch.

Make him remove his contacts and slide them into the little blue and white plastic container.

Put him in bed and place his glasses on the nightstand.

Play gentle rain sounds on his phone and pull the blinds so he can sleep.

Back in the kitchen, the microwave clock reads twelve-fifteen. This time tomorrow, I'll be ready to walk down the aisle. Right now there's no time to muse. I need help. I gotta start a phone-a-thon. But before I do that, I text friends and favorite church family members to tell them John had a small bike accident, and he needs healing prayers. I also ask them to please pray and not text me back because I'm frazzled enough.

Nikki's up first for a phone call and she answers right away. "Chablis?"

"Yeah."

"You can't be done at the spa already."

"No, I wish I was." I sigh. "John had an accident biking on the trail this morning, so I'm home taking care of him."

"What? Is he all right?"

"He's scratched up and bruised, but he'll live to bike another day. Can you contact the rest of the bridal party? Remind them we're meeting at nine in the morning at Mariah's house. After that, call Terry and ask him to check with the groomsmen to make sure they picked up everything they need and are ready to meet John at Rise."

"What about the rehearsal?"

"Nik, I think we're going to attend the world's first virtual wedding rehearsal. You and Terry, I want each of you to connect with us on FaceTime so we can see all the directions."

"You think that will work?"

"It has to. Luna and Pastor Downes can talk to us as they walk through the motions. We'll see it all, we just won't be there in person."

The BFF and I work through the rest of the plans for the virtual rehearsal. When I end my call with Nikki, I call my Mom and Dad to tell them about John's bike accident. I stay on the phone extra-long while Mom calls John a fraganackle fool, but insists she loves him with all her heart and is praying for him.

One quick call to Luxurious Events and Luna confirms she's on top of all other details related to the Gerald wedding. No worries there.

After Luxurious Events, I dial Mariah. I tell her about John's accident, that he'll be fine, but I won't return to their home until close to midnight. Then I text Binky to tell her I remember where every makeup container is in the guest room, and she should keep her hands off.

By the time I finish being communications commander, ninety minutes have passed. I haven't eaten anything all day and my hands shake.

My man is fine. The wedding will be beautiful. Both of us will be okay.

This is what I'm thinking, but I still kneel on the kitchen floor and pray over everyone and everything. After, I get up and wash my face, force myself to eat some tomato basil soup and then I get practical and...

Wash and dry John's dirty laundry.

Clean our kitchen and mop the floors.

Direct John back to bed after he wanders out to see what I'm doing.

Answer all my texts because *none of my friends listen.*

Let Nate and Terry in when they stop through to check on John before the rehearsal.

I talk to Mom when she and Daddy arrive at Rise Church. I assure her John isn't in a wheelchair, doesn't need crutches, and can stand next to Pastor Downes tomorrow.

Before the rehearsal starts, I curl up on the bed next to my man and place my hand on his head, praying for healing.

At six-thirty, John and I have identical smiles on our faces when we use John's iPad to FaceTime Terry at the wedding rehearsal.

"Loved ones," he says to our people sitting in the pews, waving at the screen. "We went through a lot to arrive at this day and no accident's stopping me—"

"Or me!" I wave with both hands.

John turns and winks at me. "Or us."

○

Even though I said Ms. Pat could come over, it surprises me when I answer the door at nine and she's standing there, smooth brown skin glowing. Those spa treatments must have worked their magic.

"Is it too late to visit?" She displays the first toothy smile I've ever seen her direct towards me.

"Not at all, come in." I open the door wide. "John's resting."

She follows me and I lead her into our humble abode and down the hall to our spare room.

"Bae, your mom is here." I step aside to let her through.

John struggles to sit up and lean onto his right side, but he still smiles when he sees his mother in the doorway. "Hey, Mom."

She puts a hand on my shoulder. "Bless you for the spa trip, and it looks like you took good care of my son."

"I did my best. John, I'll be out here if you need me." I back away so they can talk without me intruding on their conversation.

"Lord, thank you." I whisper when I walk back to the living room.

I run a hand through my hair. These curls are truly dry and unruly, but Quinsara will transform me tomorrow. When I woke this morning, I couldn't have imagined any of this. And while I could've done without John scaring the mess out of me, all things worked out for our good.

When we marry, our friends and family become part of a larger collective. There's truly a purpose in us being in one another's lives. My family is forming... with me. I'm not locked outside this sacred bond any longer. My brand-new family members are here, talking in my new home. And right about now, the joy in my heart gives all that rejection pain a total knockout punch.

I'm healing.

And I'm home.

Mini backpack in hand, I sit next to John on the bed. "This has been one *looooong* day."

"You're leaving now?" He peers at me through his black-rimmed glasses.

"It's past eleven. If I don't leave soon, I'll turn into a pumpkin." I trail my finger over his bandaged hand. "Hey, we switched places. Remember New Year's Eve? After the ball dropped?"

"I'm never forgetting that. I never had such a hard time leaving anyone."

"I kept running my fingers through your beard and every time I tried to stop, you put them back."

"What else do you remember, Miss Shields?"

"I'm demoted to Miss Shields now?"

He pulls my bag from my hands, gently dropping it to the bed. "It's the last time I'll ever say it. Lay next to me for a minute."

I slide down and we lay side-by-side. "You asked what I remembered?"

"Yes."

"You told me you'd love me forever."

"And you shouted it back."

"Cause I meant it." I roll over to face him. "I can't wait to live and grow with you."

"We're already growing with one another on the daily. I mean, look at you today. You took care of everything. See, that's the champion side of you and I always knew you had that. I'm so proud to have you by my side, and I'm hoping you love your surprise, if you haven't figured it out."

I raise up on my elbow. "Figured out?"

A smile spreads across his face. "I used Travis' road bike because I sold both of mine last month on eBay. I used that money to pay off the tropical garden honeymoon hideaway suite in St. Lucia. Now the suite itself is beautiful, but you're going to love the private pool and our outdoor bathtub for two. We have an open view of island nature and a butler to serve us the entire time. It's complete five-star luxury."

"No! You sold Samantha for our honeymoon?"

"Yes. For us."

"No."

"Yes, the third level of intimacy will happen for us in the closest thing to the Garden of Eden I could find."

"You know we're broke, acting like rich folk."

"Nah, we're not broke." He lands a warm kiss on my left dimple. "Think about the celebrations—our church family's houses and eatLARGE. God provided what we needed, and he showed his love through our friends and family. Those providential relationships? If you ask me, we're so rich Warren Buffett should ask us for advice."

pit bull

I'M an idiot with no dress.

Well, I have *a* dress, it's just that in the middle of my crazy week, I didn't take it out of the garment bag and the one I have is the wrong one. I didn't delegate to Nikki, Luna, or anyone else to pick it up. All I did was drive over Wednesday after work and the distracted shop assistant thrust it at me. I unzipped the bag this morning and instead of my gown, I pulled out a similar-looking size two dress meant for someone other than me.

"Why didn't you try it on earlier this week?" My mom asks this. She sits across from me, wrapped in a red floral kimono, steaming, while Raven curls her salt and pepper hair.

I keep my head down while Quinsara braids the hair around my kitchen. "I worked like crazy every day except Friday. I would have tried it on yesterday, but I forgot about it after John had that bike accident."

"He ride motorcycles?" Quinsara asks.

Smoke from Raven's curling iron floats over and I fan my face. "No. He fell off a road bike. The kind with pedals."

"Oh." She keeps braiding.

Luna, in a sleek champagne-colored pantsuit, a tablet in one hand and her smart phone in the other, walks into Mariah and Oscar's dining room, which we've transformed into beauty central.

She adjusts her earbuds. "We can handle this. Is there someone here we can send to the bridal shop to retrieve Chablis' actual dress? Someone not in the wedding party?"

Mariah, who's sitting by the entrance to the kitchen, waves her hand. "My husband, Oscar. He can drive there and pick it up."

"Fantastic." Luna taps her tablet screen. "Can we send him now?"

"Elegance Bridal Shoppe in the Northeast. The Boulevard. Close to the Chick-Fil-A." I keep my head down so I don't get burned. "Mariah, can you give him the address?"

"Sure." She stands. "I'll be back in a minute, so don't let Binky take my turn. I'm in that hair chair after Aunt Charlene."

Luna pats my shoulder. "Don't worry about your dress. Everything else is on schedule. My assistants set up the Rise Hall for light refreshments. And..." She swipes her tablet again and reads. "The flowers are entering the church now."

"The cake?"

"The delivery van should arrive there soon."

"Cool." I close my eyes and exhale.

Hot hair tools click. Tamela Mann croons "Feels Like" through Pandora.

This moment of peace gets pierced by a dog barking like its tail is on fire.

"What's all that noise?" My mom slides away from her chair, narrowly escaping getting burned by Raven's curling iron.

Quinsara steps away from me as I jump up and race to the window.

Mom, Nikki, Binky, and Stacey stand with me to stare at Mariah's side lawn. I blink three times because I cannot believe there's an overactive brown pit bull my beloved cousin Aaron does his best to tie to the sycamore tree.

A pit bull? On my wedding day?

"Mariah!" I yell. "Get your cousin!"

"You get him!" She hollers back. "I'm on wedding dress duty."

Mom ties her silky robe tighter, shaking her head. "I'll talk to him. Only my crazy nephew would think to bring his pet to the wedding."

She stalks outside and we watch her fuss at Aaron, telling him he can't keep the dog tied up here because what if it gets loose?

He waves at us standing at the window. "I'm sorry, cuz. He just a puppy! I wanted to stop over and introduce the fam to my new lady. We're going to brunch before we see y'all at the church. Markia, say hi to my auntie and cousins."

A pretty brown lady waves at us and we wave back. When I told Aaron he could bring anyone he wants, I didn't tell him to just bring his date. Who knows why my cousin decided his puppy needed to come.

Six warm arms surround my shoulders and Nikki, Binky, and Stacey walk me back to my chair.

I shake my head. "I have no dress and now there's a pit bull barking on my wedding day."

"No, my dad just left for your dress." Binky reminds me.

"Chablis, your dress is on the way." Nikki rubs my arms.

"The pit bull isn't a bad omen. It's just a dog." Stacey tells me.

Mom returns. "Aaron's taking the dog away."

I try to stop jogging my legs up and down. "Can somebody call and check on the guys? Tell Nate to wrap John in bubble wrap before the ceremony."

Luna strides over and takes my mom's place. This time she pats me on the knee. "Bad news."

"Is there any other?" I ask.

"Our baker doesn't have all the cake layers ready for today."

"So what can you do?"

"Cupcakes."

"Cupcakes?"

She moves to my eye level as Quinsara starts sewing in my tracks.

"The top tier of the cake, the part with the flower decorations on it, that's done and in the delivery van. I sent my assistant for white-frosted cupcakes, and the bakers can arrange those into a tiered design. It will work."

What choice do I have? "Fine. Nikki?"

"Uh-huh."

"Please get Terry on the phone. Ask him how John's doing and if he knows about the cake situation?"

Nikki, in a white robe, with her phone to her ear and a paisley-patterned silk scarf around her head, paces in front of me. "Okay... oh!"

That doesn't sound good. "What?"

She holds up a hand. "Yeah, I'll tell her. Do what you can, because we don't want to see any blood."

Blood?

I stay calm until she ends the call. "What, what, what?"

"First, John is okay. He got upset when he heard about the cake, but Lorenzo assured him it's being taken care of. He had to lie down for a minute, but the guys are with him."

"You said blood, though. I heard you say blood."

"That cut above his eye?"

"Yeah?"

"John took off the hospital bandage. He said he didn't want to look like he'd been in a car wreck before his wedding. So he and Nate tried to put a transparent adhesive patch on it, like he puts on his tattoos when they heal and that worked fine until he got upset and his wound re-opened. They just sent Travis to the CVS for bandages. But John doesn't have his suit on yet so there won't be any blood on his clothes."

My dress is MIA.

My cake is unavailable.

Future hubby is bloody.

"Loo-rrrrd!" I wail. "Fix it!"

"Girl, stop," Stacey says. "Keep your head still before you end up with your tracks all janky."

While my friends soothe me, Luna talks on the phone. She gets off, leaves the room for a few moments, then returns with a fake smile plastered all over her face. When she kneels in front of me, I brace myself.

"What now?" I ask.

"The singer scheduled for the ceremony, Gwen Bryland... she can't make it."

"But she practiced the song at the rehearsal last night. What happened?"

"Her father had a stroke, so she had to travel to Virginia this morning."

I move my eyes around the room. Quinsara and Raven stay busy working their magic on our hair and makeup. Luna, Nikki, Binky, even my mom—all of them look like they expect me to snap at any second.

I don't flinch. I can handle this through our village of Christian friends. "Luna?"

"Yes."

"Check the RSVP list. Did Rev. Alex Robinson RSVP for himself and a plus one? Please tell me he did."

She taps her tablet a few times. "Yes."

"Good. Rev. Robinson will bring D'Londa. She's a professional singer. She did off-Broadway work and everything. Someone needs to be in front of the sanctuary when they sign the guest book. Ask her if she will sing during the ceremony, even if she has to sing a cappella."

"What should she sing?" Luna asks.

"Any song about genuine love."

Mariah walks back in. "Cousin, the pit bull is gone."

"I know."

"And did you hear about John's head?"

"We know." Everyone says.

. . .

Quarter after eleven, I sit by the dining-room window in my lacy undergarments and my white terry robe. God bless Quinsara because my hair *slays*. She's hard at work styling Nikki's curls when the front door slams shut.

Finally! My dress! "Oscar?" I call out.

"It's not Oscar. I believe I'm much more fabulous than him."

Towanda, Binky's godmother, struts through the doorway in a black-and-white striped wrap dress, smelling like a cloud of Gucci No. 3. After she motions air kisses to all of us, she stares at me. "You're getting married in your bra and panties? That a new idea? Something you found on Pinterest?"

"No, I'm waiting on my dress."

"Why isn't it here?"

"The bridal shop gave her the wrong one," Mariah says.

Towanda gives me the side eye. "How come you didn't check it before?"

I'm tired of answering questions. "Mariah?" I whimper.

"I'm on it." She taps her phone. "Os? What's going on?" She listens for a moment, then puts the phone down in her coral silk-covered lap. "The shop can't find your actual dress. They've been looking for the past hour."

My skin feels electrified. "They lost my dress? So even if I'd have tried to get it, it wouldn't have been there?"

Mariah talks to Oscar again. "Did you tell them to look through every rack? Maybe someone mistakenly put it back on the floor?"

Towanda rushes over and hugs my shoulders. "What type of dress is it, Ms. Sunshine and Rainbows?"

"A white strapless tulle ball gown. Full skirt with bling through the bodice."

"Thank you." She takes Mariah's phone. "Oscar, put the shop manager on the phone, please." She plants her feet in a power stance. "Yes, Elegance Bridal Shoppe, Towanda Mathis speaking. I have the bride here and she's about to cry. She needs her gown."

Pause.

"I see. This is the solution. Chablis wears a size four, and she's a curvy four, so please make that a six. You have ten minutes to find us a white strapless ball gown with crystal detailing that matches the description."

Pause.

"I understand. Here's my response: You have ten minutes to locate a gown that matches that description, or in twenty-four hours, a video of the bride crying and a picture of your bridal shoppe will broadcast on every social media channel my corporation controls. And on Monday, the Pennsylvania Better Business Bureau will contact you. And on Tuesday, Channel 6ABC will contact you. Locate an appropriate dress and hand it to the friendly businessperson in front of you. We expect you to comply. Thank you."

She ends the call and passes the phone back to Mariah.

I dab my eyes. "Thank you."

"You're welcome. Just remember me when you have your babies and name one of them after me."

Towanda strolls out with Binky trailing her, and my mom walks back in, mature and regal in her salmon-colored suit and matching heels.

I wave her over. "You must have FaceTimed Daddy by now. Give me a report. How's John?"

"Chablis, how come he's not in the hospital?"

"The hospital discharged him."

She adjusts her gold earrings. "The whole left side of his face is scratched up."

"His face fought with a wooden board and the board won. Mom,

275

you saw him on screen last night. Don't make me worry about how he looks this morning."

"Can we send Raven to put some foundation on him?"

"Mom!"

"Anyway, other than his face, my son-in-law looks dapper. And the rest of the men? That's one handsome group in sharp suits."

I grin. "I'm nosy. What's everybody doing?"

"Hanging out at the front of the church greeting folk and listening to your daddy tell your pastor all about his gun collection."

"No, not my Pastor. Stop Daddy!"

"Why? They're having more fun there than we are here. I like your pastor. He's a riot."

I wrap my arms around my bare shoulders and speak to myself in my head so my family won't think I've lost my mind.

I am whole. I am loved. I am strong.

My love waits for me.

If I have to get married in a bathrobe, doggone it, I will do it.

dearly beloved

"YES!" I scream when I peek out the front window.

Oscar pulls his F-150 into the driveway and a bridal gown relay race kicks off.

Towanda darts from the porch to the truck. She pulls the gown from the passenger side and runs it to Binky.

Binky carries the garment bag into the living room and mom unzips it and extracts the dress.

Mom holds the gown open.

Nikki slides my robe from my shoulders and steadies me when I step into it.

Stacey drags the photographer over to snap pics while Mom zips me up.

I grin at Nikki. "Nik, am I jiggling too much?"

"You're jiggling. Ms. Charlene, pull her in more!"

Mom grunts. A tug here. A pat there. "All right, take a deep breath."

And I do, and one, two, and three and I'm zipped. Mom shifts the front a little more for modesty's sake, and ta-da, the dress fits. Strapless. Bling through the bodice. My cleavage seems a little prominent, but I can't do anything about that now.

Mom spins me around to the full-length mirror Mariah brought from her room. This dress is gorgeous. Raven's makeup transformed me into a superstar. The tracks Quinsara sewed in are perfect romance curls about my head.

"Turn this way." The photographer directs Mom and me and we pose for three serious shots and two with us, smiling.

Tears well up in my mother's eyes when she places the sparkling tiara on my head and attaches the sheer white veil.

Even Mariah is a little misty when she walks around me. "Chablis, you look beautiful. And I think we need to leave now."

I glance at the grandfather clock as the photographer snaps what might be my last picture as a single woman.

Twelve-fifteen.

Time to roll out.

We become a female circus of white, coral, and gold in perpetual motion. I step into my shoes and make my way towards the door. The ladies grab their bags to take in the limousine. Mom and Binky hold the bottom of my gown so I don't get it dirty as I ease into the soft seats of the luxury car. Months ago I had thought this moment would feel ultra-glamorous, but now that I'm here, I feel giddy and a little scared. Like that time I climbed the high dive ladder at summer camp. Moving further away, up into the sky, about to take the gigantic leap.

The ride to Rise ends in about six seconds. Mom's eyes go wide when we approach the curb in front of the church.

"You have celebrity friends?" she asks me.

"What?"

"Isn't that one of those Marvel movie actors by the banister? Nice-looking man with the tablet?"

I laugh. "Oh no, Mom, that's Lorenzo. Luna's husband. He's with Luxurious Events."

She touches up her berry-colored lipstick. "Oh, I knew my son-in-law traveled to California sometimes, but I didn't think he trolled around Hollywood."

I love my mom.

And my feet are killing me! Why didn't I break these shoes in? I smile and blow kisses at the folk who watch me and my bridesmaids climb the stairs to enter the church, but I'm afraid all my face communicates is ouch.

Luna leads the bridal parade across the atrium and stops us when we reach the sanctuary's closed doors.

Rise.

Spiritually, I grew up here, and so did John. The prayer rooms and pews and sanctuary walls hold whispers from our prayers for personal strength and change and discipline and maturity and fruitfulness. They possess the memories of who we used to be.

Used to.

Because this is also where we both let things go. Bitterness. Worldliness. Flesh-based viewpoints. All of it got nailed to the cross. It's only right that this is the place where we join in covenant.

Butterflies play fight inside my belly and I close my eyes and deep breathe, listening to Luna's assistant direct wedding guests to take the long way around to the side of the sanctuary.

Luna positions the women and children.

I bow my head and thank the Lord.

And why does it sound like Mom is about to fight someone?

"Not today! This is her day and you will not ruin it!" Mom yell-whispers. "My daughter has been through enough."

"I understand, but I need to give her this. It belongs to her."

Fake eyelashes weigh down my eyelids, so I'm not fluttering them on purpose, but that's what they do when I open them and see my bridesmaids turned around looking at me while Mom stands toe-to-toe with Ms. Pat.

"Mom, please let her through!" I step toward them. "It's fine."

Ms. Pat wears a light gold skirt suit and church hat. The flowers on her lapel match my mother's. She reaches for my arm. "I'm so sorry this took so long."

I glance down at my wrist as her slim fingers work fast to clasp Grammy's blue and silver bracelet around it.

Her eyes meet mine. "Daughter, you are lovely. This belongs to you now."

All I can do is swallow and nod. She exits as quickly as she arrived, moving fast down the side hallway.

Nikki clutches her bouquet and shoots me a look like *yes, that was a touching Hallmark movie moment, but right now you are slaying and you better not cry and mess up your makeup.*

Mom returns to the front of the wedding parade and takes my cousin Adrian's arm.

Luna arrives at my side. "Are you all right? How are you doing?"

"Good. We're on time?"

She peeks at her tablet. "Yes. Right on time."

"No pit bulls here?"

"None."

I finger the cool bracelet on my wrist. "The singer? Did D'Londa arrive? Is she able to sing?"

"Yes, we worked that out an hour ago, and she said she'd be honored to bless you all today. She's singing "I Promise Wedding Song.""

"God, please bless that lady in triplicate!" I ask my last question as two ushers move into position by the sanctuary doors. "How's John?"

"Lorenzo told me that John said he loves you, he took his pain medication, and he can't wait to marry you."

Music plays in the sanctuary and here comes my daddy.

"Baby girl!" He holds out his arm.

"Daddy!" I take his arm and hold tight to my cascading bouquet of dahlias, fern leaves, and coral-colored roses.

He leans down and kisses my cheek. "There's no more beautiful daughter on earth than you."

One o'clock and Luna raises her arms, the ushers open the doors, and it begins.

My mother walks inside first. One at a time, Luna sends the rest. Nikki. Stacey. Mariah. Binky. Rashida and Rae-Ann with their baskets of rose petals.

My feet are still killing me! We stand behind the door so no one can see me and Daddy. Luna is the only person who can advise me at this moment.

I wave my bouquet at her. "Luna! Help! These shoes don't work with this dress and my feet hurt."

She reaches behind me and pulls my sheer veil over my face. It lays, weightless, over my front.

"Go barefoot. No one will know." She whispers. "Please, its time for you to go marry your man."

I kick my heels off and abandon them behind the sanctuary door. Then Daddy and I step out and I stare at all the guests as they smile.

Muted gold and coral glittered pew bows catch my attention. Coral roses perfume the air where they tangle with cream ribbons and plenty of bling. I inhale. Amazing. Perfect.

I move along and feel Daddy try to slow my pace when I rush toward the front of the sanctuary. By the time I'm halfway down the aisle, my ladies are lined up in their places and Binky waits to hold the twins' hands after they drop white rose petals along the carpet. D'Londa's jazzy alto voice is what I imagine angels sound like.

My heart dances when I see them at the altar.

Nate. Terry. Travis. Dr. Jones. Pastor Downes.

John.

His dark beard trimmed, hair cut low, and rimless glasses grace his face. Tears wet his cheeks. He's also scratched and bruised, with a transparent bandage stretching over his eye. With the permanent scar on my cheek, now we match.

So yeah, we're a real good couple.

Each step toward the altar, I'm more buoyant. Daddy transfers me from his arm to John's and I always thought I'd cry at this moment, but I don't want to. All I wanna do is laugh because so much joy fills my heart.

Pastor Downes wears his black robe with a multi-colored Kente cloth scarf.

"Y'all nervous?" He whispers.

We nod.

"Nothing to it family." He says with a warm smile. "I haven't lost a couple yet. Relax and let's do the darn thing." He raises his head and speaks loud and clear.

"Dearly beloved..."

the unlocking

...AND YOU ARE *by his side. He whispers he's seen no one more exquisite than you. This handsome man with the smile of a best friend and the tender touch of a future lover. With eyes wide open, you watch him with anticipation.*

He does the same with you. When you turn your attention to the pastor, he mimics your motions.

Holding.

Listening.

Your pastor speaks words of wisdom and love. He leads you and your lifetime partner into a set of timeless vows. This journey you're going on is not to be taken lightly. You agree. Of course you agree. Yes. You will love, honor, and obey this man for life. Yes. He will love, honor, and cherish you until the end of days. Neither of you would have it any other way.

And so it goes with your friends and your family displaying their support as you both stand together under God. There's a break for a prayer of blessing. And another break for a sweet song. And yet another for both of you to light a candle you'll take home and eventually show your grand-children.

Maybe you'll light it together, years later, when both of you have hair gray with age.

Or perhaps you'll take it out on anniversaries as a reminder of the last minutes that ticked away at the end of your journey as singles.

And then...

It's a tiny colossal moment. Eyes wide open. Two hearts exposed. Hands holding tight. You wait for it, wait for it, wait for it. With a single sentence, you cross, seamless, into your unknown world. His kiss becomes a key that opens a lock buried so deep in your soul you didn't know it existed.

You feel honored.

You feel treasured.

And most of all, you feel loved...

party up

AFTER PHOTOGRAPHS IN THE SANCTUARY, our noisy wedding party sweeps down the corridor to the Rise Hall. And its quiet here. Too quiet.

Something's wrong.

Not with me or John, but something is *clearly* out of order with this setting.

I don't hear footsteps, voices, chairs scraping the floor, or people moving around. And I smell nothing. Okay, yeah, we're having a light spread, but I should get a whiff of turkey meatballs or chicken wingettes or something. If not for the rose and ivy arrangement decorating the wall beside the doorway, I wouldn't think anyone got married today.

I tug John's suit jacket. "How come I don't smell any food?"

"Don't worry about it." He pats my home-manicured hands. "When Luna announces us, we walk in just like she instructed last night."

I raise an eyebrow at the sight of Nikki and Terry's backs when they turn into the Rise Hall. No applause? "Okay?"

John stops me when I try to walk further down. "Come on now, wait a minute, then follow me."

285

Nikki and Terry's footsteps sound like they move faster behind the door. That's weird. I take a deep breath and let it out slow. One thing I've learned on this journey—I can trust God and my husband.

We're holding hands in the hallway when Luna calls out, "Ladies and gentlemen, announcing for the very first time anywhere, Mr. and Mrs. John Gerald."

John leads me alongside him and we reach the end of the corridor and Rise Hall.

We turn inside the doorway and... nothing.

No food. Empty tables. Empty chairs. Guests? Family? Clergy? Nothing. There's no one inside this multi-purpose room except Luna, who giggles, in her champagne-colored pantsuit holding her trusty tablet.

Oh. And John. Who stares at my horrified face and has the nerve to laugh.

I cross my arms. "You think this is funny? Is it too early for *Divorce Court*? Somebody call Judge Mathis!"

"Calm down." He points. "Luna, take a picture of this please? This needs to go on the Gram."

"John! What happened to our people and our refreshments? I'm calling a lawyer in five four three..."

He pulls me into his embrace. "I have it covered. Trust me."

"What's happening?" I try to wriggle away.

"I said trust me."

What else can I do?

Luna waves us toward the double doors. "Mr. and Mrs. Gerald, your ride awaits you outside."

John puts out his hand. "Follow me."

I shut up and grab his hand. He runs and I pull up my skirt so I don't trip when I run beside him.

I've memorized the layout of this church. The doors at the opposite end of the Rise Hall open to the side parking lot, which is reserved for clergy only. It's against the rules to have a small black party bus parked there. Especially with our entire wedding party hanging out of it waving.

"Surprise!" They yell and clap.

And they all need a whooping for scaring me so badly.

Terry calls to us. A broad smile creases his caramel-colored face. "Come on, come on. You're wasting time. Let's get to the party!"

"Party?" I'm in a daze as John guides me to the bus.

"More like a reception."

I step inside. "Reception?"

"Actually," He leads us to the carpeted seats reserved for bride and groom. "This might be like a... like a what Terry? Help me out."

"An extravaganza. That's what I'd call it." Terry slides aviator sunglasses onto his face. "Because I've never seen a wedding reception anything like what's about to happen."

"Nikki!" I shift around in my seat. "You better tell me what's going on, future godmother."

She pats her perfect hair. "I have clothes for you to change into when we get there."

I turn back around. "John? Who paid for this?"

"Poppy paid for this party bus. He wanted us to ride in style."

"And the extravaganza thingy?"

"Everyone contributed something. You'll see." He glances down, eyebrows raised. "Now I have a question for you. *Where* are your shoes?"

 ✦

The party bus stops once for the Gerald wedding crew. The photographer has our party crash into Philly with a photo session right in the middle of Broad Street, using City Hall as the background. Then we're back on the bus, and John places his hands over my eyes when we ride away from the city.

We're traveling through nature when he removes his hands. Trees. Grass. Trees. Golf course. I know this neighborhood. We're in Radnor. Minutes before we approach to the black iron gates, I see cars parked along the road. John holds me so I don't jump up and scream as we turn into the long driveway.

He has to hold on tight because I plan to be the first one out of the bus so I can hustle my bare feet over to Daisy and hug her good.

The Worthington home backs up to a large golf course, which means their land goes on forever. Plenty of space for people to picnic. Daisy waves when the driver pulls up to her front door. I climb past John, and when the bus stops, I step out and right over to her.

Daisy's face lights with warmth. "Are you surprised?" She wraps me in a tight hug and strands of her brown hair stick to my lipstick. "Congratulations Mrs. Gerald!"

"How? Just how?" I ask.

She grasps my hands and pulls me into her house. "Don't worry about how, you have to change. I'll get your bag and you know where the bathroom is."

"But everyone else... and I don't know what to do and..."

"John knows what to do. All you have to do is get dressed."

I can't believe all this. "Thank you."

"Thank the Lord, because he sure loves you a lot." She plops a Macy's bag into my arms. "Now get dressed!"

I'm not lucky, I'm loved.

And when I'm dressed in my long white skirt, matching bedazzled BLESSED WIFE t-shirt, and blingy white sandals, I feel doubly so.

Outside the bathroom, Daisy takes my borrowed dress and hangs it on a wooden hanger. John waits against the wall, in dark pants and a BLESSED HUSBAND t-shirt. Millennial newlywed picnic style.

"Walk up there and to the right." Daisy points to the staircase. "The third door opens to stairs that lead you to the balcony."

John hands rest firm on the small of my back. "Thank you for being my wife."

"Thank you for being my husband."

"I love you in that outfit."

"Thank you, hubby."

"Know what else I'm going to love?"

"No, what?"

"When I get you out of that outfit."

I'm still laughing when we emerge on the balcony and wave to our loved ones on the sprawling lawn. Applause and shouts of congratulations meet my ears as I gaze at what seems like a super-sized version of the co-ed wedding shower. Nature provides the greenery through the trees and beautiful landscaping. Beneath us the red stone patio holds floral-decorated chairs and tables. Our closest family and the wedding party sit there. Guests on the lawn rest brought picnic blankets and chairs.

This. Is. Extraordinary.

This. Is. Everything.

I turn to John. "How are we feeding these people?"

"The caterers are still doing the light spread of food. The eatLARGE crew had the idea of donating restaurant food for advertising, and Chef Gabriel convinced a few other small restaurants to do the same. Lorenzo and I made up a letter, and we told guests they are welcome to attend if they bring their own chairs and picnic blankets. We told them the truth—when the food is gone, it's gone, but they can stay and celebrate with us for hours. Aaron's DJing all afternoon and evening, so thank him for doing it for free."

That pit bull! "So you didn't pay for anything?"

"I paid for our picnic clothes and once Daisy and Tripp donated their patio and the golf course gave their okay, I paid for contractors to clean up tomorrow."

This man. "I could kiss you."

"I hope you'll do more than that." His eyes twinkle in the afternoon sunlight. "But we should eat something first."

Our wedding extravaganza isn't anything like I'd expected. It's so much more, but not because I tried to pay for it. Like John said, our family and friends—our relationships make us rich. Thank God for all of them.

A video of all our dating life photos plays on a large TV on the patio. People crowd around, smiling at our personal romance movie.

It blesses me to see Ms. Pat and my mother talking on the red stone patio. I hope they aren't scheming on grand babies too soon.

Because this is a wedding picnic, Lorenzo cues the talking and music to stop long enough for all the official toasts. My parents toast us first. Then Nate takes over.

"Congratulations, Chablis and John," he holds his glass high and smiles at us. "Chablis, I knew you'd be perfect for John the day we met, and you gave me a big hug and smile and challenged me to Assassins Creed. You are truly my sister. John, you're the little brother I love with all my heart. How wonderful and glorious it is that you both now have one another forever. What God has joined today, let man not separate. I wish for all of God's blessings to be given to you."

I blow kisses to Nate and pass John a napkin so he can wipe his eyes and glasses before we head to the portable dance floor on the lawn.

We dance to "Nobody" by Brian McKnight. Slow and sure, we hold one another for the first time as a married couple.

The music changes and our guests join us. My heart beats double-time when Terry and Nikki dance beside us. I reach out and squeeze Nik's hand real quick. When I let go, she links hands with Rashida and Rae-Ann. Terry opens his arms to include all three of them, and they dance together.

Love. Just blooming.

When the sentimental moments end, the party starts with DJ Aaron on the 1s and 2s. Family. Friends. Church members. Music and laughter. Hours pass and folks clear the floor when my line dancers perform *You're My Star*.

Then.

My eyes widen when Aaron plays Mario's "I Choose You" and John follows Jamie to the middle of the dance floor. Who knows when that man had the time to learn and practice *SOSU Deasey*. The chorus has the line, 'and if you feel like dancing, you don't have to dance alone' which is perfect for me. Halfway through, I join them and we finish together. The song ends and I leap into my beloved's arms and kiss him hard.

John *is* my husband.

I *am* his wife.

And this is our best day *ever*.

all things new

WE'VE COME A LONG WAY.

For real, we're about a football field away from the party people on the Worthington's lawn.

Hand in hand, John and I stroll the lawn perimeter at dusk. This outdoor space is kind of like the art museum park, but different. Here, no joggers, cyclists, or strollers pass us. No purple azaleas or mounds of mulch or metal drones buzzing above. Just the golf course grass beneath our feet and a sharp woodsy smell in the air.

Seasons change and October reigns with new tree leaves throwing their colors into the mix. Summer green to red, brown, orange.

Gold.

John's left hand feels rough, but I still can't stop clutching it. I let my fingers dance against the warmed metal on his ring finger. On my left hand, my thumb rubs the circle of jewelry that matches his. I'm in step with my husband, and we're alone, gazing at nature making its gentle turn into fall. We're moving into the season of abundance.

Harvest.

I touch his bandaged forehead.

"What are you thinking about, Sunshine?" His fingertips caress the make-up covered scar on my right cheek. "What's on your mind?"

"March seems so far away, it's like it happened decades ago. We're in a different season."

"Funny. I was thinking the same thing." He lifts my hand. I feel warm lips and a kiss. "I have my wife by my side. My wife! I can't believe we're finally here."

"I know, right? Only birds and trees, white clouds and blue skies. We've arrived. And no drones?"

John leads me up a short, steep hill. "Nah, I mean, I thought about a drone again, but then you'd run away and I'd have to chase you and I learned my lesson the first time. Tonight, we can just look at what's in front of us."

He wraps his arm around my shoulder and gives a gentle tug until I face the opposite direction. We're elevated and staring at the Worthington back lawn. Though the crowd has diminished, a small group of dancers move across the portable floor doing *The Electric Slide*.

Illustrating joy.

"Close your eyes," John asks.

I don't even question him. I just do what he says.

He steps away for a few moments then returns. "Now open them."

My eyelids part and John, smiling, hands me two burning silver sparklers. He holds two for himself and scattered sparks of light flicker and bounce before us.

"You asked me for shine for this day, and I'm a man of my word. Enjoy your shine," he says.

"Put yours with mine," I say. "They'll shine together."

And we press the sparklers together and they sputter and glow and spill light. These sticks of temporary light will burn out, but I don't think John and I will.

Oh no, we're just getting started.

If I could hold on to each tiny spark in front of us, I'd place them, shining, around our nude bodies tonight. Since I can't do that, I might open the blinds of the honeymoon suite to let the moon and stars cast their light upon us. Or maybe those guardian angels will show up again and cradle us with heavenly wings.

Whatever happens, the moment will be sacred.

And I know, it will be all that I need.

epilogue

THE ENGLISH LANGUAGE doesn't have enough adjectives to describe the piece of heaven on earth that was St. Lucia. Hummingbirds greeted John and I each bright morning when we opened the suite curtains to let in sunshine right before our private breakfast in a tropical garden. Every day became a Caribbean adventure. We walked through thick mud beneath a volcano, bathed in a hot mineral spring, and sailed a Hobie Cat around emerald green waters.

And everything we experienced after nightfall?

Well... ahem... blessings abound.

I texted Ariana a picture of us enjoying our candlelit dinner on the beach, and she messaged me back. We were her favorite couple to counsel. Pastor Downes must have paid her to say that, but it's okay.

Back in the Delaware Valley, my parents replaced their aged furnace and water heater. After our honeymoon, John helped Daddy upgrade their kitchen with new flooring and fresh paint. My father added a coffee nook for Mom, and she immediately posted pics of her personal java bar on Instagram and Pinterest. I've taught her well.

John and I typed our little hearts out, giving multiple five-star online reviews for Luxurious Events. Luna and Lorenzo sent us rainbow roses for helping restore their local rating.

Grammy and Poppy celebrated their fiftieth wedding anniversary with a party at the New Barber Hall in North Philly. They wore matching white outfits and danced together all night. Poppy threw his back out, attempting to impress the love of his life with a spin move during the Isley Brothers "Shout".

Mom Patty cried through the entire event. I brought her Kleenex and took videos with her iPhone so she'd have them to look at later on. What else would a darling daughter do?

Nate brought his new girlfriend to the celebration. He met her through eHarmony and her name is Ana. She's divorced too, three years older than him and a sixth-grade history teacher. He must be determined to marry a woman who can also homeschool his future kids.

Nikki and Terry give me headaches. He's determined to keep seeing her, even when she dips out for long South American mission trips. Before she set off on her last journey, she let it slip she has indeed fallen in love with him. John and I predict she'll return from Asuncion, Paraguay, drive straight to his job and tell him that using a combination of Spanish and Guarini words.

After pushing hard and paying off a whopping forty-thousand dollars of debt, John's efforts rendered us homeless and broke.

JOKES! HA!

No, the HUSBAE and I have a great financial advisor *and* a place to lay our heads. Palo Alto works well for us and John loves his new job. We've lived here for six months. For the first three weeks, I primped and posed and generally acted like I was auditioning for *Housewives of Silicon Valley,* but now I have a nine-to-five. Yes, in software testing. Yes, I still love it.

I changed my hair. Now it's cropped close to my scalp, with curls the color of ripe blueberries. John and I share the same barber: a burly guy named Big Reggie. He used to be heavy into thug and gang life in Oakland, and his neck tattoos tell the story. We've already witnessed to him, and he might visit our new place of worship soon.

We found an awesome non-denominational church. We took Pastor Downes's advice and we serve with a youth-oriented ministry. I also volunteer with the nursery ministry once a month. When I told Mom, she clutched her chest and hyperventilated until I said I'm only getting used to serving people with kids. We are *not* having one.

Yet.

Yep, one more thing in God's hands.

California real estate is no joke. We pay $3000 a month for a one-bedroom unit. It's funny. Our apartment includes stainless steel appliances in a newly constructed building. However, the square footage is only one and a half times the size of my old place back in Philly. But it's not too bad being so close to John on the daily.

Not too bad at all.

We only have one bookcase in the living room, but we managed to cram all our books onto it. The *Forever Together Faithfully* workbook sits right in the middle. That way we can pull it out and look at our notes any time.

My husband and I are genuine weekend warriors and we explore, driving up and down the coast. Everything out here is so new to us, and we love discovering the west together. San Francisco. San Luis Obispo. San Jose. Life is a highway, and we jump in the Jeep and ride it all weekend long.

John found a cycling club, and he rides twice a week. Yep, he still bikes. It proves the accident didn't give him PTSD.

After multiple Facebook group searches, I located my line dance tribe in the Bay area. I country line dance now too. Oh yeah, I can boot scoot boogie with the best of them.

What do I *know* about all this? That God *is* great, and its best to trust Him to work out all things. If it's not worked out, it's not over. Make no mistake, God carefully guides the life of this newly married line-dancing blue-haired Jesus chick and her tattooed, glasses wearing, exercise-addicted husband.

And how do I *feel*?

Well, I no longer feel like a banged-up, washed-out victim. Oh no! I understand I'm a woman chosen and saved through Christ, *and* fully treasured by her man.

And I feel blessed!

reader's guide for "engaged"

1. When the story introduces Chablis Shields, she runs from a drone, then bounces into fighting stance and will tackle the drone if needed. What do you think her actions say about what she might do when she faces resistance in the future?

2. John Gerald's extensive love life prior to dating Chablis becomes a sore spot between the two of them when they become engaged. Should Chablis have thought more about John's dating past before she accepted the ring?

3. John avoided sharing the full truth about his debt load while the couple dated, but felt pressure to inform Chablis about his money situation days after they committed to marriage. Was that fair to Chablis? Should John's lack of financial transparency while dating have been a deal breaker?

4. Aside from John, Nikki is Chablis' best friend. While she maintains that role during the story, their relationship shows signs of change. Discuss the relationship between married Christian women and single Christian women.

Can a married woman and a single woman successfully maintain their close friendship?

5. Social media allows a couple to show themselves at all stages of their relationship. John and Chablis fill their Instagram accounts with pictures of their courtship and engagement. Do you think that was wise?

6. Why do you think the author told the story from the perspective that she did?

7. For personal and faith-based reasons, John and Chablis abstained from sexual activity while dating. After engagement, Chablis attempted physical intimacy, but John encouraged them to wait for their "blessing". In today's world, do you think that was realistic?

8. Ms. Pat/Patricia Gerald clearly rejects Chablis as John's future wife and continues to give her a hard time throughout the story. Yet, when Chablis almost attacks Ms. Pat negatively, she refrains and practices forgiveness and sacrifice. Do you think she made the right decision?

9. John loves long bike rides. Chablis loves urban line dance. Should a couple share the same hobbies? What do you think the author is saying about couples who stay physically active while they grow and age with one another?

10. When the book begins, Chablis states that she's fine with her future husband's eyesight, even if it gives him problems later in life. Likewise, John proposes to a young woman who experiences panic attacks. What do you think this says about their ability to accept things about one another as their relationship continues?

11. Ariana Thompson serves as Chablis and John's premarital counselor, and she gives them insight into building the foundation of their marriage. Do you know married couples who attended premarital counseling? How do you think it affected their union?

12. Chablis sometimes describes people she meets as though they are celebrities. If you were to cast the movie version of this book, who would you cast as the main characters?
13. What feelings did this book evoke for you?
14. If you had to choose one lesson the author tried to teach with this story, what would it be?

the honeymoon journal

The Honeymoon Journal offers a glimpse into a modern garden of Eden as the newlyweds capture their St. Lucia honeymoon through dual journal entries and intimate verse. This short fiction piece follows the couple as they discover sensual pleasures, cherish their companionship, and look forward to a lifetime of love. *The Honeymoon Journal* is available as a digital download from Apple, KOBO, Everand, and Smashwords. Read it today!

Reader advisory: While alluding to sexual situations, the narrative maintains a tasteful approach reminiscent of the *The Holy Bible, Song of Songs*.

acknowledgments

This is the best part of the trip!

Thank you, Lord, for allowing me to write to your glory. *When I do not know what to do, my eyes are upon you.*

Chris Broomes—thanks for reading every single chapter and providing your comments. I still think a Dave & Buster's unicorn scene would have worked, but I trust your judgment. Speaking of judgment, a particular "dope conversation" only made it back into the narrative because you insisted on it. If the church police come after me, I will send them to see you.

Stacey Strickler—thanks for providing the wedding and event planning details. That colorful co-ed wedding shower scene? All you, sweetie!

Samantha Alexander, I couldn't have written about a cycling enthusiast without knowing one—thanks for providing the bike and local trail information. There's a Cervelo Caldonia out there with your name on it.

Janee Corbin, bless you for the late-night conversation about how men who genuinely love their women will hold their hands, buy them gifts, and go totally public with them.

Blessings to my place of worship, CareView Community Church. I appreciate your prayers and support for my creative writing ministry. I offer a special thank you to Deacon Alice Swinton-Brown, whose prayers, daily texts, and encouragements pulled me through a dark time as I wrote this novel.

Thank you, Paige Reed and Richard Allen, for serving as my

critique partners through this long and messy novel journey. I will never forget your lessons about settings and vulnerability. You never left me, and you helped me bring real heart to my main characters.

To my early readers: TashaJuanna Renee Muhammad, Pam Everett, and Tim Pietz, thanks so much for your valuable insights!

And thank you to the men who came through with support when I thought this novel might sit on the shelf for another year: Maurice M. Gray, Jr. (author of *Like a Brother*) and Dion Ringgold. My brothers in Christ, you are simply amazing!

Dear reader, thank you for buying and supporting contemporary fiction for Christian readers.

subscribe to my newsletter

How will you find out about my latest releases, read reviews for recommended books by other Christian fiction authors, and more? By becoming an author newsletter subscriber! You can sign up on my website at klgilchrist.com. As a gift, all newsletter subscribers immediately receive the free short story collection *Five For The Journey: Stories*

This eBook is not published publicly. It is only available to subscribers. So sign up today!

about the author

K.L. Gilchrist crafts true-to-life contemporary tales for women of faith. The author of *Broken Together* and other stories enjoys bringing order to chaos and dancing whenever and wherever she can. She and her family call the suburbs of Philadelphia, PA home. Feel free to visit her online at klgilchrist.com.

f facebook.com/402435140151793
X x.com/KL_Gilchrist
instagram.com/klgilchrist